SUNDOWN SERENADE

DAVE LOPARDO

Cover Photo: Sunset on Lake Nasworthy, San Angelo, Texas, 1977

TABLE OF CONTENTS

FOREWORD

It took a while, but my fifth collection is finally finished. The stories are longer and richer in detail than most of my previous works. Seven of the ten stories were written in a six week creative frenzy in August through October of 2017.

My reflective tendencies once again have pushed their way to the forefront. I often find it more satisfying to look at where I've been than where I'm going.

That being said, I've brought back the old gang from my story "Hillwalkers" and given them two encores, "Redmont Field and "Backfold." Although fictional, these characters strongly resemble the boys with whom I shared my childhood, teenage, and early adult years.

The rest of the lineup is comprised of what I usually produce when I let my creativity wander off unsupervised: mystery, crime, (with or without punishment) a novel look at an American movie classic, and the truly bizarre situations I sometimes think only I am capable of visualizing, a belief that is both wrong and pretentious, of course. Still, they are the serenade that played in my head the past few years.

There remain some unidentified melodies that surface briefly, seemingly out of nowhere. Perhaps I will be able to orchestrate them in the future.

Until then, I hope *these* stories serenade *you.*

"PINE ISLAND"
8/14/14—8/20/14
Garrett Cove, Washington, 1991

Chief of Detectives Mel Wagner carried two cardboard boxes into the office of the newest member of the detective bureau, Clancy Robillard. The boxes contained the files of the department's oldest unsolved cases.

It had become tradition that the newest detective got the cases as his first assignment. It was also tradition that no one actually *worked on them.* Clancy Robillard was generally well-liked among his peers, but not respected. He hadn't done anything *wrong,* he just didn't have that swagger that gets a ten-year patrolman promoted. Wagner had his misgivings, but he was the perfect "compromise candidate" at this time. Victor Tillis was a hothead, and Paul Reynolds did not have that inquisitive nature. Robillard, often referred to as "Mama's boy" behind his back, still lived in the house where he grew up, even after his mother's latest stroke had landed her in a nursing home.

Clancy's father had been killed in a mill accident when he was eight, possibly initiating his overly-strong ties to his mother. The mill paid a generous settlement to Mrs. Robillard. His older brother Richard was a desk sergeant in the Seattle P. D. Clancy seemed to be on the right track in his early twenties, but the death of his fiancée in a car accident sent him into a tailspin, withdrawing from most social circles. It was shortly after that he applied for and was eventually accepted into the Garrett Cove P. D.

Now a ten-year veteran, he had done his job efficiently and quietly. He was the quintessential *plodder,* meeting all the job requirements without distinction or dereliction.

As Mel Wagner opened Robillard's office door and let himself in, there was one nagging thought in the back of his mind: *if there was anyone who would take these cases to heart and work on them instead of ignoring them, it would be Clancy Robillard.*

Robillard sat at his new desk, a yellow legal pad and pen in front of him. His sandy reddish hair was already beginning to thin, accentuating the pudgy face beneath it.

"Morning, Clancy." Wagner wore the smile of one about to let someone in on a private joke.

Robillard looked at the two boxes Wagner carried under one arm. "Are those the cold cases that the new detective gets?"

"Right." Wagner sat down in the chair across from Robillard. "I am required to give you an overview of each case."

Wagner still had that "going through the motions" expression, but Robillard did *not,* and had grabbed his pen and positioned the pad in front of him, ready to take on the two cases that nine detectives over the past fifty years had been unable to solve. "Ready," he said.

"You don't actually have to take notes," Wagner said reassuringly.

"I hardly know anything about them, Mel. It might help."

Wagner's smile evaporated. "Clancy, you don't actually have to *do* anything about them, either. It's just a tradition we keep up." Wagner studied Robillard's face for any hint that the new detective was kidding along with him, but he knew better. No one had less of a sense of humor than Clancy Robillard.

"But they're actual open cases, Mel, and you're assigning them to me, right?"

"Well, yes, Clancy, but no one expects you to solve them, or even *work* them. It's just a kind of initiation."

"I understand. But I don't really *have* anything else right now. I can at least read them over after you brief me, right?"

Wagner sighed in resignation. "Right." He opened a file folder which overviewed each case.

"On December 29th, 1941, Eugene Traust, his wife Monica, and their two sons, Lawrence, age four, and Frank, age two, disappeared without a trace. Their home was left neat and orderly, their car was still in the garage, and almost all of their money had been withdrawn from their bank account. Suitcases and clothes were also missing."

Robillard jotted down notes while Wagner stared in dismay. He continued.

"On October 21st, 1944, Han and Sammy Lee, two American-born brothers of Korean ancestry, disappeared while on an all-day hunting trip out to Pine Island. Their boat washed ashore half a mile from here with all their gear, supplies, and shotguns in it. Their bodies were never recovered. Their parents contended that they were murdered, and that this department did not do a thorough investigation. The consensus is that they drowned."

Robillard looked up from his notes. "Isn't Pine Island Indian land? What would they be doing out there?"

Wagner exhaled impatiently. "The island still belongs to the Swinomish, but they abandoned it in the 1930's after they got new fishing rights and a settlement out on Lopez Point." He gave Robillard a stern look. "Look, Clancy, I know you mean well, but don't go wasting my time. Read the files if you want to know about the cases. And," he added with finality, "these cases don't carry any weight any more. So do what you want. Work them, don't work them, I don't care. Just make sure you take care of 1991 before you get too involved. Better men than you and I have taken a crack at them and gotten nowhere." He nodded at Robillard and exited purposefully.

It had to be done, Wagner told himself as he returned to his desk. Patrolman Victor Tillis caught his eye and strode over, indignation on his face.

"So, did Mama's boy cry when you dumped two impossible cases on his desk?"

"Lay off, Victor. I know you're pissed you didn't get the promotion."

"My issue, Mel, is that this guy just isn't detective material. I wouldn't have minded if Reynolds had gotten the promotion, but *him?* He's a sad sack schlub. You and the other detectives are gonna find yourselves carrying his weight. And that's all I got to say on the matter."

Victor Tillis stomped out of the building, muttering to himself.

"Hothead," whispered Wagner.

***

Clancy Robillard was not brilliant, but with most problems he worked his way through methodically; *plodding,* so to speak. He *was* smart enough to know that he could not just jump in and expect to get anywhere until he was properly versed with not only the people and places involved, but the time period, also.

For a few weeks he read and reread the case history and files, enduring the sneers of Victor Tillis and Paul Reynolds, and the pitying, sometimes exasperated looks of Mel Wagner.

The Traust home at 41 Mallory Lane had been left neat, their Christmas tree taken down, all the ornaments still in boxes in the living room. Eugene Traust had been an engineer with a reputation for unbridled brilliance, his wife Monica a simple homemaker. Mr. Traust had been employed by *West Coast Innovations,* a cutting edge firm back in 1941. Most of his friends and co-workers, if they could be located, would be in their late 70's.

The Lee brothers, Han and Sammy, were American-born Koreans. They were twenty-one and nineteen respectively and worked as trash collectors in Painted Rock. They had lived there with their parents and younger sister Sophia. When their boat washed ashore the day after they set out on their illegal hunting trip, it was assumed that one of them had fallen overboard and the other had jumped in to save him. The weight of their heavy hunting clothes and boots would have made swimming impossible once they were soaked.

Clancy looked at this information, and while he accepted facts as facts, he reasoned that no one had ever solved these cases because all the theories were wrong to begin with.

There were assumptions in both cases that he quickly dismissed. Why would one of the Lee brothers jump into the ocean to save his brother when all he had to do was hold out one of the oars for him to grab? Why did Eugene Traust leave twenty-six dollars in his bank account, taking the other eight-hundred? If they were kidnapped, why were their suitcases and clothes missing? If they had decided to run off and start a new life, another popular theory, how did they get there with the family sedan in the garage? What *reason* was there for a happily-married man with two young boys to attempt such a difficult undertaking?

In 1941, disappearing and *resurfacing* somewhere else was much more difficult. The man was not a criminal, and his work did not make him a key target of any enemy of the U. S.

None of the usual theories made any sense to Clancy, so he decided to cast them *all* aside. He was convinced that incorrect assumptions had led to incorrect conclusions. He would not fall down that same hole.

And one last thing: Pine Island. Seventeen square miles of wilderness one- and- a- half miles off the coast.

Inhabited by the peaceful Swinomish for nearly two centuries, they abandoned it in 1934 when given exclusive fishing rights on Fidalgo Island, and up the road in a seaside village called Lopez Point. But there had always been whisperings that the Swinomish had left behind warriors to guard the island and keep any unwanted people away. The whites called them the "GI's"; the guardians of the island.

***

"That Traust fellow was so friggin' smart, you could start tellin' him a procedure, and a minute later, he'd be tellin' *you* the rest of it," said Angelo Infante, jabbing his finger for emphasis.

Clancy Robillard nodded and took notes. Infante had been Traust's immediate superior from 1937 to 1941. Robillard had visited the former *West Coast Innovations,* now under new ownership and renamed *Washington Dynamics, Inc.* Their records had given him several names of Traust's co-workers still alive.

"Let me tell you something," continued Infante, "if Eugene Traust had been around during the Space Race, Werner Von Braun would have been his errand boy, that's how smart this guy was."

"Did he ever give any indication that he was unhappy?" asked Robillard.

"We were *all* unhappy. We just got sucker-punched by Japan and Germany declared war on us."

"I realize that, Mr. Infante, but did he ever talk about just picking up and leaving?"

"No, never. But the whole family just disappeared, right?"

"That's what I'm trying to find out."

Infante chuckled. "You must have ticked off somebody to get handed a case this old."

"Well, it's complicated. I'm also trying to find out what happened to the Lee brothers."

"Who?"

"Two brothers who were going hunting on Pine Island and—"

"Oh! The two Korean guys they say drowned. Never found them, did they?"

"No, but I don't think they drowned."

Infante looked around like a TV spy and lowered his voice. "I don't either. I think they got to the island and—" he made a slashing gesture across his throat.

"You think the GI's got them?"

Infante smiled and shook his head. "Not the *GI's*, son, somthin' else."

"What?"

"Ghosts. That place is haunted sure as I'm sittin' here on my porch. Those Indians made sure no one would set foot there and live to tell about it." He paused. "And don't go believin' any of that GI crap. That's all a myth."

***

Clancy's interviews with Angelo Infante and others had established Eugene Traust as a man supremely gifted in raw intelligence and resourcefulness. A man like that *could* possibly pull off a disappearing act, but burdened with a wife and two pre-school age boys, it would take a near miracle to be able to reappear somewhere and not raise suspicion. The nation was preoccupied with its new involvement in the war, but in 1941 people were much more vigilant. That was what Clancy had to keep reminding himself: put this case in the context of 1941.

He dismissed as hearsay a good deal of what he had been told by Traust's peers: he had developed a new weapons system and the government had whisked him away for national security; he was to be a witness in an upcoming trial against organized crime, he had fled to the mountains of Idaho to found an alternative society. There were others, but none seemed to fulfill the requirement for *motive* that would push a gainfully-employed man with two young children to uproot his family just weeks after his county was facing all-out war.

War? Was that the determining factor? It certainly was a life-altering variable. He filed it away with a thousand other thoughts pertaining to Eugene Traust and family, and Han and Sammy Lee.

Shortly before the fiftieth anniversary of the Traust disappearance, he got around to visiting the house on Mallory Lane. It had changed hands five times since it was auctioned off in 1942 for non-payment of mortgage and city taxes.

Sitting in his car across from the house, now owned by Mr. and Mrs. Howard Reidy, one thing did catch Clancy's eye: the garage. It seemed very old, and in fact exactly matched the photos in the original case file. He knocked on the door of the house, and within a few minutes an intrigued Evelyn Reidy had given him permission to look there.

First inspection revealed the usual: lawn mower, clippers, various tools, chairs, an old table. Clancy wasn't sure what he was looking for. Then, for no apparent reason, his eyes fixed on a small wooden ladder built into the side of the interior, right by the garage door. After getting permission from Mrs. Reidy, he prepared to climb it and inspect the upper level of the tiny garage. After closing the automatic garage door to get the support cables out of the way, he started up, then realized he had a problem. Mrs. Reidy's inquisitive face appeared outside the door.

"Mrs. Reidy, please wait inside. By the way, is anything I might find up here yours?"

"No, Detective. Howie and I have never been up there." She disappeared back inside.

Although Clancy had made it sound "official" that she could not observe, it had nothing to do with police protocol. The opening to get up to the second level was so small he knew he would never fit unless he stripped to his undershorts and socks. He remembered photos of Eugene Traust, 5' 10'' and barely 140 pounds. *He* could fit up there with no problem.

As he was about to put his arm onto the floor of the upper level, his eye-level still below it, he recalled the times his older brother Richard had scared him as a child, yelling 'watch out for spiders' or 'is that a snake?' whenever he reached into some unknown place in their basement or attic.

A wistful smile bloomed on his face as his hand came down on the garage's upper level. There was a sharp snapping sound, and intense pain in his middle finger. Every childhood fear came back at once as he recoiled and stumbled down the ladder. *What bit me? A rabid bat? A poisonous spider?*

Clancy looked at the injured finger, expecting some ferocious vermin to be clinging there. Attached to his middle finger was a mousetrap, the kind he had only seen in cartoons.

He removed it, laughing and cursing. He ascended the ladder more carefully, and with some effort managed to pull himself onto the floor of the upper level of what was once Eugene Traust's garage. In his mind he was prepared to find four human skeletons.

What he actually found were a few old child's toys, more mousetraps, a deflated beachball, and two old notebooks. There was no name on them, but part of him felt as though he was finally on the trail of Eugene Traust. The notebooks were full of procedures, drawings, and sketches. Clancy was not sure at first what any of this meant, but he took the time to examine them. He did not want to look like a fool if they turned out to be nothing more than trivial lists that most people made.

In various sections of the notebooks were detailed drawings and instructions regarding irrigation and drainage systems, waste disposal, farming, hunting, and trapping. In back of one notebook were detailed building plans for both an elaborate tree dwelling, and a tunnel system. He *knew* that these were Eugene Traust's notebooks, his getaway blueprint.

"That clever son-of-a-bitch," he whispered.

The final days of 1991 did not find Clancy Robillard in Mel Wagner's office, showing off the journals. With the disapproving looks of his colleagues in his mind, Clancy took the journals home and dissected them, along with the case files.

He had made no headway on the disappearance of the Lee brothers, a part of his sometimes childish mind remembering the warning of Angelo Infante that Pine Island was haunted by evil spirits.

1992

Clancy spent the early part of the year combing through the case files at work and what he believed to be Eugene Traust's notebooks at home. He kept getting the uneasy feeling that Eugene Traust and family, like the Lee brothers, had headed out to Pine Island.

It was the perfect spot in many ways: uninhabited, large enough to allow one to remain undetected, and rich enough to sustain them. A good number of the Swinomish tribe had thrived here. Certainly, four people could.

Clancy knew he was going to have to get permission from the Tribal Council to go out there and look, but first he had to pay a call on the Lee family in Painted Rock.

***

Mel Wagner started throwing a lot of routine investigations his way. He knew Mel had to keep his critics at bay. He continued to ask questions he felt had not been addressed. The main one was: did anyone search Pine Island for clues that the Lee brothers had come ashore that October morning?

In early April he finally got the opportunity to drive to Painted Rock to interview Sophia Lee Darwish, age 61, the only living relative of Han and Sammy Lee.

Sitting in her dining room that morning, it was obvious she remained bitter over what she considered to be a minimal effort to solve the disappearance of her two older brothers.

"Those policemen in Garrett Cove, they don't care about Han and Sammy," she stated at the outset of the interview. "They think we are like the Japanese. The war was still going, so we had to watch it. My mother and father decide not to say anything when the police tell us they drowned."

"Do *you* think they drowned, Mrs. Darwish?" Clancy asked softly.

"Of course not," she replied with a quiet defiance. "My brothers good swimmers and could handle a boat. They did it many times."

"I wasn't aware of that," Clancy replied.

"No one asks," she said with disgust. "I told you my parents not want trouble. A detective comes here the next week and tells us they drowned. He just too lazy to find the truth. And now, years later, here you come. Why do *you* care?" Her voice wavered, and she fought back tears.

Clancy looked squarely in her watering eyes. "I care because that's what *my* mother and father taught me.

And to tell the truth." He paused. "And to find it when it's missing."

She stood and wiped her eyes. "So *you* gonna find out what happened to my brothers, after all this time?"

Clancy handed her a card. "Here's my number if you think of anything that would be of help. Otherwise you won't see me again until I can come here and tell you what happened to your brothers. I promise you I will be back . . . with the truth."

***

It was time to update Mel Wagner on his findings.

He laid out all his information, including the notebooks and his discussions with Angelo Infante and Sophia Lee Darwish. Mel's face did not change expression, but he seemed to be phrasing a response in his head.

"Clancy, you do realize that Eugene Traust was a top-notch engineering designer, and those notebooks are probably nothing out of the ordinary for someone like him."

"But Mel. Farming, irrigation, waste disposal, hunting, trapping. Those sound like things someone would have to know to *survive*."

"They also sound like things *West Coast Innovations* would be working on for various clients. That Lee woman sounds bitter because she lost her brothers in a tragic accident. Can't blame her. And Angelo Infante has always been given to exaggerating. He was a friend of my father's when I was a teenager." There was a brief pause, then Wagner leaned forward in his chair. "Am I making any sense to you, Clancy?"

"Everything you said makes sense, but maybe the reason these cases have never been solved is that people made sensible assumptions, then stopped."

"Clancy, I've run interference for you, given you enough jackass duty to keep you busy, and made excuses when you weren't at your desk. It's about time—"

"Mel, I want to go up to Lopez Point and talk to the Swinomish. I think they know about the Lee brothers, and may have had something to do with their deaths."

"God damn it, Clancy," said Mel curtly, "I thought you had at least *some* sense. Why do you want to go there and stir things up with a tribe that fishes and sells souvenirs to tourists?"

"The GI's, Mel. They stayed behind to guard the island." He noted the grim look on Wagner's face. "I suppose you don't believe they existed."

Mel exhaled. "They existed, Clancy. But no one who was around then is going to give you the time of day. So go ahead if you want. Go talk to the Swinomish, flash your shiny badge at them. Think any of them will give a shit? They've been under the white man's thumb for over a hundred-thirty years. You needing to know what happened to two guys nearly fifty years ago is not gonna make it to the Tribal Council's agenda, if you get my drift."

Clancy flashed a devious grin. "Thanks, Mel. Can I go tomorrow?"

***

The sign read, *Lopez Point, Swinomish People Conservatory.* "I guess 'Reservation' isn't politically correct any more," Clancy mused. He stopped at the first building he saw. A sign over the window cutout read, *Joseph Smits: Souvenirs, Snacks, and Sundries.* Leaving his car and going over to the window he found a Swinomish man. Clancy had trouble determining the ages of Native Americans. This man could be forty, or seventy.

He *did* flash his 'shiny badge,' identified himself, and asked the man's name.

"I go by Joseph Smits."

Clancy's face wrinkled in confusion.

"It's for business purposes. We don't use our tribal names any more when dealing with the whites."

"Oh."

"What can I do for you, Detective?"

"I'm investigating the disappearance of Han and Sammy Lee in 1944. I have reason to believe they got out to Pine Island and something happened to them."

"What kind of something?" asked Smits.

"I think they were killed there. I think the GI's were involved."

Smits shook his head in disgust. "I have heard the term before. There *are* no GI's. There *never* were. As usual the whites have taken half a truth and made it the whole truth. Young men were sent to the island three times between their fifteenth and twenty-first birthdays to live off the land as our ancestors did."

"So there would have been Swinomish on the island in 1944?"

"Yes, certainly."

"I need to ask your chief for permission to search the island for the bodies of the two men."

"He will not see you Detective, but I am on the Tribal Council and will pass your request along."

"Were you by any chance one of the young men who would have been on the island during that time?"

"Why do you want to know about such things from so long ago?"

"I seek the truth for the sister of the two men. And I am looking for a missing white family of a man and woman and their two young boys."

Joseph Smits studied him for perhaps a full minute. "The others that came just asked silly questions, hyena smiles on their faces. You are not like them."

Clancy smiled at the compliment and asked, quietly, "So Joseph, I will ask you again, were you on Pine Island in 1944?"

"Come back in two or three weeks. Give me some time to talk to the Head of the Council. Maybe I can convince him to answer your questions. Until then I can give you no answers myself." He smiled and stuck out his hand. "I admire your quest."

Clancy shook his hand and smiled, then turned and began to walk back towards his car.

"Detective," called Smits.

"Yes?"

"Can I interest you in any genuine Swinomish souvenirs?"

***

There was no point in going to Mel Wagner with his latest findings, courtesy of the enigmatic Joseph Smits. For the next three weeks he played the good soldier, doing routine tasks and investigations. He still read the case files at his desk and Eugene Traust's notebooks at home. He had become a bit complacent, going through the notebooks as though they were schoolbooks, and realized that he needed to look as though seeing them for the first time.

One question bothered him still: why would Traust take eight-hundred dollars with him if he had gone to Pine Island? Maybe he *did* go to Idaho. If so, why leave twenty-six dollars (a week's pay for some wage-earners) in the account?

One evening, while leafing through the notebooks for perhaps the hundredth time, he noticed two of the pages stuck together. Further inspection showed that the corners had actually been glued. With a razor blade they came apart easily, and revealed yet more of what he believed was Eugene Traust's master plan. They were designs for the building of what were then called 'walkie-talkies.' They could come in handy on an island two miles wide by eight miles long.

Or, they could be for communicating with someone on the mainland. Did Traust have an accomplice, maybe someone who brought him out there? Did he need the radio to call this person?

At the bottom of the page with the radio specs, there were three words, nearly unreadable. Clancy got out a magnifying glass he used with the notebooks. He wasn't sure at first he was seeing correctly, but after a longer look he knew he was. The three words were *LION, TRANSFER, RADIO.* As satisfied as he was at having found something new, it frustrated him to no end. He was on the trail of a man determined not to be found.

"God damn you, Traust," he muttered.

***

Clancy Robillard was a devoted, dutiful son, but visits to his mother at McCutcheon's, a nursing facility, had gone from daily to twice a week. It took too much out of him to see his mother weakening, slowly forgetting basic information. After the latest frustrating find in the notebooks, he immediately got in his car. It would be therapeutic for him to tell her everything about the double mystery that had consumed him for eight months, knowing she would understand little of it, and forget the rest.

In her private room, he rambled on for nearly twenty minutes, starting with the September day he made Detective and Mel Wagner dumped two baffling cases on him. His mother seemed to be listening, but he assumed she was just glad to see him.

She spoke up so suddenly it startled him.

"I used to see Monica Traust with the two boys, even in cold weather. Then, I didn't see her any more. Did that strange husband of hers move them someplace?"

Clancy was astounded at the clarity of the statement and question. "We don't know, Mom. We're looking for them." He added, as an afterthought, "I think someone helped them disappear, maybe got paid to do it."

Surely *that* would not register, but it felt good to say it out loud to anyone other than Mel Wagner.

"You should check with Hugh Potts, then. Back when we were young, he was a guy who would do anything," she rubbed her thumb and fingers together, "if you gave him enough money."

""Yeah, right, Mom. Would he help Eugene Traust disappear?" Clancy said, with as much tongue-in-cheek as possible.

"Sure. They were friends, Hugh and that other guy."

"Eugene Traust."

"No, not *him*. The *other* guy, Monica's strange husband."

Clancy knew enough to play along. "Yeah, Monica's husband." Almost playfully, he asked, "Is Hugh Potts still alive, Mom?"

She pointed at the ceiling.

Another one dead and gone, Clancy thought.

"He's upstairs, Clancy. You can go ask him yourself."

His eyes nearly bugged out of his head. "I'll be right back, Mom."

"Don't get your hopes up, son."

"Why not, Mom?"

"That Hugh, he doesn't like the police, you know."

The patient ID placards outside room 205 read *William DeFoley* and *Hugh Potts*. Clancy stepped inside to find the near bed empty. In the other lay a man in his late seventies, large glasses, and thinning silver hair, reading a magazine.

"He's in physical therapy," Potts said, thinking the stranger in his room was here to see his roommate.

"I'm here for you, Mr. Potts. I'm Detective Clancy Robillard. I'm looking into the disappearance of Eugene Traust and his family back in 1941. I was hoping you might be able to help me."

Potts put down his magazine and frowned. "Robillard. Was Jack Robillard your dad?"

"Yes."

"Too bad about what happened."

"Yes, thank you. About Eugene Traust."

"Well, I knew the guy, went to high school with him. Smart son-of-a-bitch he was."

"What can you tell me about his disappearance, Mr. Potts?"

"Nuthin.' He just vanished."

Potts did not appear to be lying, but Clancy pressed on. "You two were friends, right?"

"Not after high school. He went to college. I dropped out and worked in a gas station. Smart one, that Eugene."

"Didn't he seek you out, Mr. Potts, to help him secretly get out to Pine Island? Maybe he paid you to help him. Do you remember any of that?"

"No, no, I don't remember nuthin' like that."

Potts was fidgety now, looking uncomfortable. Clancy decided to play his trump card.
"Mr. Potts, does this mean anything to you? Lion, Transfer, Radio."

Hugh Potts' eyes and brow lifted noticeably, then he looked down at the bedspread. "Nope. That don't mean nuthin' to me."

"Thank you, Mr. Potts. Sorry to have taken up your time."

***

Clancy went directly to the station and looked up anything they might have on Hugh Potts. As a teen and until he was thirty-two, he had several arrests and convictions for illegal gambling and selling stolen car parts. A small-time miscreant who had been an unmarried loner his entire life. Now he was suffering from a bad heart and lungs, and clogged arteries. There was no time to waste.

Clancy began visiting his mother every day. After each visit, he went upstairs and "visited" Hugh Potts, peppering him with accusatory questions, ending each session with the cryptic 'Lion, Transfer, Radio.' He even tried the oldest bluff in the book, hinting to Potts that Traust's notebook mentioned him by name. Potts didn't fall for it, but seemed to be wearing down.

The merciful part of Clancy reminded himself it was cruel for Hugh Potts to have to spend his final months like this. Then it hit him like a ton of bricks. Potts hadn't technically broken the law to the extent that any D. A. would give him a second look. And it dawned on him that Potts did not want any more trouble. He had enough problems now and had been clean for forty-six years. Maybe if he changed his approach, Potts would cooperate.

On his next visit, he brought him a couple of crossword puzzle books.

"What's this, bribery?" asked Potts, his defenses already up.

Clancy smiled. "Peace offering, and an apology for being so tough on you."

"Somethin's up with you Robillard. What's goin' on?"

"A deal, maybe, if you're smart enough to take it."

"I'm listening."

"I know you were involved in the Trausts' disappearance, and you *know* that I know, so I make you this guarantee." He stopped to check Potts' reaction.

"Go on," urged Potts.

"I guarantee that for your *full* disclosure of what happened, you will not be charged with *anything*. I would take your statement here, with a witness and your lawyer if you want." Clancy smiled. "Think of it, Hugh, you might even get interviewed by the newspaper or TV news."

"One condition, Robillard. If he's still on the island, don't tell him that I said anything. I promised him, ya know?"

"Hugh, do you actually think he could still be alive and on that island?"

"Wouldn't put it past him. He was one smart son-of-a-bitch."

***

If confession is good for the soul, Hugh Potts was probably the most relieved man on earth. He didn't want a lawyer present, just himself and Clancy.

The crux of his story was this: at the beginning of World War II, Eugene Traust had contacted him and asked if he would transport him and his family to Pine Island if the U. S. was drawn into the war. A non-violent isolationist, he began making plans for survival on what he believed was an uninhabited 17 square mile tract of land.

Potts said he didn't care for what Traust was doing ("that pansy-ass coward") but was promised a hundred dollars for his part. "Real good money, back then," he added.

In the two-plus years since the war's outbreak, Traust used his notebooks to develop the systems he would need to survive. The walkie- talkies he built (he was paranoid about buying anything unusual) were to let Potts know when to return to the island with more supplies and staples until he could get his operation up and running. Between December 29th, 1941, and May of the following year, (when Potts himself was drafted) Potts made trips to Pine Island once a week. Traust also allowed for the interception of his transmissions with the nonsense phrase "Lion, Transfer, Radio." It was the signal for Potts to come out to the island with the next "shopping list" of goods. If *Potts* contacted Traust with the *same* three-word message, it meant he couldn't come.

By the time Potts headed off to North Africa, Traust was completely self-sufficient, including a treehouse and tunnels in case of emergency. He also had guns and ammo for protection and a crossbow for hunting.

Potts embellished greatly, adding details and anecdotes on his fifteen or so clandestine trips out to Pine Island. Clancy found it necessary to throw in questions just to get Potts "derailed."

"What was the eight-hundred dollars for?"

"Used it to give me for provisions."

"Why did he leave money in his account?"

"Didn't want to arouse suspicion by cleaning it out. Thought of everything, he did. Even told me he had a plan for his sons if they ever left the island someday."

"Why did he leave the notebooks behind?"

"Didn't want them on him. Paranoid bastard. He memorized every word and drawing in there. I told you that son-of-a-bitch was smart."

"Did you see where he actually lived?"

"No. He wouldn't take me up there. Said it was better that way. Funny, though, we were alone there, but I always had the feeling we were being watched."

When his statement was finished, it had taken an hour and ten minutes, and filled eight pages when Hugh Potts affixed his signature to it, with his nurse as a witness.

Despite this detailed statement that answered the question of what happened to the Traust family, something inside Clancy told him it was premature to go running to Mel Wagner and drop this bombshell on his desk. In another few days, he would be heading out to Lopez Point to talk to Joseph Smits, and perhaps get the answers he needed to solve the disappearance of the Lee brothers. He would wait, hopefully get the answers he sought, and be able to drop *two* bombshells on Mel Wagner's desk.

But when he returned to Lopez Point a few days later, Joseph Smits informed him that the head of the Tribal Council was ill, and they must attend to his health before posing such a weighty matter to him. He was told to come back in a month. Clancy laid low for the next month, attending to his current tasks. When he returned, he was informed by Joseph Smits that the chief remained gravely ill, and the Council could not make a decision until his health had improved. He was told to come back in the spring.

1993

There was nothing to do but wait. Unfortunately, Hugh Potts had passed away in January, but Clancy had his statement, and a witness.

For Clancy, 'come back in the spring' meant the first possible day. So on Monday, March 22nd, he drove once again to Lopez Point. Joseph Smits met him with a look of distain. "Did spring come ten minutes ago?" he asked with sarcasm.

"It came yesterday, Joseph."

"He has not improved as we had hoped. I do not feel the Council can make a decision without him."

"Mr. Smits, I have waited for over seven months. Can't this be put to a vote of the Council, or some other procedure?"

"We adhere to strict tribal procedures, Detective. Give me your card. I can phone you so you do not have to drive here for nothing."

In response to Clancy's puzzled and surprised expression, Smits smiled wryly. "Yes, Detective, we have phones. And fire, also."

Five weeks passed with no word. He had given Smits his home phone with instructions to call after six. On April 26th the awaited call came.

"Detective?"

"Yes, Mr. Smits."

"Our chief has gone to the land of his spirit kin."

"Damn it!" Clancy shouted.

"I can tell that you are very upset at his passing," came the droll remark.

"I'm sorry, Mr. Smits. But I was hoping—"

"Detective, our Council is at full membership now. And I am the new Head."

Clancy held his breath.

"Come up to Lopez Point when it is convenient. The Council and I have decided to tell you what you have quested for many months now."

***

"Come inside my booth and sit, Detective," said Joseph Smits, "while I tell you this strange tale."

"Strange?"

"You will hear for yourself."

Clancy pulled out a yellow legal pad.

"The Swinomish left their homes on Pine Island in 1934 when we were given Fidalgo Island and the land here, along with exclusive fishing rights."

Clancy nodded.

"But until 1952 Pine Island was still used by our young men as a test of their abilities to live off the land.

We were there to learn, not harm anyone who came there illegally. When some did, we turned them away peaceably. Never any trouble.”

“I understand.”

“One day in October of 1944, two Asian men came ashore, carrying guns. We told them it was our land, and they should leave. They refused, and went inland to hunt. We had no boat to go to shore and inform your police. We were stuck on the island until the elders decided to come for us.”

“Were you there, that day, Joseph?”

“Yes, I was young, maybe fifteen or sixteen.”

“What happened?”

“We followed the men without them knowing. They went up the hill leading to the summit. One of them fired his gun at something, and they laughed. Sometime later, we heard shots from the summit, and both men dropped down dead. We continued to hide and watch. The white man who had lived there came out of the woods, holding his own gun.”

“Wait a minute!” shouted Clancy. “You *knew* about him but allowed him to stay?” Clancy was astounded.

“We watched him from the first day he came, brought here by another man. We saw that he was pure of spirit and only wanted to live in peace. After a while we decided to leave him and his family alone. We *never* let him know we were here.”

“How the heck did you do that for almost three years?” Clancy asked, again dumbfounded.

“Detective, when a Swinomish does not want to be seen, he is *not*. We left the other man alone, too, who came out here to bring supplies and tools.”

“What happened after he shot the brothers?”

“At first he exclaimed to his wife that he had killed two Japanese soldiers, but after he examined them and found that they were not soldiers, he cried.”

"Then what?"

"He and his wife took their guns and went down to where their boat was. They put the guns in the boat and set it adrift. They made a stretcher and carried the two dead men to the west end of the island, where there is flat land and little growth. The man dug two graves and buried them while the wife and two young boys watched. They prayed, then returned to the summit. And that is what happened, Detective."

"Holy shit," was all Clancy could manage.

"Holy shit, indeed, Detective."

"It all makes sense now," Clancy whispered.

"The truth, Detective, has a strange habit of making sense."

***

Clancy Robillard was not used to writing long, detailed reports. A page or two detailing forged checks or breaking-and-entering offenses were all he had done. The report he was now preparing was more like a doctoral thesis, but he was determined to include every detail, right down to the mousetrap in Eugene Traust's garage attic.

When he was nearly finished, he realized that what was missing was *evidence*. All he had was *testimony*.

On May 28th, he paid a Swinomish fisherman two-hundred dollars of his own money to take him to Pine Island. Joseph Smits and two others from the Tribal Council accompanied him.

Ashore, all four men, armed with rifles, ascended the hill that led to the summit. Clancy was both scared and exhilarated. Joseph Smits was in rare humor. "It isn't every day we have permission to kill a white man."

Clancy reminded them that they were dealing with people who might do anything not to be found, even though

Eugene Traust would now be seventy-eight, and his sons in their fifties.

At the summit, structural remains were discovered, along with tools, smashed walkie-talkies, garden plots, and a massive, elaborate tree dwelling that no one could figure out how to get to. A huge concave firepit had been dug, nearly fifteen feet deep. Terraced steps had been constructed to get down to it.

"A clever man," remarked Joseph Smits. "No passing ship would ever see a fire up here."

A nearby tunnel was discovered when Clancy tripped and fell over the plywood cover, much to the delight of Joseph Smits and his companions. The tunnel was searched but proved to be a very tight fit. "Traust, you skinny bastard," muttered Clancy. Nothing was found inside.

They descended and traveled to the west extreme of the island. "Show me the gravesites, Joseph," Clancy directed.

Joseph Smits' face grew stern. "We will not allow you to dig without a proper search warrant, Detective. This is not a treasure hunt. A person's grave is sacred."

"I understand."

The expedition had lasted all day. On the trip back, Clancy wondered what Mel Wagner's reaction would be when he learned that he had indeed solved both cases. But Joseph Smits' objection to random digging resonated in his head. There was now another step to be taken, one that could not be accomplished by the small-town police department in Garrett Cove.

***

"Richard, I need a big favor, and only you can help."

Sgt. Richard Robillard seldom heard from his younger brother. There had always been a rivalry between them, especially now that they both worked in law enforcement. "So what can the Seattle P.D. do for little old Garrett Cove, Clancy?"

"I need your people to fly over the far west quarter of Pine Island. I'm looking for the exact co-ordinates of two gravesites."

"You mean a plane with GPR, don't you?"

"Yes."

"Why don't you just go out there and dig up the graves yourselves? Surely the Garrett Cove police department can come up with a couple shovels and body bags."

Still an asshole, thought Clancy. "The Tribal Council doesn't want random digging. We can get a search warrant, but it would be a lot better if we know *exactly* where the bodies are."

"Glad to know you guys have heard of search warrants, little brother. Whose bodies do you want us big-city Seattle cops to find for you?"

"Han and Sammy Lee."

There was respect now in Richard Robillard's voice. "Very impressive. So you guys finally found those two, huh?"

"No, *us guys* didn't find them. *I* did, myself."

"You don't say. Well, I hate to burst your bubble, Clancy, but we got some budget problems for the remainder of the fiscal year. Call me in July, and I'll see what I can set up, okay?"

Clancy did as his brother directed, but was told that there were complications, and the GPR airborne unit was booked, first priority going to their own jurisdiction. This continued for months, with one excuse after another from Sgt. Richard Robillard.

1994

Clancy was well-off for a police detective. For many years, living at home, his mother refused to take a penny from him. He occasionally bought things his mom wanted for the house, but he had to practically beg her to let him help. Even after this, he was still quite well off. He was reminded of this as he made another call to his brother in April of 1994.

"Richard, this is Clancy."

"Clancy who?"

Still an asshole, came the silent reply. "Richard, I was wondering if your GPR airborne unit would be available if someone was to write a check for its services." He paused purposefully. "Or even cash."

"Well, Clancy, you may be in luck. I might be able to *rearrange* the schedule."

"I need the *exact* co-ordinates of anything on the west quarter of the island mailed directly to me at home."

"And where might that be?"

"Still an asshole," Clancy mumbled aloud. "Deal?"

"Of course, *Detective*. Always glad to help out. It will cost you four-thousand five-hundred dollars."

"I'll send it to *your* home, *Sergeant.*"

Clancy hung up, and wondered how much of the money would actually get to the plane and its crew.

***

The flyover of Pine Island occurred two weeks later. The report arrived at Clancy Robillard's residence as promised. Clancy expected to find two anomalies at the west end of the island. But there were actually *four*, the co-ordinates placing them seventy-one yards from the ocean.

Clancy wondered who else was buried there. Had Eugene Traust killed two more intruders after 1952, when the island had been truly abandoned? He had killed the Lee brothers, thinking they were enemy soldiers. Would he have done the same to anyone? Clancy didn't think so. Most likely the other graves were two members of the Traust family.

And where were the other two?

Clancy now added to his report for Mel Wagner. There would certainly be a body recovery operation now. Who they actually found out there with the Lee brothers would merely be an appendix in his report.

On May 24th he turned in two reports. Including sworn statements from the late Hugh Potts and Swinomish Tribal Council Head Joseph Smits, they covered forty-one pages, not counting the notebooks used by Eugene Traust to plan his disappearance.

Wagner was so overwhelmed, all he managed to say was, "I thought you just petered out on those cases, Clancy. I had no idea. But it all makes sense, now."

"The truth, Mel, has a strange habit of making sense."

On June 2nd, nearly every Garrett Cove off-duty police officer, along with Clancy, Mel Wagner, Garrett Cove Police Chief Franklin Gates, and a delegation of Swinomish, including Joseph Smits, landed at the west end of Pine Island. The co-ordinates from the GPR log were used, along with a yardstick, to locate a section of ground to be dug. Within two hours, four sets of remains had been unearthed. While forensic technicians tended to this grim task, police did a final search of the island.

Joseph Smits accompanied Clancy to the summit. "Sometimes," he said with a wry smile, "you people actually do the right thing."

The next day Mel Wagner and Chief Gates held a news conference. From there the story went national, earning space in newspapers across the country, as well as radio and evening news on most major networks. Clancy had asked for permission not to be at the press conference. The request was granted.

The following Monday, Wagner taped another report on the cases to use as an instructional tool on cold case investigations. Victor Tillis, who was actually making himself ill over the attention given Clancy Robillard, walked through the office and spouted, "Big deal. Just goes to show that even a blind squirrel can find a nut now and then!"

Mel Wagner turned to Tillis. "Tillis, why don't you get your ass on the street where it belongs and see if you can find a couple of nuts yourself."

As Tillis slinked out of the office, the news report was announcing that the bodies found on Pine Island were of Han and Sammy Lee, killed in 1944, and Eugene and Monica Traust, who had been dead five to seven years. In addition, it showed photos of Lawrence and Frank Traust, their sons, who were unaccounted for. The program made an educated guess, with the aid of age-enhanced sketches, as to what Lawrence, now 57, and Frank, now 55, might look like.

Wagner made sure he took care to record the show in its entirety so that Clancy could see it when he got back to the office. He was currently in Painted Rock, paying a courtesy call on Sophia Lee Darwish.

***

Virginia Beach Daily Press, June 18, 1994

'Gap Brothers' Possibly Identified

Staff at the Virginia Beach Adult Care Facility think they may finally have discovered the true identity of Mitchell Layton and his brother Dennis, believed to be in their fifties. Popularly known as the 'Gap Brothers' because of the huge gap in their knowledge of the world, the pair have lived at the facility for six years

Fluent in English and German as well as reading, writing, advanced mathematics and physics, they have no knowledge of history or world events from their own lifetime.

Psychologists have questioned them repeatedly and tried to find clues as to their upbringing, but the brothers claim they do not remember their childhood, who their family is, or how they got to Virginia Beach, causing some to theorize that they were on the run from the law. A police check turned up nothing on the two men.

The recent solving of two cold cases in Washington State two weeks ago, however, may shed new light on this mystery. Among four bodies recently unearthed on coastal Pine Island were Eugene and Monica Traust, a couple who mysteriously disappeared with their two sons Lawrence and Frank, age four and two at the time, in the weeks following the attack on Pearl Harbor.

The Trausts, estimated to have died sometime between 1987 and 1989, fled to the island to escape World War II.

Concerned social workers, along with government agencies, took the men into protective custody several years ago when they were seen in Virginia Beach wandering aimlessly. They had no identification and were hesitant to co-operate or answer any questions.

The two have lived at the facility without incident, showing an interest in the events of the second half of this century.

Extremely shy, the brothers have been observed communicating secretly over the years, leading staff to believe they have knowledge they are not sharing.

And although they continue to be uncooperative regarding their past, a recently-discovered method of identification known as DNA may reveal their true identity.

"STICK-PILE"
A Midwestern Memoir
12/10/15-12/15/15
Prelude

Sometimes you gotta go *back* to actually move forward. At least that's what I told my wife Melissa while trying to convince her to let me drive back to my hometown, about six hours from here. I left there nineteen years ago in 1965, when I was about to enter my senior year of high school, and have never been back.

There was a very special event about to occur in my boyhood hometown, and I didn't want to miss it. I was fortunate that I had kept in touch with one of my childhood friends by long distance and postcard. He was the one who had told me.

In the process of convincing Melissa, my ten-year-old son Raymond piped up and begged to go with me. Before I could even ask Melissa if Ray and I could take a road trip together, she was urging me to take him.

So we started planning our father-son getaway. The major event I mentioned was scheduled for August 10th, so we planned to leave early in the morning two days before, get there by afternoon, check in at the place we were staying, and make the rounds of the old home town.

I'm sure you've noticed that I have not mentioned any specific places by name. My friend who informed me of the event also knew I liked to document things in writing. He *strongly* suggested that I keep things as anonymous as possible. He didn't give any specifics, and I knew enough not to ask. I was grateful to be invited.

The Stick-Pile

So just what is this event I was driving six hours to a quiet little Midwestern town? It was the dismantling, or destruction of the Stick-Pile. I write it in capital letters, like a proper noun. And for us, it was a specific thing, both then and now. We would no sooner have put it in small letters than we would have written our own names in small letters.

And now, in August of 1984, the Stick-Pile was to be no more. In the nineteen years since I left, I had thought about it fondly on many occasions. But of course, land is constantly being developed; nature pushed aside.

Some corporation, I was told, had bought the land containing the Stick-Pile and the Dark Forest (more on that later) and was going to "develop" it for housing or possibly a shopping center.

So what exactly is the Stick-Pile, and why all the fuss over its impending demise? To fully appreciate this phenomenon, you need a little history. The land in question, back in my former hometown, was mostly farmland when first settled in the mid-1800's. There were fourteen farms in the area, and as the families cleared their land, they used wood from the trees for firewood, to build things they needed, or to sell to logging companies. But there was a proliferation of *sticks,* small branches, that were deemed useless. As it turned out, the farmers in the area put their heads together, and ended up bringing all their branches to this one spot, and piled them up.

As generations passed, the farms were no longer. A few of the families stayed on the land, while most moved on, selling out to new tenants.

If you ask why the original families didn't dispose of their scrap branches on their own, I simply don't have an answer. I don't think they were *trying* to create something unique. There is no written record of what possessed these otherwise normal people to do something that is now thought of as *bizarre.*

The town has grown in the nearly twenty years since I left, and now has a population of nearly fifteen thousand. Many of the amenities and luxuries of the 1980's are filtering their way in. But the Stick-Pile remained.

The Dark Forest

Earlier, I mentioned The Dark Forest (yes, this one gets capitalized, too) and stated that there would be more on it later.

Not fifty yards from the Stick-Pile was a large wooded area known as The Dark Forest. As kids, of course, lots of things scared us, most of which we outgrew. The Dark Forest was not one of them. It was as scary to me at seventeen as it was when I was five. The trees there grew so close together, and were so tall, that sunlight had to fight its way in. There was a perceptible darkness there. There were small brooks and clearings in there also, but *no* paths or trails. So few people went in there that nothing got worn down. I still couldn't tell you how big The Dark Forest was, but the railroad tracks that cut through town ran along one edge of it. It was as big as the distance between our town and the next town.

And if The Dark Forest wasn't scary enough: on October 30, 1951, an eight-year-old girl named Joanne Neddles was seen by friends going into The Dark Forest. She was never seen again. I was a toddler at the time, and I don't remember it, but it was a story that we were all made aware of as we grew. Police from our town and the next claim they searched every inch of The Dark Forest.

Posters were put up with her description, and that she was wearing pink gloves, hat, and scarf, gifts from her grandparents. Parents did not let their kids out of the yard for over a week, fearing a kidnapper.

Every hobo (yes, we had hobos back then) and derelict in a ten-mile area were hauled into the police station and interrogated. There was one hobo who actually had a crude shack out in the middle of The Dark Forest. The police hounded him constantly, brought him in several times.

He was eventually released, but story has it that he had been traumatized by being a suspect. He abandoned his shack and rode the rails from then on. He was found dead near some railroad tracks about a hundred miles from here seven years later. *That,* I do remember.

Death was still fairly new to me in 1958, and I remember asking my father how he died.

"Hobo-itis," he replied.

I'm still not sure what he meant.

I'm told Joanne's parents still live in town. Growing up, I used to see Joanne's grandmother occasionally. She always carried a rag doll they were going to give her for her birthday, about two weeks after she disappeared. She hugged it, talked to it, everything.

Boy, the things grief can do to you, huh?

The Ride Over

With most ten-year-olds, a six hour car ride would be an ordeal. Not so with my son, Raymond Andrew Calloway. I wanted to name him Devon, after me, but Melissa convinced me to "let him have his own identity."

Not to brag, but Ray is very unique. His likes and dislikes are normal for his age, but when it comes to one-on-one conversation, he is like a miniature adult.

He knew very little of the story of the Stick-Pile and The Dark Forest, and in the first half-hour of our drive I had given him the history of it and the terrible disappearance of Joanne Neddles. Questions rushed out of him.

"They *never* found the girl?"

"No."

"Did the kids back then stay out of The Dark Forest after that?"

"Pretty much."

"They just played at the Stick-Pile from then on?"

"Actually, Ray, the kids that grew up ahead of me never played on the Stick-Pile to begin with."

"Why not?"

"I'm not really sure. They did other things, I guess." I had to think a little. "Ray, the older kids grew up in a different world than we did. I don't think they saw the Stick-Pile as a place to play, or pretend."

"Then what was it to them?"

"I think they saw it as a huge pile of sticks that they had been told to stay off of and stay away from." I paused, trying to get a phrase that would summarize it. "I don't think they had the *imagination* that we did."

He thought a moment, trying to process the concept. "Oh," he finally said.

There was a lull, and then a new round of questions started, mostly about the town itself. I did the best I could with what I remembered, and got a laugh when I told him how both the library and high school burned down within a year of each other.

"Somebody in your town hate learning, Dad?"

"Could be, Ray. They never found out the cause of either of those fires."

He pressed on, asking about town history, and if we would find anything interesting in the library, then paused. "They *did* rebuild it, didn't they?"

"Of course. *And* the high school. I went there through junior year. But I don't think you'll find anything interesting."

"Why not?"

"They hadn't really foreseen it *becoming* a town, I guess."

"Where are we staying, again?"

"The Meadowview Bed and Breakfast. It was actually where one of my friends lived back then, but the family moved, and some older people from back east bought it and made it into an overnight place for travelers."

There was another lull, so I tried to change the subject over to football, which Ray loved. "So who do you think will be in the Super Bowl this year, Ray?"

"Forty-Niners and Dolphins," he said without hesitation.

"Really?"

"You'll see. 'Niners and Dolphins."

"Okay, let's say it's "Niners and Dolphins. Who wins?"

"The 'Niners, easily. By three touchdowns."

Kids, right?

(I just realized I slipped up and named the Meadowview Bed and Breakfast, but I don't think it's any big deal. My friend just didn't want any geographical *locations* named, and as I already said, was *very* insistent on that point. It's not like somebody will ever be able to type in "Meadowview Bed and Breakfast" on a computer and find the old town.)

The Meadowview

It was surreal, to say the least, entering the old home town, driving on roads I had not seen in nearly twenty years. Ray suddenly turned into a five-year-old, asking if we were there yet seemingly every thirty seconds.

I had walked and driven on these streets so long ago. We were a good three miles from the Stick-Pile, and I didn't want to go there just yet. I headed west and found the Meadowview with no problem. Even that didn't seem right. The large gray house was now white, with a statue of a deer in front. The driveway had been extended, and there was a small white cottage in back. Four cars were parked in a paved area between the garage and the cottage.

After I parked, Ray and I got our bags, and feeling like big-time travelers, entered the front door of the house where my friend Tommy Lind once lived. The seventyish couple was very friendly, asking what we were doing in the area.

"I grew up here. Moved away nineteen years ago."

"So what brings you back to your old stomping grounds?" the old gent asked. He had a definite New England accent.

"The Stick-Pile."

His face was blank for a second. "Oh, the huge mound of branches they're gonna finally get rid of."

"The huge mound of branches is called the *Stick-Pile.*" My face felt hot and red.

"Well," he said, "I'm sure it has special meaning for you."

I just stared at the floor.

"Here's your key. Number four. Upstairs, first room on the left. There's a community bathroom there. You can park anywhere in back. My wife and I live in the small house back there. We have a common area in the next room. Magazines, TV, and a phone. Make yourself at home. We serve breakfast from eight to nine."

"What do you have for breakfast?" asked Ray. I had almost forgotten he was standing right next to me.

"Oh, we usually serve bacon and eggs. And coffee."

Now *Ray* was staring at the floor. He hated bacon and eggs and didn't drink coffee.

We got to our room and unpacked our few belongings.

"What's the plan, Dad?" Ray asked. "We gonna go see the Stick-Pile and The Dark Forest?"

"I gotta make a call to my old friend, the one that told me about this. He'll come over and take us on a tour of the old town."

"Sounds good. What's his name?"

I had to think a moment. "Kenny Carpwell. I don't think I had ever used his actual last name.

Kenny arrived at the Meadowview a few minutes later. After our initial handshake, we stood back and took a long look at each other. He had sandy-blond hair and now had a bushy moustache. But he was still "Crapwell" to me. He was my best friend. Heck, he was *everybody's* best friend in those days. Just one of those people you couldn't help liking more than anyone else. I introduced him to my son, and while they shook hands, asked if he could just leave work on a Wednesday afternoon.

"No problem, you old rattlesnake. I own the biggest car repair shop in the county. I can take off any time I have to."

Yes, he called me an "old rattlesnake." He got it from a *Maypo* ad on TV. *Maypo* was an oatmeal cereal, sickeningly sweet, but oddly popular back then. I tried it once and nearly threw up in my bowl. Kenny loved the stuff.

We called him "Crapwell," a juxtaposition of the letters in his last name. It was used so often that there were times I went over his house to get him, and his mother would yell, 'Hey, Crapwell, Devon's here.'

Ray and I followed Kenny to his car, a dark red Toyota, and off we went. He took me to the center of town first, and I got to see the new version of the old town. A few old buildings were gone, with new ones in their place, and the usual refurbished look one might expect after nearly twenty years.

"That the high school you went to, Dad?" asked Ray.

"Yeah, that's it. Let's go over to Schibi Road," I suggested. My old house was there.

Kenny sighed, then looked over at me. "Sure thing," he said.

We turned off Centervale Lane onto Schibi Road. About halfway down, he slowed, then stopped.

There was a small apartment building where my house had once been. A lady was sitting on her porch, looking intently at the strange car in front of her building.

"Sorry, Devon," Kenny said softly. "Things change, you know."

"How long has *this* been here?" I asked, trying not to show my dismay.

"About eight years or so. The people you sold your house to moved to Florida, and some developer bought it and threw up this building."

"Yeah, 'threw up' is the word for it."

Kenny slapped my shoulder. "Waddaya say we head over to the greatest place we ever knew?"

"Yes!" Ray hissed from the back seat, making a victorious fist. "The *Stick-Pile!"*

Miscellany

Before I bring you to the Stick-Pile, I'm going to take a break from events as they unfolded August 8th, and mention some things that Kenny and I had talked about, as well as some other stuff I had told Ray.

First off, I was the only one from the old neighborhood invited back for the removal of the Stick-Pile. Everyone else was long gone, or lived nearby.

It was interesting how it was decided to get rid of the Stick-Pile. The first proposal was to remove it and dump it somewhere else out in the middle of nowhere.

"Wouldn't that just create *another* Stick-Pile?" Ray asked.

"Didn't make sense to you either, huh?" I replied.

At some point, the people involved realized that you could not get *any* type of machine on top of it, so much of the dismantling would have to be done by hand, with loaders and dump trucks at ground level.

It's time to tell you how gigantic the Stick-Pile actually was. As kids, we used to measure it constantly in between our many adventures there. The Stick-Pile was **131 feet long, just over 67 feet wide, and at its top was 17 feet, 3 inches high.**

It was sloped, so there was little danger of actually falling off, but you could roll all the way down, theoretically. What usually happened was you got caught in something and never got all the way to ground level.

Because of its sloping nature, it was easy to climb. We found it best to use a crawling motion. You could scale it in less than a minute, and would find yourself nearly two stories up, walking on a spongy-type surface. My first impression was that it was like being in another dimension.

I sometimes wondered, as a teenager, if maybe the town should have put up a billboard advertising it: *World's Largest Stick-Pile,* like tourist attractions they have in many small towns in the Midwest. But then we wouldn't have been allowed to play on it, so I guess it was for the best.

Old Man Parker was the grandfather of one of our friends, John Parker. He seemed to be the only adult who was willing to talk about the Stick-Pile. In my childhood he was in his late 60's, and whenever we asked him about the Stick-Pile, he rambled on about 'The Depression.'

We knew he wasn't right in the head anymore. He had been in combat in World War I and was never the same when he came back. We tried to get him to tell us anything he knew about the Stick-Pile. But whenever we asked, his eyes got wide and he would say, 'Yeah, the Great Depression.' We all knew what *that* was, our parents having lived through it as kids. So the only thing we heard from any adult back then about the Stick-Pile didn't even have anything to *do* with it.

I asked Kenny if he was still around, and surprisingly, he was. Still lived in the same house with his now-grown grandson John, who took care of him as best he could. Good old John Parker.

The Stick-Pile Revisited

I wish I could say that going to the Stick-Pile that afternoon warmed my heart with fond memories. But that was not the case. For one thing, you could almost *drive* up to it now, on one of the many new roads. The famous "jumping tree" was gone. In those days there was a large tree about twenty feet from the Stick-Pile. If you climbed nearly all the way up, and had the nerve to edge out on this one branch, you would be right *over* the lower part of the Stick-Pile.

It was kind of risky, since there wasn't a lot to cushion your twenty foot drop, but many of us did it anyway. Over and over.

One of those orange and gray construction site fences surrounded it, the kind that if you lean on it, it bends down nearly to the ground.

Kenny was strangely quiet. I looked over at Ray to see his reaction. He had a transfixed stare on his face. He finally spoke. "I thought it would be a lot . . ."

"Bigger?" I said, further disappointed.

"No, *smaller*. This is the most . . . *immense* thing I ever saw. Dad, this is unreal. You guys actually *played* up there?"

Kenny and I smiled with pride. "That's right, Ray," I said.

I have to admit, that construction fence seemed to give the Stick-Pile an aura of significance, like something in a museum.

In the distance stood The Dark Forest, looking as ominous as ever.

Interlude (August 9th)

Kenny drove us back to the Meadowview, and told us the dismantling would be at 9:00 on Friday morning. He had business to attend to the next day, and asked if we could manage on our own.

"Of course, Crapwell. Waddaya think? I got my car, I got my son, I got my old town. What else would I need?"

He gave me a wistful smile. "How about a time machine?"

There was next to nothing of interest to see or do in the town that Thursday. Ray and I drove around, ate dinner in a diner that wasn't there in the sixties, and took another trip to the Stick-Pile. Even that wasn't fulfilling. The beauty of the Stick-Pile was being *on* it, not *looking* at it.

The greatness of the Stick-Pile lay in *what we did there, what happened there,* and most of all, *who was there with me.*

Dramatis Personae

There were probably a couple dozen kids that played regularly at the Stick-Pile, and most of them I can see in my mind, even if I no longer have a name to put with the face. There were a few that still stood out in my memory.

Kim DeAngelini was the tomboy of the group. She played baseball and football with us, and whenever there was a massive group bike ride, she was there. She handled herself on the Stick-Pile pretty well; no screams or shrieks when things got a little hairy up on top. She *never* played basketball with us, seemed to avoid it noticeably. My theory is that when she was little somebody hit her in the face with a basketball.

Hassan Tribek was a Moroccan kid, born in Tangiers but raised in England. We always kidded him about his name and being foreign. This was when you could do that without being accused of a hate crime. He wasn't good at American sports, but he was a whiz with a soccer ball. We would kick one around once in a while just to shut him up, but even then we called soccer "dirt hockey." Again, no counselors or social agencies were called in, nor did any of us have to undergo sensitivity training. He was a good guy and could speak five languages, *none* of them fluently. He moved back to England shortly after I left.

Louis Farnham was an odd-ball who tried to fit in, but never quite did. He missed school two or three days a week, saying he was 'sick.' He would always return with all his assignments completed. We called him "P. T. Farnham," both as a play on the circus guy P. T. Barnum and short for "Part-Time" because of his erratic attendance. He *participated* at the Stick-Pile, but never seemed really *into* it.

Gary Nowlen was the one kid who I thought would become famous. He lived in his own imaginary world when he wasn't up on the Stick-Pile. He wrote these amazing, creative stories about this made-up town, Garyville, where he was the mayor. The stories involved all kinds of conflicts: natural disasters, monsters, alien invaders, and criminals, among other things. By the end of the story he had solved the problem and was the hero.

He also had stories of a superhero he had created: "Chemical Man." A timid shoe store clerk with a chemistry background, Chemical Man had created pills to cover any situation a hero would need. One pill made him fireproof, one made him super fast, one made him invisible, etc. It was very entertaining, I'm not kidding.

Like Hassan Tribek, he was still around when I left, but in the time since, no one knows what became of him.

To this day, when I see something creative or weird on TV, I always check the credits for the line, '*Based on the story by Gary Nowlen.*'

The most memorable character was a chubby blond kid named Ainsley Tourloupis. With a last name like that why did his parents paint a target on him with the first name 'Ainsley?' This kid was paranoid about dying. Any bump, bruise or scratch he got and the first words out of his mouth were 'Am I gonna die?' We just scoffed at him and said, 'Yes, you are.'

The funniest story I ever heard involved Ainsley. His parents wanted him to get in with the upper crust, so they used to drive him to this country club about forty miles away so he could caddy and make connections. One day greed got the better of him and he offered to caddy for two guys at once. Their bags were heavy, and old Ains' was having a hellava time even walking. There was one hole where you had to cross a bridge over this stream. There were no railings, and that, of course, is where Ainsley lost his balance and fell. God, were those two guys *pissed.* Ainsley had to clean and dry everything. The two men actually finished the round, but refused to pay him for falling in the water with their bags and clubs. I picture that and I laugh till I cry.

Carl and Joe (I *cannot* remember either of their last names) were the daredevils of the group. They started jumping off the tree onto the Stick-Pile. They also started the "dives" *off* the Stick-Pile onto the bottom branches, where there was less cushion, and you had a pretty fair chance of getting hurt. One time Joe landed near the bottom, and a stick caught him just above his eye. Blood was everywhere. Carl yelled that it was an "emergency," so Jimmy Masselli went over to the tree and brought back a piece of rope. (explanation later) We all laughed so hard, even Joe, that we forgot all about the injury.

And to Tommy Lind, John Parker, Augie Notte, Vincent Dibben, Jack Conley, the Sileo brothers, Ron Yurashes, Lenny Lovetere, Dave Daigle, Ken Carpwell and many others, it was great to have made your friendship at the Stick-Pile.

The Stick-Pile Revue

It was a strange feeling up there on the Stick-Pile. Like I said, it was best to crawl to the top, as it was a gradual slope to the summit. One odd characteristic was that at the very bottom, the sticks just mushroomed out another ten or fifteen feet, like a welcome mat.

Once up there, we did whatever we felt like. There were days we ran around up there. There was the aforementioned tree jumping, and the dives off, usually confined to those who had little regard for their own safety. We wrestled, had chicken fights, races, you name it. Every once in a while we would have a list of events, almost like a decathlon. The "Stick-Pile Olympics." We even played games of tackle football.

One day we tried to get our bikes up there. It was impossible. We gave up trying after a few tries, all except Carl, the daredevil. He must have spent almost an hour trying to get his bike up there; pushing it, dragging it, throwing it, etc. The other activity we could not do up there was baseball. We tried a couple times, and lost the balls. It was like they got swallowed up.

So we lost baseballs in there, and somewhere inside we figured it was *possible* for one of *us* to go down, too. But we made allowances. You see, the Stick-Pile was always changing slightly. You figure, one section got a lot of weight on it, and the *properties* of one area might become firmer or even more brittle.

We lost a football in there one day. It went down about two or three feet and we couldn't reach it. How did we get it out? *We used a STICK.* There were *plenty* of them around.

The scariest thing that ever happened was the day Peter Sileo dropped through a "fragile" area. He had to have been six feet below us, screaming for his brother John to go get his parents. We couldn't have *that.* We kept John with us, while Jack Conley and Lenny Lovetere ran to Lenny's house and came back with a rope. We lowered the rope to Peter, and had him out in no time. We all swore each other to secrecy, of course. It was decided then and there that we would keep the rope over by the jumping tree "in case of emergency." Now you see why it was so damn funny when Joe was bleeding all over the place and Carl yelled 'Emergency!' and Jim Masselli went and got the rope. It *did* serve a purpose, though. Joe bled all over *it* instead of ruining his handkerchief.

The 'Why' Of It All

Why was the Stick-Pile so important to us? After all, it *was* just a huge pile of sticks where we did things we could do other places, like the road, a playground, or somebody's back yard.

To us, the Stick-Pile was some kind of magical phenomenon, a metaphysical marvel. Is that the right word? I don't know. It defied all the rules of the way things *were,* or were *supposed* to be.

We pretended to walk on another planet years before the first men walked on the Moon. When I watched Neil Armstrong and Buzz Aldrin that July night in 1969, I was as much in awe and wonder as anyone. But in the deepest recesses of my being, a part of me was saying, 'I know *exactly* how you guys feel.

Maybe I'm the only one who would put it this way, but I sometimes viewed the Stick-Pile as a gentle monster who could kill us at will if it chose to, but instead chose to share itself with us, and give us experiences and friendships to last a lifetime. Like I said, maybe it's just me.

August 10th: Surrender and Revelation

If you're into the logistics of the Stick-Pile dismantling, the branches were being conveyed to a wood pulp plant upstate. There were uses for them that didn't exist years ago. So the company that bought the land, Midwest Acquisitions Incorporated, was going to make a decent profit.

Ray and I arrived at about 8:30, as the crew was getting their machines into position. Little by little, people started showing up, most of them of the age that had played on the Stick-Pile until it was fenced off months back. Kenny found us and stood by our side. My throat and eyes felt funny. *Time to grow up, Devon,* I kept telling myself.

An attractive mid-thirties woman came over to Kenny, and he pointed at me. She looked, her face blossoming into a smile.

"Devon Calloway! Is that you?"

"Well, it's either me or Rory Glover," I joked. Rory and I were the only black kids in the neighborhood at that time.

It was Kim DeAngelini, of course. She laughed, and we exchanged encapsulated bios. She was Kim Webber now, married with two kids, who were at the lake with her husband. I commended her for attending and complimented her on the great athlete she had been.

"Except for basketball," I added. "We couldn't get you near a basketball."

"Funny thing," she said. "When I was five my cousin hit me in the face with a basketball."

(NAILED IT!)

The workmen started promptly at nine, a dozen or more throwing down branches which were loaded onto huge dump trucks, which took off for their storage facility nearby. Several loaders were brought in, and the guys on top were tossing branches down at a high rate of speed.

I thought it would be sad, but it was actually kind of boring. Kenny and I started walking around, visiting people from my past. It was turning into more of a high school reunion than anything else. Of course, *I* was easily remembered by almost everyone, while Kenny had to identify several former friends.

At the edge of the crowd of nearly two-hundred stood a man in a dark sport coat and gray slacks. *Him,* I recognized right away. I grabbed Kenny and strode over to say hello.

"Louis Farnham!" I said, extending my hand. "I'm . . ."

"Devon Calloway," he said, smiling shyly and returning my handshake.

At least he didn't think I was Rory Glover.

"P. T. Farnham," I said, laughing. "Come to say goodbye to the Stick-Pile?"

"Actually, I'm supervising its removal."

Kenny and I stared at him blankly.

"I'm Executive Vice-President of Midwest Acquisitions. I'm responsible for making sure everything goes smoothly for however long it takes to clear this."

'This?' Louis referring to the Stick-Pile as 'this' ticked me off.

"Executive Vice-President, huh? I bet you have to show up *every day* for that job, huh, 'P. T.'?"

He looked embarrassed and uncomfortable. "C'mon with me, guys," he said. We followed him over to the fencing as he whispered something to the foreman.

The foreman raised his arms and yelled out, "Midwest Acquisitions would like to give anyone who wants one a small piece of the Stick-Pile as a remembrance."

For the next twenty minutes, he did just that. I got four pieces.

Ray was getting bored. "Dad, if we go around all the machines, we can go see The Dark Forest."

"That is *not* happening!" End of discussion.

Amazingly, the Stick-Pile was nearly at ground level. And it hit me, for some reason. The mighty Stick-Pile, the gentle monster from my youth, had been forced to surrender. It felt like a living thing was being *diminished,* even *killed.* I looked around. Kenny stared at the ground, biting his lip. Kim DeAngelini brushed away tears with both hands.

I put an arm around her shoulder. "Almost as bad as getting hit in the face with a basketball." She laughed through her tears.

A husky, blond guy with yellow-tinted sunglasses had come up to me suddenly.

"Rory Glover?" he asked.

"No," I said, sighing. "Devon Calloway."

"Oh, okay. I remember you. Long time no see. How you been?"

"Fine, thanks. And you are . . .?"

"Fred Tourloupis. I grew up here, too."

I was laughing inside as I asked, "You related to *Ainsley* Tourloupis?"

"That's *me!* I use my middle name, now."

Wise choice, I thought. "So what do you do now, uh, *Fred?*"

"I'm the golf pro at (name omitted) Country Club."

I stifled a laugh, again picturing him falling off the bridge with two huge golf bags. "So all that caddying back then paid off, huh?"

"I guess it did. Well, gotta get back to the wife. Nice seeing you again, Rory." He rushed off.

"I'm not . . ." Ah, never mind.

They were *at* ground level now, and the mat of sticks that had spread out from the Stick-Pile was being gathered up. "Oh, Christ!" yelled one of the workers. Everyone craned to see what the problem was. Because of the fencing and workers in our sightline, we could not see anything on our side. So we looked *across* at the other side. With all the "welcome mat" branches gone, it was obvious. *The **workers** were at ground level, but the **Stick-Pile kept going BELOW ground level.*** It was covering a huge hole.

"Maybe *that's* why they piled them up *here,"* offered Kenny.

I overheard the foreman, who was on a walkie-talkie with someone, probably P. T. Farnham. "There's a huge God damn depression where we thought the bottom of this pile was. This could take another day, sir."

Did he say 'depression?'

Kenny and I looked at each other. "Old Man Parker," we said at the same time. The guy might not have had all his marbles, but he actually *knew* that the Stick-Pile covered a huge dip in the land. A 'Great Depression.'

The work went slower now, but we had renewed interest. Everyone wondered how deep the depression was. Ladders and pulleys with large baskets attached were now being used. It got to the point that afternoon where the workers on the other side of the Stick-Pile were below eye level.

At about 2 P.M. the foreman was handed something from the crew down below. He held up two incredibly old baseballs. "These belong to anyone?" he said, laughing.

About ninety people raised their hands. He tossed them into the crowd.

I poked Kim. "I wonder if they'll find a basketball down there."

"Will you please stop with that?" she replied, smiling in spite of herself.

Somewhere around 2:25 we heard an exited shout from down below. Workers on the rim looked down, and the foreman ordered everyone out of the hole. None of us could figure out what the hell was going on. When the crew came out, one held up a pink hat. There were a few gasps, but most of us just stood with an unbelieving, stunned expression.

Aftermath

The police were called, and everyone had to clear out. I drove to Kenny's auto-repair shop, where we spent the rest of the afternoon. The old town had doubled in size, but it still had that small-town mentality. Rumors, theories, and facts spread through the community. Customers at Kenny's place had their share of them.

Facts: the pink scarf was found shortly after. Just below it, the nearly intact skeletal remains of Joanne Neddles, still wearing what was left of her pink gloves.

Rumors and theories: 1) the old hobo *had* killed Joanne and used the Stick-Pile to hide her body. 2) She had fallen in a semi-bog on the edge of the Stick-Pile (it could not be determined if there had been such a thing) and had suffocated, with the forces of gravity sucking her into the Stick-Pile. (I repute both these theories. I *know* what probably happened.)

You had to understand the nature of kids, and dealing with *the forbidden,* the Stick-Pile. Joanne Neddles and her schoolmates had been warned their entire lives to stay away from the Stick-Pile. But it's a late October afternoon, the day before Halloween, and cute, innocent Joanne wants a scary adventure to tell her friends. After a brief foray into The Dark Forest, she goes up on the Stick-Pile, and somehow falls through. It would have had different properties back in 1951 because it had never been tamped down, and would have been much more brittle and unpredictable. She panics, thrashes around, and that causes the branches beneath her to give way, and she sinks even lower. It became a fatal, repeated progression: panic, sticks breaking, sinking lower, more panic, more sticks breaking, etc.

I will never believe it was anything else.

Her parents were called, and identified the clothing after viewing the skeletal remains.

An autopsy would not turn up any traumatic injuries. The police would locate and question as many of her friends and acquaintances as they could, including the girls who said they saw Joanne going into The Dark Forest that Tuesday afternoon. The police were left with a "death by accident or misadventure" label on their oldest unsolved case. But like I said, I could have solved it for them.

Several unfortunate circumstances led to Joanne Neddles' disappearance becoming a tragedy. Kids did not play on the Stick-Pile back then, so there was no one around the next day, or *any* day, to hear any possible cries for help. (All children were kept at home, besides, due to the general panic of a possible kidnapping.) No one thought to search at or near the Stick-Pile, as authorities and volunteers were deep in The Dark Forest, busy questioning the vagabond nomads who rode the rails in those days. And finally, there was no one to report a terrible odor that would have arisen from the Stick-Pile in the days that followed.

Epilogue

The ancient Greeks would have said that poor little Joanne was a sacrifice. In return for her life, we would all be safe from the Stick-Pile. A creepy, unsavory thought, considering the fun we had there, while thirty-five feet below us lay Joanne Neddles.

There was a special edition of the town newspaper that afternoon, which included photos of Joanne Neddles standing by the family Christmas tree in 1950, and her parents going into the hospital to identify her clothing.

An out-of-towner, I was not consulted. The story eventually reached all one-hundred-plus counties in our state, which made all the anonymity I exercised unnecessary. But, like I said, I could have put it all to rest in a few short sentences. I'm sure that in time, someone else will figure it out.

Kenny and I said our good-byes later that day, and promised to keep in touch. He also said he would let me know what "progress" was being made in the case. I told him that wouldn't be necessary.

The ride home was very quiet. Ray turned to me several times as though he had something to say, but nothing ever came out. He held one of the pieces of the Stick-Pile in his fingers, and I could hear him whispering to himself.

In another week or so, when the investigation was done, they would finish taking away the Stick-Pile, and that would be that.

I thought about the Stick-Pile the entire drive home.

Funny, the things you hold on to.

"UNSCATHED"
Aug. – Sep. 2017

Gilbert Moody and Tony Cooke peered at the dark clouds rolling their way from the dugout at Killiany Field.

"Your mother was right," said Gilbert, an eleven-year-old with long brownish hair. "I guess that's why she made such a fuss."

"By afternoon all the big kids will be here and we won't even get on the field," Tony replied with conviction. "At least now we can pitch to each other. The guy who hits goes and gets the balls, then he pitches to the other guy."

"Sounds like an *awful* lot of trouble just to hit a few balls."

"Never mind," Cooke snapped. "Let's just get out there before we get drenched."

"I'm hittin' first." Gilbert grabbed the two bats they had brought and ascended the dugout steps, squinting at the sky where the sun had emerged from the blackening clouds.

Both youngsters now looked toward the sound that had suddenly taken precedence over nearby birds and insects. Somewhere among the blackness that now dominated the California sky came the sound of an engine; an engine straining to operate: cutting out intermittently, and restarting, seemingly under protest, sputtering and laboring.

"Is that a plane up there?" Tony asked, nervously fanning his hand through his brown crew cut.

"Sounds like it," said Gilbert. "I think it has engine trouble."

The sputtering sound now grew louder. As the two eleven-year-olds watched and listened, a white, single engine Cessna 150B appeared suddenly through the cloud cover, then immediately rose once again, engulfed by the dark sky.

"Holy shit!" shrieked Gilbert. "Did you see that?"

A shocked Tony Cooke moved involuntarily forward. "Think it's gonna crash?" he asked.

The plane's stricken engine faded into the distance. The boys stood still, straining to listen. Less than a minute later they could hear it getting louder, coming right towards them.

"I think he's looking for a place to crash land!" shouted Gilbert.

"The outfield!" yelled Tony. "I bet he tries to land in the outfield!"

"What the hell do we do? He might miss the outfield and land *here!*"

The plane appeared again, facing them, in a downward arc towards center field. A line of smoke was now visible from the tail.

"It's on fire!" shouted Gilbert.

The plane rose with a jerk, and circled again, heading west, its pilot obviously determining that there was not enough room in the small field for a safe landing.

"He's heading towards the state park," shouted Gilbert.

"That's almost two miles," Tony said softly. "He'll never make it."

"C'mon!" Gilbert dropped the bats, grabbed Tony by the arm, and started running towards a path in the woods beyond left field. The three baseballs Tony held joined the bats on the infield grass. Tony took off his glove and tossed it over his head as they ran.

As they ran on the path they stumbled often, falling several times. Looking up, trying to follow the sound of the engine, they collided with tree stumps, tripped over vines, and ran into pricker patches. At the end of the path was a hilly clearing. The boys emerged, dirty, disheveled, with their legs and arms a mass of bloody scratches.

They stopped and looked up, the sputtering engine still audible. Like a large white bird swooping down, the

Cessna plunged from the overcast a quarter mile ahead of them. Both boys stood dumbfounded as the plane and a steady rain fell to earth. A loud, dull thud was heard. All of nature around them was silent, except for the sound of the rain.

. . .

Eleven-year-olds often put themselves at the center of a universe of their own creation. Gilbert Moody and Tony Cooke were by no means the only people who saw or heard the small white Cessna develop engine trouble, drop down, rise, circle franticly, and eventually crash on a small hillside near a wooded area, halfway between Killiany Field and Gauthier State Park in northern California.

Motorists along Route 571, campers, and dozens of people in Gauthier State Park saw and heard the same sequence. Many rushed toward what they believed to be the crash site.

Some abandoned their cars and ran nearly a mile uphill through brush, some dashed through woods bordering the state park. The first arrival was a Sanitation Department worker, Tom Lobracko, aged 48. He had pulled his pickup over on Route 571 and dashed uphill toward the crash site. A distance runner most of his adult life, the uphill mile was merely a moderate workout for him, and not the arduous trek it proved to be for most of the twenty-seven souls converging on the spot.

Lobracko crested a final ridge and saw the ruined Cessna, its tail broken, folded into a rocky hillside. It was no longer smoking, mostly due to a steady rain that now fell. On a large smooth ledge about fifty feet away sat three boys, ten or eleven years old. One had his arms around his knees and shook with silent sobs. The other two stared at him, eyes wide.

Lobracko ran first to the two wide-eyed boys. "You guys all right? You got some scratches on you but that looks like it."

"We weren't *in* the plane," one of them answered. *"He* was. We got all scratched and dirty running here from the baseball field."

Lobracko now fixed his attention on the third boy. An inner voice yelled to him: *How could **this** kid have been on the plane? There's not a mark on him!*

From the north and east of the crash site people now stumbled out of the woods or up the hill. A woman in her late thirties, dressed for an outing, identified herself as Lila Radocy, an RN. She immediately went to Gilbert and Tony and started a preliminary examination, asking them where they hurt, urging them to lie down, and asking them questions about the crash.

Gilbert looked at her, wide-eyed. "We weren't *in* the plane. *He* was."

Nurse Radocy turned to the third boy, still sobbing, silently. She now asked him about *his* injuries. He shook his head violently and pointed to the plane, holding up two fingers.

"There's two other people on the plane?" she asked.

He nodded, still sobbing.

By now at least a dozen people were nearby, as the rain abated to a soft sprinkle. Two men grabbed the half-open hatch and stepped inside, then exited immediately. They looked at the grief-stricken boy, then at the others. One shook his head solemnly.

"God, it's awful," the other said in a stage whisper.

A man who identified himself as an EMT also entered the plane. He remained inside for a few minutes before exiting. He came over to the boys sitting on the ledge. "I don't know how you boys survived this. The grace of God, I guess."

"We weren't *on* the plane," explained Gilbert Moody for the third time. "Just *him!*"

"Christ," said the EMT, "he hasn't got as much as a bump or bruise on him. He's . . . *unscathed!*"

The scene was soon awash in onlookers, emergency crews, and several reporters, who questioned, among others, Gilbert Moody and Tony Cooke, the first on the scene, nurse Lila Radocy, Tom Lobracko and an unnamed EMT. The boy who survived the crash uninjured did not speak, shaking his head when questioned.

. . .

The *Daily Echo's* front page headline the next morning read, *Husband and Wife Killed in Crash; Son Unscathed.* The article gave the couple's names as Robert and Dorothy Shumter of nearby Follento, on their way to visit Robert Shumter's parents. The cause of the crash was under investigation, but bad weather or engine failure was suspected. Nearly half the article focused on the survivor, Michael Shumter, age ten, who had walked away from the crash without so much as a scratch. It was reported that although seemingly unhurt, Michael was badly traumatized by the incident and had not spoken a word the entire time he was at the hospital, undergoing a thorough medical check, which found absolutely no injuries of any kind.

When his grandparents came to get him the next day, he ran to them and indicated by pointing to the nearby elevator that he wanted to leave. He still had not spoken a word.

. . .

A small plane crash with two fatalities is not that uncommon. In most areas of the country there are several in a year. Some of them have survivors who *are* able to walk away reasonably unharmed. But *no one* had ever heard of a crash where people died horribly and another came out of it . . . *unscathed.*

Thus began the groundswell of publicity and follow-up stories on the crash of a Cessna on August 27th, 2017, and the miraculous story of Michael Shumter, age ten.

The story was soon picked up by many television stations across the country. The dual focus of these stories was the almost unbelievable fact that Michael Shumter had come away from the crash without as much as a scratch, and that he had not spoken a word since, now nearly a week later. He was currently living at the home of his paternal grandparents, Morris and Helena Shumter.

A multitude of requests for interviews with the boy were turned away by his grandparents, who stated that Michael had not recovered from the trauma of the accident and did not seem to be able to speak, although he could communicate in other ways.

Follow-up sessions with psychologists and psychiatrists had yielded nothing; the boy either did not answer their questions on the notepad they had given him, or simply refused to with a shake of his head.

He was given a battery of intelligence, psychology, and emotional exams, all of which he passed easily. There was, apparently, no physical damage to his learning or comprehensive abilities. It was determined, at last, that he was suffering an extreme traumatic after-effect of the crash.

As for Gilbert Moody and Tony Cooke, they had a level of notoriety that they could   never have achieved with their typical eleven-year-old lives. Peers and adults alike came up to them and asked what it had been like to be the first on the scene of this miraculous event. They seemed to revel in the retelling of the time sequence that morning, even adding how they had come out of the woods so beaten-up that no fewer than three adults assumed *they* had been on the doomed plane.

The new school year began a couple of days later. Gilbert and Tony found themselves the co-stars of their sixth grade class at the Green Hollow Elementary School. One new member of the student body, who had been whisked into the building a half hour after the opening bell, sat in a small conference room with a one-on-one tutor, Mrs. Greene. At noon, a cafeteria meal was delivered by Miss Failla, who took over the academics for the remainder of the day. Fifteen minutes before the final bell, Michael Shumter was quickly escorted from the building into the waiting car of his grandparents.

While this kept the curiosity seekers away, and allowed Michael, an above-average student to get specialized instruction, it may have been the worst-kept secret in the history of secrets. So many well-meaning students happened to wander by Room 117 that construction paper was put over the oblong rectangular piece of glass on the door.

And it wasn't long before students, including Gilbert and Tony, had gotten a fix on Michael Shumter's arrival and departure times. To his credit, Michael took the staring in stride, and when a few kids worked up the nerve to yell 'Hi, Michael' and other encouraging words to him, he acknowledged them with a wave and a shy smile.

His tutoring progressed nicely; Michael communicating with Mrs. Greene and Miss Failla by pointing, nodding, and writing short notes on a small erasable white board. An end-of-the-month assessment was made and it was determined that he was exactly where he should be in English and history, and was at the very top end in math and science.

Over the next four weeks there came a dramatic increase in his inclusion into the normal flow of the school day. The first such immersion was a weekly gym class, where Michael participated in whatever ball and cone game was being played. Next came recess on the playground, where he either participated in running games or watched with interest.

Another noteworthy incident occurred here, when one day he walked up behind Gilbert and Tony and put a hand on each of their shoulders. He smiled an appreciative smile, seemingly in gratitude of their effort on that August 27th. Gilbert and Tony turned and clapped him on the back, returning the gesture of friendship.

. . .

Four months passed. Michael Shumter was gradually placed in all the classes he normally would have been in, including the highest group in math and science. The school made every effort to place him, wherever possible, in classes with Gilbert or Tony, since he had shown such a liking for them. One of his tutors accompanied him to all such classes. Although almost a year young for the grade, he continued to thrive.

. . .

Despite numerous attempts to get Michael to share details of the accident, he continued to refuse. This led to questions of his actual memory of the event. He wrote that he remembered everything clearly from the time the engine faltered (engine failure was the official cause of the crash) until the plane actually hit the hillside, which seemed to be in the neighborhood of ten to twelve minutes.

He had developed a close relationship with his grandparents, who were now his legal guardians, and considered Gilbert and Tony to be his best friends. The three boys spent the majority of their free time at each other's houses, playing ball, board games, (a big favorite of Michael's) building forts, riding bikes, and all the other trappings of friendship at that age. They had fallen into a happy routine, or as happy as one can be who was in a plane crash that killed one's parents and left one as a human curiosity. But it was plain to see that Michael had a resolve to live as close to a normal life as possible.

A week after Christmas Tony and Gilbert had the conversation they both had suppressed since that day in August.

"I'm gonna ask him," stated Gilbert.

"Don't. He's our friend."

"Maybe a friend is who he needs to talk to about it. A whole bunch of doctors and school shrinks already asked him, and he won't tell *them.* "

"You'll bring back bad –"

"I'm *gonna* ask him, and you got to be there when I do."

So the next time all three were together, playing a game of *Life* on Gilbert's computer, he gathered his resolve and asked, "Michael, did you walk away from the crash because your parents covered you with their bodies? Is that why you feel so badly about it? Because they sacrificed themselves to save you?"

This was perhaps ten times more direct than all the professionals who had taken pains not to trigger a traumatic reaction in the miracle boy.

Michael's shoulders sagged. He grabbed his nearby pad and pen and wrote briefly: *That's not what happened. Dad was at the controls. Mom tried to get to me but we were in too steep a dive by then.*

Gilbert and Tony looked at each other in fascination. Another first for them: they were the first to get Michael Shumter to relate anything of what had happened. Gilbert was more comfortable now in questioning Michael. "So if no one was shielding you, why didn't you get hurt?"

Michael paused a moment, then wrote, *I can't tell you that, guys.*

Gilbert interpreted the answer to mean that Michael didn't *know* why he was unhurt. But Tony's mind worked differently. His thought was that Michael *did* know but chose to keep it to himself. It didn't really make sense to him. Why would you *not* tell how you miraculously survived a crash?

Michael scribbled on his notepad again: *Guys, don't tell anybody what I just told you. It'll get in the papers and I don't need to relive it, okay?*

Gilbert and Tony nodded, and that was the end of it. They finished their game of *Life,* and went outside to toss the football around.

. . .

With the warmer weather late in March, the boys went for a long bike ride to Gauthier State Park. The park was still closed to campers and swimmers, but you could enter and ride on the many trails there. They skirted the parking lot by the beach, then headed down a steep trail unfamiliar to them.

Rounding a bend, they suddenly came upon an extremely steep drop, fitted with crude wooden steps for the benefit of people on foot. For someone on a bicycle, it was an accident waiting to happen.

Gilbert saw it at the last instant, and purposely ditched his bike in some nearby brush. It was too late for Michael to react. His bike, with him still aboard, pitched down the drop. Michael was thrown over the handlebars and tumbled violently down the remaining four stairs, the bike careening after him and landing on his head. The pedal gashed his temple, and blood poured out as he rolled onto his side.

Tony, aware of the havoc in front of him, threw his bike down at the top of the incline, He and Gilbert dashed down the steps to their friend, just getting up. Gilbert grabbed a handkerchief from his pocket. Michael held his hands towards them, and wore a slight sheepish smile. He shook his head and shrugged his shoulders as if to say 'It's okay, guys. I'm not hurt.'

"You're bleeding, Mike." Gilbert pressed the handkerchief against Michael's head. Michael took it and held it there, a smile of resignation on his face. He removed a small pad and pen from his pocket. He wrote briefly and held it up so both boys could read it. *Since the accident I can't feel anything.*

"Not *feel* anything?" shouted Gilbert. "Are you *serious?* You aren't in *any* pain right now?"

Michael shook his head and wrote, *Not a bit. Watch.* He picked up a nearby stick, about fourteen inches long and two inches around. He proceeded to strike himself sharply on the knee, elbow, and the back of his hand, all sensitive areas. Gilbert and Tony knew such blows should have had someone screeching in agony.

"You can't be *hurt,*" shouted Gilbert. "What the *HELL!*"

It comes in handy sometimes, Michael wrote. *But I do have this gash on my head. We better get home so my grandparents can take care of it. And guys, you can't tell anyone about* **this** *either, okay?*

"We won't tell," promised Gilbert. "Jesus Christ, this is unbelievable." He paused a second. "Wait a minute. Why can't we tell?"

Michael gave him an 'isn't it obvious?' look. He wrote, *First off, some idiots will do all kinds of things to me to see for themselves. And second, I'll be even* **more** *of a freak than I already am. Who knows where they might take me. I just wanna live a normal life like everybody else!* He gave Gilbert and Tony time to read it, then put the pad and pen back in his pocket.

They rode back to Michael's house, where his grandfather looked at the gash on Michael's head and made a 'here we go again' expression. As Gilbert and Tony rode home, Gilbert's mind was agog with thoughts of his mute friend who seemed to be part superhero, but Tony fretted inwardly about the seemingly evasive answer from Michael about the crash, coupled with this bizarre and somewhat disturbing revelation from the beloved miracle boy.

. . .

Long before their first encounter with Michael Shumter, Gilbert and Tony sometimes met behind one of their houses and had a "pow-wow" if there was a person or situation they needed to discuss and exchange ideas or to make sure they were in agreement about something. Up to now, any adult overhearing one of these "pow-wows" would chalk it up to kids making a big deal out of nothing. Even Gilbert and Tony could look back on these discussions and admit that most, if not all of it was "kid stuff." But this seemed to be much, much more. There were many adults involved in the Michael Shumter situation, but *they* had information unknown to anyone else. Heck, Michael, *their friend,* had been a national news topic on occasion. This was definitely *not* kid stuff.

"He can't talk *and* he can't feel pain," stated Gilbert. "What do you make of it?"

"It's very strange," replied Tony. "And he's not the 'poor kid who lost his parents' anymore. He's got this . . . *attitude* about him now. *And* he keeps reminding us not to tell anybody about the accident details he told us and the not being able to feel pain."

"Well, it seems like he's okay with things now. Isn't that a good thing, Tony?"

"You just don't get it, Gilbert. I know he's our friend and all, but something is really not right. Don't you see it?" Tony had been down this road before with Gilbert, not being able to see beneath the surface of people's behavior. Tony had had to bail Gilbert out of several uncomfortable social situations. He was in his own world when it came to evaluating people, their motives, and agendas.

"I wonder if he's indestructible," said Gilbert, once again not really paying attention to what Tony was laying out for him. "Maybe he's like . . .*supernatural,* like in the movies."

Tony was deep in thought and likewise not paying attention to Gilbert's enthusiastic assessment of the situation. "Those two things don't make sense. They don't *go* together."

"What two things?" asked Gilbert innocently.

Tony shook his head and sighed. "Never mind. Let's go back inside."

"Good idea. Hey, let's call Michael."

. . .

Gilbert and Tony were true friends to Michael Shumter. It was part of the 'friendship code' they and everyone they knew had grown up with. They continued to keep secret the things they knew that no one else in the world did, namely the exact details of the crash and Michael's inability to feel pain.

A week later during geography class, the door opened and Mrs. Greene, Michael's tutor for advanced math, came in, looking like she had seen a ghost. She handed a note to their teacher, Miss Alicky, who read it, her eyes now wide with shock.

"Gilbert, Tony, could you come up here, please?"

As the boys approached, Gilbert thought, *My house burned down,* while next to him, Tony thought, *My dad got in a car accident.* Neither of them had done the math on this note, which would not have included both of them.

"Boys, would you read this note, please?" asked Miss Alicky.

Oh, my God, we're both in big trouble, so big Miss Alicky can't even repeat it! thought both Gilbert and Tony.

The note read, *Gilbert and Tony: Michael has **finally spoken**, and has asked to see you.*

Miss Alicky smiled through her welling eyes. "Go ahead, boys. But come right back. And don't run," she added, but Gilbert and Tony were already halfway down the hall.

They burst into Room 117. Michael sat at one of the two desks, a big smile on his face. "Hi, guys," he said in a hoarse whisper. "I can finally talk."

His two emotionally-charged visitors both went for the one empty desk, Gilbert landing in it, while Tony landed on the floor.

A rasping laugh came out of Michael Shumter.

Within an hour the entire school knew the news. By late that afternoon the entire town, including local news reporters, knew.

Morris and Helena Shumter kept Michael inside and reporters away. Only Gilbert Moody and Tony Cooke were allowed to see him. They spent the afternoon talking about anything and everything. By suppertime both boys noticed that Michael's voice was becoming closer to normal.

Morris and Helena must have known that the sooner they let Michael tell his story, the sooner everyone would accept it and move on to the next set of circumstances that would pass for news. And that is exactly what happened. The boy who survived a plane crash without a scratch on August 27th and could not speak until the following April 8th told his story. Local, regional, and national press sent reporters to the Shumter home over the next week, and Michael Shumter had an *additional* fifteen minutes of fame. Questions were restricted to the crash and Michael's remarkable social and emotional recovery. And after that, everyone, indeed, moved on.

Everyone except Tony Cooke. Anthony Charles Cooke was a very observant and perceptive twelve-year-old. He had noticed a change in Michael even before he finally spoke, and an even greater one after. Long gone was the timid, shaken boy who could not even speak. There was a sureness to him now, almost an arrogance. It went beyond his gradual adjusting to his new life and surroundings. The interviews he had finally given seemed almost *orchestrated* to Tony. All the right questions. And all the right answers by everyone's miracle child, who had escaped certain death, *unscathed.* There was no mention of his bizarre, unearthly inability to feel pain. A person who could not feel pain would continue to be a side-show attraction for the rest of his life. No, Michael Shumter just wanted to *appear* normal, Tony thought, and still be someone who had the sympathy of people and would be given the benefit of the doubt by everyone.

. . .

And things *did* go back to normal. There was no fuss over Michael Shumter. Not even when he accidentally got hit in the head with a whiffle ball bat on the playground. He grimaced, rubbed the spot, and even managed to cry for a few seconds. Nobody gave it a second thought. Except Tony. He knew Michael's game here. *Just fit in like everybody else.* And there was no Gilbert to commiserate with this time. He was home sick on this day.

But Tony went over to his house after school that day and related the bat to the head incident.

"He *had* to pretend, Tony. You remember what he told us the day he crashed his bike at the park. If people knew he couldn't feel pain he'd be analyzed by doctors, shrinks, everybody!"

Tony once again told Gilbert about all the observations he had made regarding their friend; the change in demeanor, the way he carried himself, everything. But Gilbert once again would not believe a word of it.

"What's the matter with you, Tony? Look what he's been through. Lost his parents, couldn't speak. So he's trying to move on and be normal, and *you* think he's some *evil mastermind.* What's his plan? Is he gonna take over the *world* someday?"

Tony exhaled deeply. "Let's sneak down to our spot behind your house"

"You wanna have a pow-wow over *this?*"

"That's right. Well?"

"No, Tony. No way."

Tony left without saying another word. He had gotten down to the next street when he saw Michael Shumter walking toward him, a pleasant *normal* smile on his face.

"Hey, Tony. How's it going?"

"Fine."

"So, were you just at Gilbert's?"

"Yeah. He's feeling better."

"Great."

That smug, confident look Tony had observed was all over Michael's face.

"So what did you guys talk about?"

"Nothin' much."

Michael Shumter's eyebrows seemed to come together. "C'mon, Tony. I bet you had a lot to tell good old Gilbert."

Maybe he can read minds, now, too. I wouldn't be surprised at this point. "Okay, I told him about you getting hit with the bat and pretending to be hurt."

"Tony, I told you about that. I don't want people knowing I can't feel pain. It would ruin everything. I'd be famous again. And I don't want that, you know."

"Yeah."

"Ya know, Tony, I bet you told Gilbert a lot of other stuff, too."

"What stuff?"

"Oh, the kind of stuff you been thinking lately." Michael paused and raised an eyebrow. "Stuff about me, Tony."

Tony was very uncomfortable now, almost scared. "What stuff would I be thinking about you?"

"Tony, my good man. Let me lay it all out for you. After the crash I couldn't feel pain, I was suddenly a genius in math and science. They had to go to the high school and get me eleventh grade textbooks, did you know that? And when someone is next to me, like you often are, I can *sense* their thoughts. Well?"

"And you couldn't talk for months," Tony added, without knowing why.

"Nah, that was fake."

"What?"

"Yeah, that was something I threw in on my own. To gain sympathy. You know. 'Poor kid. Lost his parents. Can't even talk.' Worked pretty well, but man, that was a real bitch. I didn't even talk when I *knew* I was alone. Couldn't take the chance."

Tony's head was swimming. He looked side to side and behind him confusedly.

"Nobody's around, Tony. That's why I'm tellin' you all this. After all, I *am* still a kid. I just can't keep all this crap inside any more."

"I was right about . . ." Tony's thought and voice faded to nothing.

"Yeah, Tony, you were right. Congratulations."

Tony held his hands out in front of him. His face showed both fear and total disbelief. "What's going on, Michael? What's this all about?"

"I'll tell you what it's *about,*" Michael said sternly. "It's about the deal I made when the plane was going down. I prayed to God, Tony. I didn't want to die at age *ten.* I told God I would do *anything* if I survived. All I could hear was my mother screaming and my father saying it would be all right, and the engine choking." He paused, a faraway smile on his face. "And then, a moment later there was a voice *inside* my head, it seemed. And it said '*I'll save you.*'"

Michael paused again, as if for dramatic effect. "And down we went. I could see the side of that hill getting bigger. And the plane hit. There was a loud crash, and a huge jolt. Then everything got quiet. And the voice inside my head came back. And it said, 'You're *mine,* now.' Through the window I could see you guys running toward the plane, and I figured I better get out there so you wouldn't have to see what was left of my parents."

Tony had just heard so many incomprehensible concepts it was as though all of his powers of comprehension were shot. He struggled to speak, and when he finally did, could not form a coherent thought. "You – but – who . . ."

Michael clapped his hands sharply in a show of impatience. "C'mon, Tony. I thought you were *smart.* I asked *God* to save me but he was willing to let me *die,* unfulfilled. And yet I *was* saved. So do the math, Tony, old boy."

Tony stared at Michael for several moments. "A *power* saved you from death. But it wasn't God. So it had to have been—"

"*All* right, Tony. You get it now. There's no need to name names." He walked over to Tony and put an arm around his shoulder. "Ya gotta admit, I was given some great gifts. I can't feel pain, I can basically *sense* people's thoughts, and they still don't know how far off the charts I am in math and science." He paused, and smiled in anticipation. "And who knows what else was is this deal?"

Tony's next question came out before he realized he was asking it. "Do your grandparents know?"

"Are you *nuts?* I wouldn't lay any of this on them. They're nice people. They're better off ignorant of the whole situation."

Tony dared to bore into Michael's happy face with a glare. "Are you *glad* your parents died and you came out of it . . . like *this?"*

Michael drew back as though stung. "No. I loved my parents. I felt awful that they died." His face took on a stern resolve. "But I begged to live, and I *did."* He relaxed again, then seemed to become happily agitated. "Hey, I got a theory about all this."

Tony stared blankly, his mind overwhelmed.

"Wanna hear my theory, Tony?"

Tony exhaled deeply. He appeared to nod slightly.

Tony again assumed a friendly disposition. "I have a theory that everybody that survives when they should have *died* got some kind of *deal,* like I did. Probably not the exact same one, but *something.* Something *extraordinary.* Michael's eyes widened. "You have any idea how many people that could be? People with unusual abilities and . . . *gifts. "*

Tony seemed to be completely spaced out.

"Tony, you there, buddy?"

Tony looked up and focused. "What *now?"*

"Whattaya mean, pal?"

Tony mustered his thoughts for seemed like a final question. "Michael, what are you supposed to *do?"*

Michael Shumter, the miracle boy, threw his arms out and shrugged, a winning smile on his face. "I have *no* idea, but I'll bet it's gonna be a hell of a ride." He elbowed

Tony kiddingly. "At least better than the one on my dad's plane!"

"REDMONT FIELD"
Aug. - Oct. 2017

Redmont Field, or what *was* Redmont Field, is nearly impassible now; a morass of weeds, eight-foot-high briars, trees, saplings, seemingly endless pricker bushes, and unruly meadow grass over two feet high.

But when I was a teen, and even into my early twenties, it was a *kingdom,* and my friends and I were the kings.

If you go to the end of Calvano Street and enter the woods situated there, and if you successfully plod through a hundred yards of thick (and I mean *thick*) woods without getting off course due to rockpiles, brambles, small ravines, and a brook, which over the last forty-odd years has formed a *very* steep embankment, you will come to a huge pine tree which marked the edge of Redmont Field.

And bring your machete. Because once you climb over the now-unstable rock wall at the base of the pine, you may not be able to take another step without hacking your way in.

The field lies between a large house, located about sixty yards uphill, and the rest of the lot, a steady downhill which abuts yet another tract of woods.

Back in the 60's and 70's the boys from the three hills played at Redmont Field on a regular basis. We had all grown up together on Pershing Hill, Lilac Lane, and Pratt Hill. There were perhaps as many as twenty of us, with several sets and trios of brothers. We played baseball and football on the nearly one-hundred yards of grass. Years later many of us realized how important Redmont Field had been in the shaping of who we were to become as adults.

We had no idea of the carry-over life lessons we were all teaching ourselves and each other on an imperceptible timeline.

The field was named after Redmont Ayers, the son of the couple that owned the large house and land. The owner's name was Raymond Ayers, the principal of a vocational-technical school. His wife was Dorothy Redmont Ayers. But it was known that the field was named for their *son*, not the wife's maiden name. It was obvious that the Ayers family was quite wealthy.   All we knew was that the guy, Raymond Ayers, was very accommodating in letting us use his back field to play ball. Heck, he even mowed the grass down there before we used it the first time. After that, we got a couple of lawn mowers in somebody's car up on Clearview Drive, then walked them down to the field. Twice a year was sufficient.

Before I get too far afield, let me tell you about Redmont Ayers, for whom Redmont Field is named. He was an only child of the wealthy Raymond and Dorothy Ayers, and yet was the most congenial, caring and generous person you could ever meet. He looked out for others, did all kinds of community service, and was active in the Boy Scouts and Christian Youth Organization.

But what made him stand out was his athletic ability. From the time he got involved in organized sports, he was a combination all-star/superstar in baseball, football, hockey, and track.

From fifth through eighth grade I would constantly see his picture in the papers for all sorts of fantastic sports accomplishments.

He was a power-hitting centerfielder, starred at both quarterback and halfback, and a first line right wing. In track he broke the school record in the 400 several times before graduation. He was scouted by baseball, football, and hockey teams at the college level as well as the Cleveland Indians.

I was in eighth grade when Redmont Ayers graduated (yes, with honors) and was interested in where he would attend college and rewrite *their* record books. But something else drove him, a fierce sense of duty and patriotism. He loved sports, but they were not the motivating force in his life. He excelled at them because of his unique abilities and willingness to practice, but Redmont Ayers was a *warrior* at heart.

The Monday after graduation he was in the Marine recruiter's office, enlisting for a four-year stint. They took one look at his accomplishments, and offered him Officer Candidate School.

As easily as I could picture Redmont patrolling center field for the Cleveland Indians, running a sweep for the Philadelphia Eagles, or scoring goals for the Boston Bruins, I could also picture him leading a company of Marines in Vietnam, winning battle after battle, and endearing himself to the locals. That's what he'd done here in Ohio. He won battle after battle and endeared himself to the locals, *us*.

Did Redmont Ayers ever play in Redmont Field? Of course he did. It was his *back yard*. He and his friends might play a game of 'grounders and flies.' or have a friendly game of touch football. But Redmont and his contemporaries were between four and ten years older than us, and the ratio of free time to chores and other responsibilities seemed to have been much less back then.

. . .

Redmont Ayers joining the Marines was the lead story on the sports page. He did not disappoint. He was a standout in boot camp, graduating at the top of his group and already a PFC, on his way to becoming a Lieutenant.

Meanwhile, my friends and I were given permission to play ball in Redmont Field. And did we ever.

It must have been a sight, ten to twenty of us walking down Calvano Street, then disappearing into the stretch of woods that stood between that quiet dead end and the mighty pine tree that marked the beginning of Redmont Field.

The woods back then was not that hard to navigate, but there *was* one pitfall: a rapidly-running stream about three feet deep with very steep banks, and just wide enough that it was difficult to jump. The usual result was one foot ending up in the water, and getting soaked up to the knee.

Once, I jumped across, but could not balance on the opposite bank, and fell backwards into the stream. There was no baseball game that day. I was holding our only ball, and everyone was laughing so hard no one could even hold a bat. Everyone stayed right there and gave their own reenactment of my fall, each one adding his own little flourish, including slow motion versions, and inserting some creative dialogue.

One kid, Donny Casale, made everyone forget my mishap. He decided to *pole vault* across the stream a week later. He ran to the bank and inserted a huge stick into the water. Of course the stick broke when he was halfway over and *he* went in backwards. We laughed like hell and then everyone reenacted *that*.

After that we built a crude bridge across the stream. Problem solved, except for the time Petey and Anthony were pushing and shoving each other and fell off the bridge. Anthony was sobbing as he climbed out and we were scared he got hurt and would squeal on Petey, but he was pulling soaked dollar bills out of his pocket, yelling, "You're gonna pay for this money, Petey!"

You could hear a pin drop, it was so tense. Then good old Petey started singing this goofy hippie song, "Everything Is Beautiful," and we all laughed our asses off. Even Anthony was laughing at that point.

Oddly enough, the sappy "Everything Is Beautiful" became our theme song as we walked through the woods that summer on our way to Redmont Field. Thank you, Mr. Ray Stevens.

We had all been friends for years, and cared about each other, although you could never get any of us to admit it. We had a thing called "The Brother Rule." There were two parts to it. One, any younger brother of any of us was allowed to hang out and play ball. I mean, here we were, mid to late teens, and yet Roy Temmons, barely nine, was considered one of us because of his two older brothers. And two, you didn't touch anybody's younger brother, or give them any shit, unless the older brother *agreed* with the shit. Then they would probably *add* shit to the shit that was already going down.

For example, nobody touched Frank Martin, but I swear his brother John was ready to kill him at least twice a week over a dropped pass or a strikeout. It usually went like this: "Frank, you God-damned asshole, I'm gonna freakin' kill you! Catch the damn ball!" Then John would take off after poor Frank with a bat or throw the nearest object at him, and *then* chase him. And John's voice carried. A couple of times we had to tell him he could swear at Frank and chase him all he wanted, (that was an understood part of the Brother Rule also) but to keep it down. The Martin brothers were *very* entertaining.

But, brothers *are* brothers. If anyone gave Frank too much guff, John would come to his defense, in a manner of sorts. "C'mon, he's just a puny little shit, he's not gonna be able to catch a pass that hard. I mean, look at him."

We were quite the crew. We all loved sports except for this one kid, Bobby Nichols. Cars and motorcycles were his passion, but he was good friends with my younger brother Denny, so he was with us a lot of the time. You gotta give a guy credit for playing baseball and football when he didn't even know the basic *rules*. He was a tall, skinny kid with very long arms, so during football games he got a lot of passes thrown his way. He would make these incredible reaching catches, then head directly out of bounds, no matter where the defenders were.

. . .

Well, enough prologue.

In 1965, Lt. Redmont Ayers was wounded in Quang Tri province while leading a long range patrol against the Viet Cong. The papers didn't give much detail except to say he was hit by grenade fragments and was being evacuated to Camp Zama, Japan. From there he was eventually coming home.

We were sad that he got wounded, but happy he was getting out of that shithole. Then we were sad again when we learned that he was paralyzed from the waist down and could barely use his right arm.

Redmont's parents always did things in a big way. Instead of his homecoming being a quiet, private affair, they held a reception for him at their home overlooking Redmont Field. Half the town was there. His parents put out a spread better than what you would see at a country club wedding. I was maybe sixteen at the time, and really wanted to meet him, but I knew how uncomfortable I would feel, so I did not attend. (Plus, I was not actually invited.) On my recommendation, none of us played at Redmont Field that day.

A couple of days later we were back there, playing football as usual. Bobby Nichols was catching balls five feet over his head and then running directly out of bounds. John Martin cussed out Frank for not "covering his zone," then pulled up a sideline stake and chased him with it.

Greg Duquette happened to glance uphill towards the Ayers house.

"Hey, look guys, there's Redmont Ayers."

And so he was. He was out on their semi-enclosed back porch, which was on the first floor of their massive house if you entered from Clearview Drive. But the land sloped acutely downward, and from the back he was on the second floor. His mother was with him, fixing an area for him to read, with a book and a glass of something nearby. He sat in a wheelchair, of course.

Many of us waved and called a greeting to him. No one used the term 'thank you for your service' back then, so we really didn't know what else to say. Thankfully no one said anything stupid like 'how's it goin?'

To our surprise Redmont called down to us. "Great day for a football game, guys. Mind if I watch?"

No, I guess we didn't 'mind' him watching while we played in *his* backyard in a field named for *him.*

It was summer, and in summer we played both baseball and football with no particular agenda. It was just what ended up happening after we all got together in front of my house on Lilac Lane. All through that summer we played at Redmont Field, while its namesake sat on his porch in his wheelchair and cheered us on. He was quite the fan, yelling 'nice catch,' 'nice pass,' 'good hit,' and other encouraging things to us. It made me sad to have a guy with so much ability taken away still having a positive outlook.

It was Donny Casale who brought the binoculars that day. Donny was obsessed with looking at faraway people and things and commenting on them. Most of us had some little quirk. With Donny, it was binoculars.

We were in the middle of a game one day and Donny was not with us, which was strange because he had gone into the woods with us. When he wasn't there at the field we just assumed he changed his mind and went home.

Halfway through the game Donny comes bursting out of the woods, and runs into our huddle.

"What ja see in the woods, Donny, a yellow-bellied sapsucker?"

"Shut up, Petey." He turned to me. "I was looking up at Redmont on his porch from in the woods."

"Why would you *do* that?" I asked, irritated.

"I like faraway things," he said.

It was always the same answer. "So you playin' or what?"

"Get this," Donny said. "Redmont has a bottle of pills on his tray."

"So what? You think he can just sail through the day like us?"

"He's got a bottle of booze up there, too. Maybe he'd give us—"

"We aren't doin' *that.* He's got every right to drink. Probably helps him get through another day in that chair."

"Maybe he'll—"

"Knock it off, Donny. Think about what he lost because of that war."

"Yeah, I guess."

. . .

Good old Donny Casale. Just had to 'see faraway things.' I know he didn't mean any harm. It wasn't like he was trying to *snoop,* the way *real* snoops do. He was just a curious teenager, like the rest of us.

We went on with our high school and middle school lives. Redmont Ayers watched us every time we played baseball or football in his field, and continued to cheer us on and encourage us. Just by his presence, sometimes. Maybe I was the only one who really got that, being the oldest.

Winter came, and we abandoned Redmont Field. On December 5th we played our last game of the season, or tried to. It was twenty degrees out with an inch of snow on the ground. It had been hell just trying to *get* there. Every time someone touched a branch in the woods, all the snow on the tree fell on whoever was next to it. We were miserable even before we could pick sides.

Nobody could pass the ball or hold onto it, not even Bobby Nichols. The onset of snow and cold had put all of us into a depressed frame of mind. But Redmont Ayers was out on his porch in his chair, watching us. *What a guy,* I thought. He was bundled up like the rest of us. I wondered if he had a bottle of whiskey up there to keep him warm. Damn you, Donny.

. . .

It was during that winter that my parents started not getting along. Little things at first, like leaving lights on, the cap off the toothpaste, and each of them starting to get a bit snarky about the other's personal habits. It deteriorated into the friends my father spent time with and my mother being too fussy about how the house looked.

My father's unpredictable moods when he came home a little buzzed made things worse. Sometimes he would just laugh at whatever criticism was coming his way, which made my mother even more furious. Other times he would be very defensive.

I succeeded at staying out of the way. You didn't have to take sides if you weren't in the room, I learned. But my younger brother Dennis not only was caught in the middle, he was one of the things they fought over. He was doing lousy in school, and my father was on him like flies on shit. My mother defended him, his choice of friends, and just about everything else that moron did. My father had it in for good old Donny, stating that he was the one getting my brother to neglect his schoolwork, skip classes, and act like a slovenly bum.

This situation was still going strong as winter faded into spring. And it had been a brutal winter, with all the tension, arguing, and yelling. As an escape, I began taking walks into the woods at the end of Calvano Street. When I got to the wall and the big pine, I would sit down and try to be at peace. I didn't want to go *into* Redmont Field. There was no place to sit, and I didn't want anyone from the Ayers family to think I was weird or something. From the wall I could see up the slope to their house. There was no Redmont on the back porch.

Spring wore on. The turmoil in our family got worse. They were fighting over money, now. I heard on some talk show I was trying to ignore that that was usually the kiss of death for most marriages. I could not picture my parents divorced and Dad coming around on weekends to spend some quality time with Dennis and me. Heck, he didn't do that *now.*

In a few weeks, if the weather cooperated, we would be able to start playing baseball. John Martin would get Petey Sager to bring up his dad's mower, he would get *his* father's mower, and they would run them down from Clearview Drive to the field. Every time I saw John in school I would ask him if it was time yet. I bugged him so often I think he started avoiding me.

I was in such anticipation of us being able to play at the field I started walking the perimeter of it on my visits. The cold weather lingered. Even though it was almost mid-April nobody wanted to play, and any attempt at cutting the grass would have been futile.

On one of my walks around the field I was surveying the downhill part of the land. We had lost our share of foul balls in there. While I was looking down there, I thought I heard a strange buzzing sound. I listened closely, and I was sure I could hear an erratic droning: the sound of someone's voice.

I looked up at the house to see Redmont Ayers sitting on the porch in his chair, the tray beside him. He was rocking side to side.

At first I thought he was talking to *me,* but he was looking off into space. I stopped so I could hear him. He was mumbling and ranting. I couldn't make out any of the mumbling, but the ranting and shouting was clearly audible. He would mumble, and then I heard, "It's all just a game, a big, stupid game!" He mumbled some more, then raised his voice again. "All for nothing. Everything was for nothing!"

I think at that point I guessed that he was depressed and bitter. The war in Vietnam was a big, stupid game and everything he had done was for nothing. I looked again and he was taking a huge gulp from some bottle, most likely whiskey. (Happy now, Donny?) I turned and ran for the big pine. I figured I was next, probably representing all the carefree, stupid people he had fought for. The yelling started up again, but thankfully my footfalls and heavy breathing drowned him out. I could hear Redmont Ayers' tortured voice in the distance as I hustled across the bridge.

. . .

The weather finally broke, and John and Petey took their mowers to Redmont Field. The cold weather had let up, but not my parents' marriage troubles. At least now I could get out and play baseball with the guys.

It became a crap shoot any day we played at Redmont Field. Some days he wasn't on the back porch. Other days he was, but didn't say a word. And a few times he was his old self, like a supportive older brother cheering us on and encouraging us. Even his knowledge of the game shone through: "Pull hitter! Shade him toward the line in right." Or: "Choke up with two strikes. Just try to make contact."

Unfortunately, there was a fourth category. Some days we got the Redmont Ayers I had seen that day back in April. It started with derisive laughter at every strikeout and error, then deteriorated into a tirade of personal insults and degradations at whoever was pitching, hitting, or fielding. He made John Martin sound like a life coach by comparison.

The first time it happened I called everybody in and explained what was going on.

"Where's his parents, for Christ's sake?" asked John. "Can't they get him some help?"

"I don't know, John. But we got two choices. We just let him yell and say nothing or we go play someplace else."

We decided to tough it out. On most of the bad days his insulting verbiage usually sputtered down to nothing. At that point he was usually asleep.

After a few of these "bad days" we decided to only play there on Saturdays for the rest of the school year. I mean, why antagonize the guy by our mere presence? He was tortured enough.

For the next few Saturdays, Redmont Ayers was not out on the porch. We had put a "recon" plan into effect. We sent three or four guys ahead to go in the field, toss the ball around, and kind of feel out what mood he was in. That last Saturday he was there, but in one of those mumbling to himself moods. So the rest of us came out and started a game.

It was maybe the second inning. I was about to pitch to Len Daignault, who had just changed the batting order by grabbing the bat from his brother Charlie and kicking him in the ass. I was still laughing at Charlie rubbing his rear end, when I heard Donny call out from first base, "Guys, hold up!"

Raymond Ayers was walking down the slope toward us. "Hey fellas," he called out. A couple guys stayed in the outfield, but everybody else came over.

"Guys," he said softly but clearly, "I'm afraid you're not gonna be able to play in this field any more."

"We didn't do anything wrong," Frank Martin protested.

"Frank, shut the hell up and listen," said John.

"Boys, my son Redmont is not well. He's reacting badly to his medications. Instead of calming him down, it's doing just the opposite."

I shot Donny a look as if to say, 'Don't mention the booze.'

"He gets rattled and aggressive during the day," Mr. Ayers continued. "I'm sure you all heard the mean things he said. I apologize for that."

"It's all right," said Tommy Temmons. "We know it wasn't his fault."

There was a smattering of comments agreeing with Tommy. The guys in the outfield had come in and were finding out what was going on.

"At any rate," Mr. Ayers said, "you're a good bunch of kids and I hope you find another place for your sports. Thank you for understanding." He looked grim and beaten as he plodded back up the slope to the house. We looked up. Redmont Ayers was sound asleep in his wheelchair. A bottle had fallen in his lap, and was dripping all over the porch.

. . .

So that was basically it for our wonderful years at Redmont Field. We actually did find other places to play, but most of our games were on Lilac Lane and Calvano Street. It kind of changed the dynamic when you could no longer dive for the ball, and the width of a *street* defined your football field. And since Lilac Lane was an actual *hill,* one team was always at a slight disadvantage.

There were a couple of good backyards a few streets away, but that meant we had to suck up to the Domber brothers, and no one really liked them that much. And of course they included *their* friends, and no one liked them *at all.*

But we managed. We all learned that no matter how important something is, if it becomes unattainable, you compensate and learn to be satisfied with what you *do* have.

Could that possibly be of use in real life?

. . .

Five years went by. I was in college studying to be a history teacher. Those who forget the past, you know. Tommy was in college way over in Boston. And him the biggest Yankee fan I ever knew. Lay low, Tommy. The Daignault brothers and Greg Duquette had moved. Tall, lanky Bobby Nichols, who played sports with us even if he didn't know the actual *rules,* and whom we called "Giraffe," had died in a terrible motorcycle accident the year before. Everyone else was still around, but our age differences now *divided* us as opposed to *uniting* us. Lonnie Temmons joked that if I got a job at the local high school, he *could* be one of my students. (Yikes.)

. . .

For all the friends I had, and for all the things we did together, I was at heart a solitary person who liked to take walks and just think . . . or *not* think. None of the other guys were like that.   We had come to a point in our lives where I was the odd man out.

Where I once was the oldest kid and the leader, I was now at a place where I had little or nothing in common with the old gang except *past* experiences. My time with them had come and gone, and I didn't have a problem with it anyway. But I still loved the memories of Redmont Field. And so, on my solitary walks I would head down Calvano Street and enter the woods.

The path was easy to access, and there was nothing to be afraid of, so I started taking walks there in the evening hours, three or four times a week. I would get to the wall where the big pine was and sit down. I carried a small flashlight with me, of course.

It was about mid-June on the night in question. I was about to sit on the wall by the old pine when I was sure I heard noise in the distance. At the far end of the field, where home plate had been, I could see a small light, bouncing around and moving very slowly down the hill into the tall scrub that bordered the playing field. Voices carry across that field, for some reason, and I heard people talking, but I couldn't make out any words.

The light moved down toward the bottom of the Ayers' property. I had no idea who was out there or what they were up to. I certainly wasn't about to confront them. I turned off my flashlight. After a few more minutes I could see a faint glow down at the bottom of the hill. There were two lights now, and I could hear sound coming from down there that was *not* people talking.

I was curious as to what was going on, but I was also scared shitless. My first thought was some big drug deal, but why here, why use lights which the Ayers family might see, and why move so slowly? Why would they cut through the Ayers' yard to get down there? It made no sense.

I'm not what you'd call brave or even daring, but I decided to get a closer look. Our field was no longer a field, of course. It had meadow scrub several feet high and masses of pricker bushes. These people, whoever they were, were a good hundred yards away, diagonally, if I took the shortest path, which of course I didn't. We never went in there when we used the field, and I wasn't about to start now. I crept over the wall and made a straight line for the far end of the field, about a hundred yards away. I crouched down and walked. It was very difficult, what with the tall grass engulfing me and finding myself entangled in pricker bushes. I would stop every few feet or so to look down at the bottom of the hill and listen. I could still see lights down there. There was no sound of voices, but there was that intermittent, unrecognizable sound.

After a couple minutes I looked up at the Ayers house to gauge my position. I was just about at the pitcher's mound. For you football fans, let's call it the twenty yard line. I stopped there and *did* lie down. After about twenty more minutes the sounds from the bottom of the hill stopped and it got dead quiet for maybe five minutes. Then I saw the lights pointing uphill and heard the faint sound of footsteps. It was only a matter of time before they would cross right in front of me. I knew that would be my best chance to try to see how many people there were and maybe get a clue as to what they were doing in Redmont Field after nine-thirty at night.

Minutes later they crossed in front of me, twenty yards away. I didn't move or breathe. There was no full moon to illuminate them, but my eyes had gotten accustomed to the dark. I thought I counted three people. The first person shone the light, and the other two were shuffling, not walking normally, seeming to stagger step. They were *carrying* something that was either bulky, or heavy, or *both.* They crossed the level part of the land, where we had played, and started uphill. Not a word was spoken. When they were about halfway up, I turned and began a cautious retreat.

I was wishing that Ray Ayers would pop out onto the back porch with a shotgun, yelling, 'Who's there?' I got back to the wall, climbed over, and hurried home.

I spent a lot of time that evening deep in thought about what I had witnessed. I didn't think I had any reason to call the police, but I *was* thinking of calling Mr. Ayers and telling him about what I had seen. Maybe he would invite me to show him the spot at the bottom of the property where these people had been. On the other hand, he might ask what *I* had been doing nosing around his land *at night*. But I was going into my senior year of college, and had seen some of my life's goals falling into place, so I was feeling quite proactive.

I *did* call him, the next day. When he answered I told him my name. "I was one of the boys that used to play ball in your field."

"Yes, I remember you guys. My son used to look forward to watching you."

I hesitated, but this was twenty-year-old me, now. "How is he doing these days, Mr. Ayers?"

"Ah, so-so. Every day is a struggle. Well, you saw how he was after the first year."

"Yeah, so sorry."

"Well, what can I do for you?"

So I gave him chapter and verse, from when I sat down on the wall, until the people headed back uphill.

"Oh, okay, young man." He chuckled. "I think I can ease your mind a bit. That was my brother and a couple of his friends. They dig night-crawlers down in that corner. Big fisherman. Me, I got all I can handle right here, you know"

His tone had changed from light to grim with that statement. I was a little puzzled, however. "Why would they go all the way down in the corner to dig night-crawlers?"

"My brother said it was the best spot, where you find the biggest ones. You know, no foot traffic. Some damn thing like that. He's been down there before."

"Well, what were they carrying up that was so heavy it took two of them?" I knew I had probably overstepped my bounds, but that part of it still did not make sense, unless they had dug up eighty pounds of night-crawlers.

There was an ever-so-slight pause. "Oh, okay. Yeah, they filled a burlap sack full of soil from down there. Said it was perfect for keeping the night-crawlers in."

I didn't really know what to say at that point.

"So anyway, young man, that's what you saw last night. I'm sorry you got all concerned, but I thank you for caring enough to call it to my attention. Okay?"

"Yes, Mr. Ayers. Sorry to have bothered you."

"No bother at all."

"Uh, give my best to your son."

"I will, thank you. Goodbye, now."

You know, I'm no detective, and everything he told me made sense. But what *didn't* make sense was that he let me tell this long, long story and never once stopped me to explain.

I was convinced it was because he needed time to think of a plausible explanation for something that no one was supposed to see. And that *other* pause after I asked about the thing being carried up the hill. He had to come up with a story for *that,* too.

Guess who was planning another nighttime trip to Redmont Field.

. . .

Guess who got his work schedule at Burger Heaven moved to nights six days a week. That killed the return trip to Redmont Field. That, and a conversation I had with myself. Did I really need to stick my nose into this? If I didn't happen to be there at the big pine I would never know that three people were traipsing around Redmont Field that night. Maybe Ray Ayers' brother and his friends *were* digging for night-crawlers. Or maybe they snuck down there to smoke weed and didn't want to do it in the house with Redmont around.

Whatever it was, I still had a senior year of college facing me, and a job market that was getting tougher for social studies majors. At any rate, I did not investigate further at Redmont Field.

Almost a year to the day later, I was getting my college diploma on a hot June afternoon with my parents, grandmother, and eldest aunt in attendance. Three weeks before I had luckily landed a teaching job at the high school I had graduated from just four years before. It was a weird situation, because at least half a dozen of our gang were still attending there. Luckily my own brother was at the local technical school. That just would have been *too* much.

And good old Lonnie Temmons *was* in one of my classes. Poor kid, he must have been ready to call me by my first name countless times before he caught himself.

Good news and bad on the home front. My parents had tried counseling as a last-ditch effort to save their marriage. It was actually working. They just had to remember to keep their mouths shut on about half the stuff they wanted to say. The bad news was my father had lost his job and did not qualify for unemployment benefits due to management lying through their teeth about the circumstances of his departure. (Dad's version.) He was fighting it, so there was no real money coming in, except for my first year teacher's meager paycheck. So there I was, still living at home but *supporting* my parents and brother.

One morning during April vacation, I came into the kitchen to see strange expressions on my parents' faces. They had left the morning paper at my place. My first thought was that the school had burned down and now *I* was out of a job, too.

The lead story on the front page told how the Veteran's Administration had paid a random welfare check on Redmont Ayers at his home. They did not find him there, and there was no record of him at any care facility. Big questions followed. Where was he, and what was being done with the money in his one-hundred-per-cent disability checks?

Raymond and Dorothy Ayers sat in their living room, sobbed, and told a most bizarre and creepy tale. Redmont had *died* a year and ten months earlier, his death brought on from the excess of pain medication and alcohol. His last request of his parents was that he be *buried* at the bottom of the field that bore his name. Not *cremated,* but *buried* there. Which we all know is illegal. Ray and Dorothy had never said 'no' to Redmont his entire life. They had let him have all that booze and who knows what else in his depressed condition, so I guess their guilt level was off the charts. They carried out his final request.

And *that* is what I had been witness to that June evening nearly two years earlier. The people I saw and heard that night were Ray and Dorothy Ayers and Redmont's uncle Joseph. With Mrs. Ayers leading the way, Ray and Joseph carried Redmont, still in his wheelchair. When they got to the bottom they wrapped him in his favorite blankets and dug a regulation-size grave. *That* had been the unidentified sound I heard—the sound of shovels digging.

They held a brief memorial service in the dark once they got him in the ground. That was the five-minute gap I remember. They came back up the hill, carrying the wheelchair and shovels, and passed right in front of me, lying on my stomach twenty yards away.

Had Raymond Ayers, an astute, worldly man, really thought he could get away with this? But he and his wife were blinded by their love and loyalty to their only child, who had, in effect, given his life for his country.

The Ayers had not touched a penny of the money the government had paid to their son. It was determined, after exhuming the body, that the date of death and circumstances given by Raymond Ayers was accurate. Redmont was reburied with full military honors. His parents returned every cent of the money in his son's account.

Mr. and Mrs. Ayers were charged with illegal disposition of human remains, and paid a hefty fine. They got several years' probation, and Mr. Ayers promptly resigned as principal of his school. His brother Joseph got lots of community service time.

The following year the Ayers' sold the house and moved to Florida. The ballfield itself and the land below it was purchased by a real estate corporation, and lies empty to this day. Perhaps someday they will clear it and build houses or apartments there. (I often toy with the idea of someday living where home plate or the pitcher's mound once was.)

Occasionally I take a walk through those now-difficult woods by myself, sometimes with Donny Casale or John Martin, and we sit down on the wall by the big pine and relive old times at Redmont Field, when it was a *kingdom*, and *we* were the kings.

"BIRD GUYS"
Aug, - Oct. 2017

Norman Fielding was known as "The Bird Man of Meadowlark Terrace." There *were* no meadowlarks, as such.

There *were* sparrows, though. Sometimes a hundred or more of them, congregating in the back yard of his luxurious two-story house at 171 Meadowlark Terrace. Seventy-seven-year-old Norman Fielding, widowed eight years with no siblings, children, or any other interests in life, had created what could best be described as "Disney World for Sparrows."

Scattered across his spacious back yard were nearly twenty feeding stations; on the ground, on poles, and attached to windows and windowsills. Depending on the time of year, there could sometimes be so many visitors that the green of his lawn was obliterated by the brown, gray, and black birds.

There was nothing really notable about this sight and there was *absolutely* nothing noteworthy about Norman Fielding. He was one of the legion of elderly who had faded into oblivion. This was accentuated by the fact that he had virtually no contact with anyone around him. But Norman didn't feel alone or isolated from his fellow humans. People weren't his *thing*. The only passion in him, the only driving force in his life, were the tiny creatures he called, regardless of gender, "Bird Guys."

. . .

Tommy Vallunas and Ken Linden sat at their favorite booth in *Francie's Café,* finishing their pizza and beer.

Ken knew that Debby, their waitress, would soon bring the bill, and *he* would be paying it. Tommy never offered to pay simply because he never had any money.

"You *could* ask your mom for a few bucks and pitch in now and then."

"Why ruin a good thing?"

"What good thing? The thing where every time we go out I get stuck with the check?"

Tommy hunkered down in his half of the booth and lowered his voice. "No, man, the thing where I only hit them up for dough when it's somethin' real important."

"Like what?" Ken demanded.

"Like pot, booze, and beer. The party essentials."

"So do you tell your mother you need money for pot, booze, and beer?" came the sardonic rejoinder.

"Course not." Tommy snickered and brushed back his long, stringy brown hair.

"Well, now that we're finished with the pizza, I figure I got your attention."

"What's up?"

"I think I found a way for us to make some easy money." It was fortunate, or clever of Ken to have used the word 'easy' in his pitch. Tommy Vallunas was someone who wanted no part of any venture unless it was easy, free, or dropped into his eager, waiting hands.

"How much?" came the eager reply.

"Hundreds, maybe thousands," Ken replied quietly.

"What do we have to do?" Tommy asked. All he could think of was how much pot, booze, and beer he could buy with hundreds, or thousands.

"There's this house on Meadowlark, across from the elementary school."

"Woodrow Wilson School?"

Ken raised his eyebrows. "I'm surprised you remember anything to do with a school." The mild insult did not seem to register with Vallunas.

"The guy that lives there," continued Ken, "is this old coot, like a hermit, and he's loaded."

"Loaded, like rich?" asked Tommy.

"Yeah."

"How do you know?"

"The company my dad works for cleans his yard twice a year. He heard some of the other guys talking about him. Ever since his wife died the guy hardly leaves his house or talks to anybody. No friends. He just feeds birds in his back yard."

"So how we gonna get money off *him?*"

"We gain his trust, then pull a con on him."

"Really," said Tommy, not looking impressed or convinced. "And what if he gets wise to us or someone thinks somethin' is fishy and calls the cops."

"When did you become such an analytical thinker?" Ken said, half in anger and half in confusion.

"I don't know what that means. But I know that running a con on some rich old guy can be risky."

"All you gotta do is follow my lead. Can you do that?"

Visions of pot, booze, and beer danced in Tommy Vallunas's head as he nodded in agreement.

. . .

"Act like we're looking for an address," Ken said, as he and Tommy looked at various houses across the street from Woodrow Wilson Elementary School.

"What number do we want again?"

"One-seventy-one." He paused and looked Tommy in the eye. "What are you gonna do when Fielding answers the door?"

"Just go along with whatever you tell him and not say anything unless he talks to me."

"Good."

They ambled up the sidewalk and Ken rang the bell. Steps sounded inside the house and the door opened. Norman Fielding was a short man, five-foot-seven, a bit bell-shaped but not truly overweight. His mass had simply shifted. His gray hair was parted on one side. He wore glasses and a medium-sized moustache. He almost gave off the air of an English gentleman, but spoke in an Oklahoma drawl.

"Can I help you young men?" he asked politely.

"Yes, sir," answered Ken. "I'm Ken, and this is Tommy, and we have a community service obligation that we have to fulfill."

"So what is it that you need?"

"We're taking a civics class at the community college, and our main requirement is to help out a senior citizen or a child from a disadvantaged family"

"Well, that's very nice of you boys. But how did you know a senior citizen lived here?"

Tommy shuddered inside. How *would* they have known that?

"We were driving by on Baeder Street, over there, and we saw you feeding birds in your yard."

"Yes, I feed them every day. Wonderful little creatures." Fielding paused and seemed to be considering their offer. "I would be glad to help you out."

"Great. Our instructor is Mr. Brunnell if you want to call him."

Tommy turned away and grimaced. Ken was blowing it!

"I don't think that will be necessary. I trust you boys."

"Great. What would you like us to do first?"

"Well," began Fielding, a faint smile on his face as he glanced upward, seemingly in thought. "Let me look around this afternoon and I'll make a list. I'm not as spry as I once was," he said with an apologetic smile. "How long do you boys have to do this for?"

Another tough question, thought Tommy.

"At least fifty hours," Ken answered.

Now Tommy sagged outwardly. He was twenty, like Ken, but hadn't done fifty hours of work in his entire life.

Ken thanked Norman Fielding, and they walked down the street to Tommy's beat-up Chevy Malibu.

"Jesus Christ!" Tommy shouted as they got in. *"Fifty* hours. Why couldn't you have said like, *ten?"* And what if he does call that college professor?"

"I made him up, you dip. He doesn't want to be bothered with that. The guy can't keep up anymore, and he just got two hired hands that won't cost him a cent."

"But what if he *does* call—"

"He's not calling anybody. He thinks he got it made. So we clean here and there and feed his stupid birds. *We're* the ones that got it made."

. . .

"The usual, boys?" asked Debby Watkins.

"Yes, please," answered Ken.

"So what *is* the plan?" asked Tommy, as Debby rounded the partition between the bar and booths.

"Patience," stated Ken. "We gotta spend at least a week getting' a fix on his habits. We gotta observe while we work."

"Whattaya mean, 'observe?'"

"His routines. Does he use a computer, does he pay his bills by check, does he leave money out, how does he do his groceries, where does he get all that damn bird food, stuff like that."

"Why do we have to know all that stuff? Can't we just con him and split?"

"You're unbelievable," sighed Ken. "Do you think he's just gonna hand us a pile of cash?"

"I don't know."

"Well, I *do* know. We can't just take a big bite out of the guy. He's a loner but I'm sure he's not an idiot. We gotta go slow. It'll add up in the end. I figure we got about ten weeks."

"Why ten weeks?"

"We told him fifty hours. Five hours a week for ten weeks, Tommy. Simple math."

Debby appeared around the partition with their beer and pizza slices, ending the strategy meeting. Ken had learned that when beer and pizza were around, Tommy stopped listening.

. . .

They gave Fielding two days to compile his list of jobs, then returned. As he handed them the list, he looked almost apologetic.

"I hope this isn't too much, boys, but you told me you had to do fifty hours."

Ken looked at the list. There were once a week tasks, like mowing the lawn. There were once a month chores, trimming his nine-foot hedges. And there were one-time jobs, such as cleaning out the garage. The daily chores involved emptying bird trays of chaff, hosing them out, and refilling them.

Inside his house there was a multitude of cleaning, such as the attic, the basement, and other jobs in several unused rooms.

Ken guessed that it would not take fifty hours of labor to complete the long list. Tommy looked at the same list and came to the conclusion that he would not live long enough to finish it.

. . .

"Let's do the morning feeding first," Fielding said, leading Tommy and Ken out to his closed-in back porch. "I keep a twenty-pound bag of bird food here. When it runs out, I get another from the garage. They prefer the seven-to-nine time period. You'll notice certain groups congregate at their favorite spots."

Ken and Tommy stared at each other in amazement.

"You can't really tell them apart, can you?" Tommy asked.

"Well, *I* can. They're my regular bird guys that come here several times a day."

"Bird *what?*" asked Ken, nearly laughing.

"Bird guys. Just a name I call them. They're all sparrows. That's the only kind of bird I feed. The starlings and blue jays are more aggressive and try to hog everything. At least they used to."

"Used to?"

"Yes. Sparrows are small, but they have strength in numbers. They drove all the others away." Fielding wore a satisfied expression, as though the ousting of larger birds was a personal triumph.

Ken and Tommy continued to stare.

"They are very simple-minded," continued Fielding. "Find food, find safety. That's about it." He smiled.

"So what do we have to do?" asked Ken.

"You clean the chaff from all these feeders," Fielding said, waving his arm towards the multitude of trays, "hose out the ones that need it and fill them. I'll stay here with you for today so they'll know it's okay."

"Won't they just see the food and eat it no matter who puts it down?"

"They're used to seeing me. They wait for me. But I don't think it will bother them too much if you fellows are carrying the new bags from the garage. As long as I'm here." Fielding paused, then added, "I have to warn you, there are hundreds of them now, almost like they passed the word."

Tommy and Ken exchanged slightly uneasy looks.

"When they all come, it gets loud, and they buzz right by you. They nearly cover the ground."

"Will they attack?" asked Tommy. Ken looked down and shook his head.

Fielding laughed. "No, of course not. They're just sparrows, and you're *feeding* them. They would never attack you." Fielding added softly, "Just about the meekest creatures there are."

As Norman Fielding watched, Tommy and Ken set about their first feeding of the "bird guys." They did exactly as Fielding had directed with the emptying out of the previous day's chaff, and hosed out the trays as needed. Then came the arduous task of carrying seed from the twenty and forty pound sacks in the garage to the numerous trays located on the ground, on poles, and on window sills. It was not a lengthy process, but it was tiring. Tommy and Ken walked over to where Fielding stood by his porch.

"Now what?" asked Ken.

Fielding wore a wry smile. "Take a look around you, boys. You've got company." He pointed to his hedges, which were saturated with the brown and gray birds. A chirping started, then steadily grew to a din. "Why don't we step inside the garage. We can watch from the window."

They went inside, Fielding shutting the door behind them. "Don't want any of them to fly in here by accident when they're swarming." Within thirty seconds there was a dull whooshing sound, and scores of Norman Fielding's "bird guys" covered the yard.

Ken and Tommy watched with wonder as literally every feeding station was obliterated. After a couple of minutes Tommy asked, "Is it safe to go in the house?"

"I guess," Fielding said, frowning. "I'm usually inside when they're feeding. I suppose they'll get startled and swarm away. It might *seem* like they're going to run into you, but that never happens. And they'll come right back as soon as you're inside."

Fielding opened the garage door and calmly walked up the steps to the tiny closed-in porch. He knocked on the window to get Tommy and Ken's attention, but the sound caused the nearest birds to take flight in all directions. This caused a chain reaction in the groups all over the yard. Within a few seconds the yard was empty. The chirping from all the birds whose feeding had been interrupted was cacophonous. Tommy and Ken quickly left the garage, shut the door, and strode up the steps onto the back porch.

"See, told you there would be no problem," stated Fielding.

They retired to his living room, where Fielding produced a sheet of paper with all the jobs for their "community service requirement."

Both Tommy and Ken immediately took notice of a small nightstand in one corner. On it were piles of one, five, ten, and twenty dollar bills. While Tommy was still gawking at the piles of currency, Ken moved so that Tommy was between him and Fielding, reached into his pocket, and grabbed a five-dollar-bill while stuffing the rest back.

"Mr. Fielding?" he called.

"Yes, Ken?" said Fielding, looking up from the list.

"I just found this on the floor. It was partially under your recliner here."

"Thank you, Ken," Fielding said, his voice filled with gratitude. "That is very forthright and honest of you."

"Well, it was lying here on the floor. It had to be yours, I figured."

"Thank you very much, Ken. It seems I have two capable, honest helpers. You did an admirable job with my bird guys this morning."

"Thanks, Mr. Fielding."

"It takes me the better part of forty-five minutes to do the morning feeding, and you fellows got it done in fifteen minutes."

"Glad we could do a good job for you," chimed Ken.

"I'll tell you what. Why don't you take the rest of the day off. I can handle the noon feeding."

"How many feedings *are* there?" Tommy asked, looking somewhat overwhelmed.

"Well, there's the main one in the morning, and a smaller one at noon," Fielding replied. "And sometimes around four P. M. I just add a little bit to the trays that are empty."

Tommy moved towards the door to leave, his social skills as sadly lacking as most of his others. Ken shook his head at him slightly.

"We didn't put in our two hours for the day yet, Mr. Fielding. We don't want to start fudging on our time."

"Why don't you come back around four if you can and just add a little seed to the empty ones. How's that?"

"Great, we'll stop by then." He bumped Tommy to cue him to head for the door. "We'll just do a quick refill without bothering you."

They proceeded to head out the door as Norman Fielding saw them out. "Thank you again, fellows."

. . .

As soon as the car doors had closed, Tommy began an imitation of Ken. "'I just found this on the floor, Mr. Fielding. Here, take it. Glad we could do a good job for you. We don't want to start fudging our time.' What the hell was all that? We're gonna con *him?* *You're* the one out five dollars."

"Think, asshole. The guy *trusts* us now."

Wheels were turning in Tommy Vallunas's brain. It seemed as though he actually understood. "So now what?" he asked.

"We go back there today at four and feed the damn bird guys."

. . .

They quickly fell into a routine of showing up at Fielding's for the morning feeding, then sticking around to knock off a couple of the chores from the master list.

Most of the other jobs were around the yard; mowing, trimming the edges, and keeping his tall hedges from invading his narrow driveway, which contained an old 2004 Chevy Malibu.   Norman Fielding kept a record and periodically showed it to Ken, whom he had figured was in charge. Ken pretended to have kept a duplicate record, and would say, 'Yeah, that seems about right.' when shown Fielding's time record.

Ken quickly noticed the layout of the first floor. Since the front entrance, kitchen, living room and dining room formed a circle he would use any excuse to walk around and pass by the small table with the piles of bills on them. Volunteering to do some vacuuming, he took the opportunity to take several of the dollar bills in the huge pile, assuming Mr. Fielding did not know *exactly* how many there were.

Nothing was said. That afternoon they ordered a pitcher of beer at *Francie's*, and as Debby delivered it, Ken raised his glass and called out, "To Norman Fielding, for buying us this pitcher."

"Here, here," responded Tommy.

"Okay, Tommy, listen up."

"Yeah?"

"I'm not sure we can score a big hit off this guy."

"Whattaya mean?"

"I don't think we can scam this guy out of hundreds. I been watching him. He lives *small*. No computer we can use to order stuff on. He has his groceries and all that bird seed delivered. He does his banking in person. He pays his bills by mail. There's nothing there except that pile of money on that end table. I mean, I can nail a few bucks here and there, but that's about it."

Tommy looked half devastated and half outraged. "What the hell, Ken. After all that bird seed we hauled and everything else. For what? A pitcher of *beer?* I could get an actual *job* and be better off!"

Ken spit out the beer he was about to swallow. "Let's not talk crazy, now, Tommy. You? A job? Listen, give me a day or two. Maybe I can think of something."

"Well, you better think of something fast, or I'm out!"

"Professor Brunnell would be very disappointed."

"I don't care. Wait. Who?"

Ken Linden shook his head in disbelief.

. . .

As simple-minded as Tommy Vallunas could be, he was *not* a person of habit or routine. He talked Ken into pilfering from the 'five' and 'ten' piles of money on the small table. There was no mention of missing money from Mr. Fielding, and the two scammers became slightly bolder in their thievery each time.

It was Tommy, usually so oblivious that he might not have noticed if his arm had fallen off, who called it to Ken's attention that the "bird guys" were getting louder, more agitated, and more *aggressive* each time they fed them.

"Honest to Christ, Ken, one of them suckers came so close I could *feel* the breeze."

"That's just because there's so many of them now, they get in each other's way."

Ken was right. The number of sparrows massing for the morning feeding (Fielding called it "staging") had increased noticeably. It nearly resembled mass hysteria, like a mob fleeing a disaster.

That same day Fielding led them up to his attic on the third floor. It resembled the debris piles often seen after a tornado.

"Could you boys possibly neaten this up for me?" he asked politely.

Ken swallowed and said they could, wondering how many hours it would take.

"I have a few garbage bags in the corner," Fielding said, "with stuff that can be carried to the curb. I did that before I met you fellows. The rest of the items up here would need to be picked up and put in neat piles, if you could."

"Don't worry, Mr. Fielding, we'll take care of it," said Ken.

"Thank you, boys. One of my checks came today, so I have some finances to take care of. I won't be here to look over your shoulder while you work. That's not my style," he added with a chuckle.

"We'll be fine, Mr. Fielding. Do what you have to do."

"Thank you *so* much, fellows. I don't know what I'd do without you." He descended the attic stairs and could be heard going down to the first floor.

Tommy stomped his foot. "This just can't get any wor—"

"This is *great,*" asserted Ken.

"*What?*"

"Look at all this stuff. Lots of old people have things in their attic and cellars that are worth a lot, and they don't even know it."

"Like *what?*"

"Collectibles, foreign stamps, rare coins, old recordings, that kind of stuff. He has no real idea what's up here, I bet, except for what he's tossing out. If we find something of value, we sneak it out and sell it to Joey B."

"I guess it's worth a try."

It took two hours to arrange all the scattered pieces of Norman Fielding's life. At one point Tommy found an autographed 8X10 picture of an astronaut. "Think this is worth anything? An astronaut. Neil 'something.'"

"Neil Armstrong."

"Worth anything?"

"Five bucks if we're lucky. Just put it back. We're not taking any small time stuff."

A moment later, as Tommy was tossing the signed photo of Neil Armstrong (now worth up to ten thousand dollars) on top of the nearest pile, Ken was lifting up a large old-fashioned photo album. He opened it, his eyes getting wider with each turn of a page.

"Holy shit. Tommy, you gotta *see* this."

It took Tommy a moment or two after looking at the page to make a connection. "A newspaper did a story on Mr. Fielding?"

"That's right. Sixty-six years ago he was "The Bird Boy of Painted Rock." Ken looked again at the headline from an April 21st, 1951 Tulsa, Oklahoma newspaper. The feature article showed a photo of eleven-year-old Norman Fielding sitting in his yard, surrounded by dozens of sparrows, who not only had no fear of the boy, but showed an actual *affinity,* bordering on *adoration* for him.

Ken read the article to himself. "Wow, the old man was like a 'Bird Whisperer.' He started out feeding them and they got friendlier until they were like his pets. They would perch on his arm and sit on his head and everything"

"Maybe he can get the ones we feed to calm down. Those little bastards are getting downright *nasty*. One pecked my arm today."

"Really?"

"Yeah, you haven't noticed?"

Ken shrugged. "So big deal. We feed the stupid birds and then come inside for our *real* purpose here." He flipped through the other pages of the album quickly, not bothering to read any of them. He noticed that all the pages had a common theme: Norman Fielding and sparrows. He had been obsessed with birds, and had worked for a company that sold bird-related merchandise and had a separate research division.

Unknown to Tommy and Ken, at the louvered attic windows at both ends of the attic, several sparrows had been roosting and watching both outside and inside Norman Fielding's attic.

"Hey," said Tommy, "you realize we got absolutely *zilch* out of cleaning this attic."

"Not exactly zilch, Tommy, old boy." He removed a large manilla envelope from his pocket. "I found this in the album. Fielding got some award for bird conservation and research. The letter is signed by the President of the United States."

"Trump sent Fielding a letter?"

"Idiot. It's from 1958. President Eisenhower. I bet Joey B. will pay some good money for *this*. *And,* we still have to visit the old money pile."

There was a rustling, shooshing sound by the attic windows as the two headed downstairs.

. . .

Joseph Bonatti took a long look at the letter of commendation awarded to Norman Fielding for his exemplary work in avian conservation and research. It was signed in ink, not auto pen, and had the signature of Dwight Eisenhower, 34th President. Joey B. had clients who collected signatures of notable people, and knew he could get at least five-hundred dollars for it.

"Fifty bucks," he said to Tommy and Ken. "I might be able to sell it for eighty. Whattaya say?"

"Sold," said Ken.

"Where'd *you* guys come across somethin' like this?"

"We was helpin' this old coot clean his attic. Figured it wasn't doin' *him* any good," stated Ken.

"Okay. Any other stuff like this?"

"Just an autographed picture of this Neil Armstrong guy. An astronaut. Ever hear of him?"

Joey B. *had* heard of the most famous astronaut in history. While he was alive, Armstrong's signature was the most coveted one on the market. But they were scarce, since the publicity-shy Armstrong had stopped signing anything in the early 1990's. Since his death in 2012, the value of his signature had skyrocketed. He was sure he could get up to ten *thousand* for a genuine Neil Armstrong.

"Yeah, I heard of him," replied Bonatti. "Why don't you guys bring that one in, too. I might go a hundred for it."

Two sets of eyes across from him widened.

"Give us a little time, Joey, we'll see if we can get it."

"Don't wait too long. The market on these things is kind of funny, sometimes."

. . .

"Hey," said Tommy, "maybe if we give Fielding some props for his being in the paper he can get those damn birds to calm down a little."

"Stupid," Ken hissed. "He can't know we were snooping through his stuff. He might put two and two together."

"Yeah, okay. Right."

"What we gotta do is find a reason to get back in that attic, even if it takes a while."

"Joey B. said we should get that picture as soon as possible."

Ken shook his head. "Joey B. is a greedy little asshole, Tommy. Just so you know. We play it cool on this. Nothin' to raise any suspicion from Fielding. We're just gonna feed his little birds, and clean whatever he asks us to clean."

Tommy pointed for emphasis. *"And* visit the money pile!"

"Yeah, Tommy. *And* visit the money pile."

. . .

For the next two visits, they played it close to the vest. They arrived, fed the birds, neatened things in Fielding's garage, and moved a pile of old boards behind the garage. The work itself went smoothly, but the noise level among the "bird guys" had picked up noticeably. Tommy suggested they ask Mr. Fielding to try to get them to quiet down.

"He can probably do it, you know." Tommy added. "He was the 'Bird Boy of Painted Rock,'" he added, proud of the fact that he actually remembered something that had been read to him.

"Ya dummy. I told you before he *can't know* we read that article. He might get suspicious. Now shut up,

I'm tryin' to think of a reason to go back to the attic so we can get that picture."

"How can you think with all this noise?" Tommy nearly shouted.

The words were no sooner out of his mouth when everything went silent in the yard.

"Hello, boys," said Norman Fielding, appearing around the corner of the garage with two glasses. "I brought you some iced tea. Why don't you take a little break?"

"Thanks, Mr. Fielding," said Ken.

"The bird guys sure have been noisy lately," said Tommy, trying to show that he could be 'cool' about things.

Ken shot him a look.

"I think it's mating season," said Fielding. "They get very excited then."

Ken assumed a serious expression. "Say, Mr. Fielding, I'm pretty sure I left my driver's license up in your attic on top of one of the stacks we made. Could Tommy and I go up there when we're finished and look for it?"

"Certainly, boys. You can knock off now if you want to." His cheerful look turned puzzled. "But why would you have your license out while you were cleaning the attic?"

Ken didn't hesitate. "Well, we were making your attic *neater,* and I just thought how disorganized my wallet was, so I pulled it out and made *it* neater, too."

"That's interesting, Ken. You boys head up to the attic and I'll take these glasses inside."

. . .

"Where the hell did you put that picture?" Ken asked, tossing things to the floor.

"I don't remember. *You* said to just leave it."

"Never mind. Where were we? Wasn't it over in that corner?"

"No it was right around here."

"We can't stay up here much longer. I told Fielding I left it on *top* of one of the piles."

"Looking for this, gentlemen?" sounded a voice behind them.

They turned to find Norman Fielding at the top of the attic stairs, holding the photo of Neil Armstrong.

Tommy stared at the floor, a coping mechanism he used since kindergarten. Ken flushed and reached for his wallet. "I found my driver's—"

"Please stop, Ken. You weren't looking for your license. You were looking for this signed photo of Neil Armstrong, the first man to walk on the moon."

"Mr. Fielding, we didn't mean—"

"Again, let me stop you. I am well aware of what you two have been up to."

"How?' asked Tommy, not thinking or bothering to deny it.

"Do you think a man of my wealth just leaves piles of money around without knowing how much is there?"

Tommy shrugged his ignorance. "I don't know."

"You two have *pilfered* one-hundred seventeen dollars from me. Those stacks were there in the open because I live *alone.* It's *convenient* for me to have them there. Normally there is no one around to *see* them. Ken, you gave me a five-dollar bill you claimed you found by my recliner. That would *not* have been possible. You did it to show me you were honest and to gain my trust."

Fielding paused and inhaled deeply, as though getting his second wind. "I no longer have friends, as such, but I *do* have connections. The niece of my late friend, Randall Thomas, works as a waitress at *Francie's Café*, I believe."

"Debby?" asked Ken.

"Yes, Debby. She called some time back to tell me that you two were toasting me for buying you a pitcher of beer."

Ken figured he better say *something*. "We're sorry, Mr. Fielding. We'll find a way to pay you back."

Fielding let out a loud sigh. "I sincerely doubt that. But while we're on the subject, how much did you get for my Presidential award I received at age eighteen?"

"Fifty dollars," said Ken quietly.

Fielding shook his head, laughing softly. "Well, you two are not only dishonest, you're stupid to boot. That letter has a genuine signature of a U. S. President! There are people who would pay up to a thousand dollars for it."

"Joey B.," Ken muttered.

"And what were you offered for Mr. Armstrong's photo, which I correctly assumed was your next theft?"

"Maybe a hundred."

"Maybe a hundred," Fielding repeated with disgust. "This would have sold for over three thousand when he was *alive*. It's probably *tripled* in value since his death."

"Shit," Tommy whispered.

"God damn Joey B.," Ken complained.

"And may I assume you have found and read my scrapbook?"

"Yeah, you were 'The Bird Boy of Painted Rock,'" said Tommy, proudly.

"Indeed I was. I'm going to take a wild guess that you did not actually *read* all the articles. Maybe the first one and then just looked at the pictures."

Fielding was right about this.

"If you *had* read the later articles, you would have known that I developed a method of *communicating* with sparrows. I used whistling tones that were not part of their language.

People have *no* idea how intelligent these creatures are. And how *loyal.* I have pampered the sparrows in my neighborhood for years." He paused and smiled. "What I have done for them buys a *lot* of loyalty. Watch." He proceeded to the attic window and whistled a strange melody, half yodel and half South African folk song. Ken and Tommy had never heard anything like it, and were not at all comfortable when a crescendo of sparrow sounds were accompanied by the whirring, buzzing sound of over five-hundred of them circling the house like TV Indians attacking a wagon train.

Fielding returned to the top of the attic stairs. *"They're* onto you, too. You are their enemy now, and they have just declared war."

"But we *fed* them." Ken said, plaintively.

Fielding frowned, shook his head, and tapped his temple, inferring that his "bird guys" were not easily fooled.

"What the hell, Mr. Fielding," Ken shouted. (He *had* to shout to be heard at this point.) "We said we're sorry and we'll pay you back. We'll even buy back the letter from Joey B. Whattaya say?"

"I say good luck trying to get to your car, boys."

Tommy looked at the nearest attic window. He could barely see anything other than hundreds of sparrows circling the house in a clockwise rotation. "Call 'em off!" he shouted. "Please! Call 'em off!"

"I think not," replied Fielding. "Well, you gentlemen should be leaving, now. I'll give you a week to make some form of restitution before I call the authorities."

"We can't go out there. The bird guys will kill us!" Tommy yelled.

"Shut the hell up." Ken shouted. "We're leaving. Right now."

Fielding smiled, turning back to savor the fear and consternation he had wrung out of these two, with some help from his trusty Bird Guys. His first step mistakenly kicked against the stair post and pitched him downward, head first.

Ken instinctively grabbed for Fielding, but hit him in the back, propelling him faster.

In the hundredths of a second the human mind is capable of operating, Norman Fielding, about to take the worst fall of his life, received a message that Ken Linden had *tripped* him and then *shoved* him.

Across the street at the Woodrow Wilson Elementary School, Mrs. Reiser's fourth grade class stood plastered against the windows, watching a brown blur orbiting the house next door.

"Mrs. Reiser," asked one girl, "are those bumblebees?"

"Look how *fast* they're going!" added a boy.

"Are they gonna come over *here*?" asked a third voice.

Linda Reiser did not answer. She skipped the call to her principal and dialed 9-1-1. She also skipped telling everyone to ignore the interruption, joining them at the window.

At the bottom of the attic stairs Norman Fielding lay on his side. He had no idea of *what* or *how many* bones he had broken, but he knew they were *numerous.* He still had enough of his wits to play dead when he heard two sets of footsteps descending the stairs.

"Serves you right," he heard Ken say. "See if your bird guys can help you *now.*"

"You won't be needing this," he heard Tommy say as the photo of Neil Armstrong was retrieved from where it lay beside him.

Ken headed for the back door, where the enclosed porch gave them a chance to assess the situation. That situation easily matched the bird-swarming scenes in Alfred Hitchcock's classic movie.

"My God," said Tommy. "Look at them all. Look at how *fast* they're going."

"Big deal," said Ken defiantly. "Look how *small* they are. Tommy, they're *sparrows,* for Christ's sake."

"The car is out in *front.* We gotta run all the way around the house to get to it."

"Then let's go *out* the front, jackass. "

He and Tommy made a mad dash through the kitchen and living room, flung open the front door and ran for the car. One floor above them, Norman Fielding lay in his hallway. Despite his excruciating pain, he managed to face a screened window and whistle an eerie, bizarre melody.

. . .

"Mrs. Reiser! Those two men are getting pecked and bit from all those little birds!"

Linda Reiser closed the blinds. "Everyone sit down now! No one is to look over there!"

As a police car pulled up to 171 Meadowlark Terrace, the massive flock took flight, scattering into nearby bushes, trees, and hedges on the Fielding property, as well as the roofs of the house and garage.

Ken Linden and Tommy Vallunas sat on the ground, bruises welling and streams of blood flowing from dozens of wounds. Nearby, face down on the sidewalk, lay a wrinkled and slightly torn photo.

As the two officers got out of their vehicle, a lone sparrow flew from the nearby hedges and perched atop the antennae of Ken Linden's car, chirping an odd melody.

"EDDY"
Aug. – Oct. 2017

In all fairness, we *had* been warned not to go swimming in Scobee's Pond. In fact, we had been strongly advised by our parents to stay away from its *general vicinity*.

But truthfully, we never actually *listened* to our parents. What kept us out of dire consequences to life and limb was a general application of common sense, rather than any *specific* caveats from the people who had brought us into the world.

. . .

Scobee's Pond was located on land owned by a local dairy farmer named Seb Scobee. If you've lived here for any length of time you have probably heard stories about the place. And by stories, I mean things that were both strange and unexplained, and unexplain*able*.

For example, two or three times a year the water in Scobee's Pond simply disappears. No dead animals or fish are found. No one dares to go walking where the water once was. We all know how *dangerous* that is. Just throwing in the pitfalls of rocks, soft ground, and how hard it is to safely get down there and out again is enough. But add in some of the other creepy things that were known about the place, and that decides it.

Two or three days after the water disappears, it comes back. There has *never* been a witness to the water disappearing or returning.

Why doesn't someone keep a vigil on the pond after the water disappears so they can see it come back? *No one wants to be anywhere near Scobee's Pond when that kind of shit is going on.*

One time, a *rowboat* was floating out in the middle of the pond. Luckily, a strong wind came up and it drifted in to shore. Seb Scobee himself secured it and called the sheriff. Sheriff Henry Barnaker came out to see what was what. The boat was missing an oar, and inside were a pair of cheap reading glasses and a soaked short story book by J. D. Salinger. There were no missing people for miles around, and Barnaker used that as an excuse not to send divers down there. People came to the conclusion that it was a prank by some kids.

I tell you, though, if it *had* been a prank eventually someone would have bragged, or squealed, or something. So I don't think it *was* a prank. I think it was another of those unexplainable things that happen out there.

There have been sightings of an unidentified pond creature in the water. It is a huge lizard or salamander-like thing, thirty to forty feet long, short legs, and black with some yellow markings. It is called "The Long Lizard." None of the people who have seen it are liars or crackpots, either.

Our First Selectman, Joseph McCabe, got a notion that we should *publicize* the sightings of The Long Lizard, get some notoriety, but cooler heads prevailed. Who knows what might happen with a bunch of reporters and camera crews were traipsing around where we locals know enough not to go.

Somebody would probably open their mouth about the other stuff, and we get branded as weirdos. Maybe the state makes the town drain the pond, especially if they found out about the rowboat incident. We get people here trying to capture or kill The Long Lizard, and who knows what might happen? We all dealt with Scobee's Pond and were all somewhat *uncomfortable* by it, but we knew enough to keep it "in-house."

Teenage boys trying to show off for teenage girls have been known to park there at night. A lot of them later talked about strange sounds coming from the pond. Word of *that* eventually got to the sheriff, and twice a week he sent a patrol out there around eleven P. M. to chase off the teens and do a walk-around of the pond, which is about as big as a football field, end zones included, but wider and more oblong-shaped.

The officers reported nothing but the sounds of frogs and such. Not many of us believe that such walk-arounds actually *occurred.* Like any body of water at night, the place had a special creepiness.

. . .

Craig Vernay and I had been best friends since kindergarten, eight years ago. Since I'm an only child, he was like the brother I never had. Same for him, except he has an annoying little sister. We spent entire days together in the summer, playing baseball, board games, exploring, you name it. Fall was for football and basketball, and in winter we went sledding and played hockey. Scobee's Pond, because of its size, would have been ideal for hockey if it hadn't been, well, Scobee's Pond.

Only a couple months apart, we went through the same ups and downs together, too. We were like counselors to each other. Sounds kinda corny, but it was great.

. . .

It was August 23rd. With about a week left of summer vacation, Craig and I were looking forward to being in high school, even if it was in the same building we had gone to for seventh and eighth grade.

Still, I think we were subconsciously looking to end the summer with a bang. Maybe even something *daring* or *outrageous.* And what could be more daring and outrageous than a dip in Scobee's Pond?

To be clear, Craig and I walked down by its edge almost every day. We would shout insults at it (yes, we were immature) and had brought pellet and BB guns there to shoot at frogs. We would dare, double dare, and triple dare each other to go in. Then we would defiantly throw a couple of rocks in and walk off to our next adventure.

But I felt today would be different. I could sense it. We got down there and went through the usual dare fest. Only this time, following a *quadruple* dare by me, Craig smiled and said, "You're on." He stripped off his tee shirt, kicked off his moccasins, and walked toward an area free of reeds and other growth.

Before I knew it, he was thirty feet out, the water just above his waist. While part of me was thinking *better you than me,* part of me was reminding myself of our strong friendship; the bond we had after so many years as best friends. If he would dare do this reckless thing, then so would I.

I took off my shirt and hurriedly tried to untie my sneakers. That, of course, made them knot up and I struggled to take them off without untying them. By the time I got to the water's edge, Craig was even farther out, the water up to his chest.

He turned back. "Gonna take the plunge, hey? You're a true friend, Larry." His arms were horizontal now, on the water's surface.

Right then is when I saw it. About thirty or forty yards beyond Craig, in the direct middle of the pond, the water seemed to be swirling. It started picking up speed, and got bigger. I tried to yell but nothing came out. Craig was still facing me, waving me to come out farther.

"Craig, get out! There's an eddy!"

He turned to look and that's when I ran back to the shoreline. When I turned back, the eddy encompassed nearly half the pond, moving even faster. Craig was now *caught in it,* being rotated clockwise. Only his head, neck, and shoulders were visible.

"Craig! Swim!"

The eddy picked up. Craig was moving at the speed of someone jogging briskly.

I was completely panicked now. I scanned the shoreline for *anything* I might use to help get him out. A huge, black *something* was slithering out towards shore and taking refuge in the reeds about a hundred feet from me. *The Long Lizard.* There really *is* one, a deep part of my mind reported.

For many kids, the last resort is to run and get a grown-up. I knew there were several houses across the street. I took a last look at Craig orbiting Scobee's Pond like some carnival ride from Hell. There were no shouts or screams. I wondered if he even *could* speak. He wasn't waving his arms. He was a silent passenger in the eddy.

I ran, still shirtless and barefoot, to the pond's entrance and across the road. At the driveway of the first house I came to I looked up to see a German Shepherd running down the driveway, growling and barking.

"Christ!" I yelled, retreating back down the driveway. I knew that dog never left his yard. At the next house I ran up the driveway and saw a guy standing next to a lawn mower.

"Mister, ya gotta help! My friend went in Scobee's Pond and he's stuck in an eddy!"

"A *what?*"

"A big whirlpool!"

The guy looked startled and confused, then ran into his garage, coming back with a large coil of rope. "Get in," he said, pointing to a red pickup at the top of the driveway. We jumped in and he backed up and sped down the driveway, took a sharp right, and headed for the pond's entrance, already within sight. We passed the German

Shepherd sitting at the foot of his driveway, and veered sharply left at the pond entrance.

The guy got as close as he dared, then did a U-turn and backed up. We jumped out and grabbed the rope. Neither of us had time to actually *focus* on the pond when his truck had gone screaming into the entrance. But now we both looked out at the approximate six-thousand square yards of Scobee's Pond.

It was as still and serene as water in a bathtub. A gentle August breeze moved the reeds and created a few ripples. But no eddy. And no Craig, either.

. . .

The guy, Danny Brewster, and I called for Craig, hoping he had gotten out and was lying in the reeds. We walked around the pond twice.

"Let's go back and call somebody," he said solemnly. Within ten minutes there were three police cruisers, a fire truck, and an emergency rescue unit all crowded into the pond's entrance, except for the fire truck, which couldn't fit, and wasn't allowed to park where it might get hemmed in. Uniformed people were all over the place, poking around and asking Danny Brewster and me a lot of questions. I couldn't help but notice that *no one* was actually *in* the water.

Sheriff Barnaker pulled me off to the side. Seb Scobee stood nearby. "You're Lawrence Pickard, right?"

"Larry Pickard, yes."

"What the hell happened, Larry?"

The tone was one of a parent or teacher beginning to interrogate a suspected wrongdoer.

I started with us going to the pond and quadruple daring Craig to go in.

"Why would you *do* that?" demanded Barnaker.

"We did that every day. It's no big deal."

He extended his arm toward the water. "Well, today it *is*. Today it's a *very* big deal. Your friend is probably at the bottom of this ungodly body of water. Is that a big enough deal for you?"

I started crying then, damn it. And then Craig's parents rushed over. Craig's mother Leah actually hugged me while his father went off on Seb Scobee for not draining the pond, or roping it off, or blowing it up.

I finished my story, right up to when Danny Brewster and I walked around the pond twice. What got me was that no one seemed shocked that there was an *eddy* in a damn *pond*. All anyone seemed to get was that two kids were screwing around where they shouldn't have been and a tragedy occurred. Just then *my* parents showed up.

"Take him home and keep him there," Sheriff Barnaker said to them. "I'll be in touch."

. . .

They did do a search later. Small boats were put in the water, two people in each one, and secured to the shore with a rope held by other people. I don't know what good they thought that was gonna do. Maybe they were hoping to find him near the surface, so they wouldn't have to send divers down.

But divers *were* sent down. Two men from the state showed up and searched the pond. No one mentioned securing *them* with ropes from the shoreline. We convinced ourselves that these guys were professionals and could handle it. Then we crossed our fingers and prayed.

The divers found nothing, and reported that the pond's inner depths looked like any other body of water. I bet they wondered why people kept asking what it looked like down there.

I was questioned two more times, by the sheriff and the State Police. It was ruled a death by misadventure, an unfortunate accident.

But I had blame aimed all over the place. I blamed myself. If I hadn't been such a chicken shit I would have gone in *with* Craig, and we could have helped each other to shore when the eddy started. I blamed Seb Scobee and the town for not *doing* something when all those creepy things happened. I even managed to blame the German Shepherd, who kept me from getting help sooner.

School started a few days later, and as you might imagine, I was a celebrity, of sorts. I was given sympathetic, deferential treatment by almost everyone, especially the teachers. I happened to see Craig's third grade sister Jeanne, and when she saw *me* she burst into tears and had to go to the nurse's office to calm down.

So there was some guilt, like I already said. At lunch, this big goofy kid named Schwartz gave me a hard time. "You ran out on your friend, Pickard," he said.

. . .

No one could figure out why they didn't find Craig. It was hell for his parents. My mom said they were talking about having a funeral service. God, what if they found him right *after* that? Would they have to have a *second* funeral?

Divers returned a few more times. There were no results. No one even saw The Long Lizard. And there *is* such a thing. I saw him on August 23rd, 1980, the day my best friend Craig became a victim of an eddy in Scobee's Pond.

As weeks went by and people got used to what happened, they started to get more analytical. One theory was that he was taken by an alligator, but there are no gators within hundreds of miles. How could a gator survive the freezing temperatures we occasionally get in winter? Another was that he got out of the eddy somehow, staggered down the road, and was subsequently abducted by someone. *Very* far-fetched, but possible.

At least those two theories were of this world. I don't believe he was captured by aliens, but there had to have been some reason why they didn't find his body. And of course you had the unfeeling bastards who said to just wait until the water disappeared and *then* you would find him.

Somebody asked one of the divers how deep it was out in the middle. He said it was eighty to ninety feet deep, then added, somewhat hesitantly, "It *seemed* normal down there, but it wasn't, really. Just kind of strange." Then he shrugged and said, "I don't know. It could just have been my imagination."

Nine months went by, and the first round of holidays without Craig. All the plans we had for Halloween. I wasn't even up to going out, so I didn't. Thanksgiving and the big neighborhood football game. I played, but it wasn't the same. During Christmas my partner was no longer with me, so there were no suicide sled runs. As far as the main point of Christmas, I felt a kind of *shift* in what I considered the main focus.

It *had been* presents and school vacation, now it was something else I couldn't quite put my finger on. I just felt kind of empty, incomplete. Adults seemed to put the emphasis on family and friends, and *my* best friend was gone.

Craig's little sister, on the other hand, seemed as happy as ever. Suddenly an only child, she was doted on and spoiled by her grief-stricken parents. On the playground I heard her bragging about how she got *so* many more gifts this year. Greedy little bastard. I'm bitter, I know.

. . .

And then came springtime, the first one without Craig. Baseball, fishing, all that. I did become closer with a couple of kids I already knew. They were so *receptive* to anything I did or said I had the feeling that they had been *encouraged* by their parents to *adopt* me as their new good friend.

Their names were Devon Kramden and Greg Isola. They had been friends since third grade.

I noticed as the school year was getting short that I was being included in more things they did, which wasn't much different from things I did before. With one exception. Craig and I had gone down to Scobee's Pond on a regular basis. I hadn't set foot there since that day in August. I don't think too many other people had, either. Seb Scobee had put up signs around the pond: "No Swimming or Wading." Big deal. Nothing about The Long Lizard, the creepy vibes the state divers got, or the killer eddy in a body of *pond water.* I would have at least mentioned those in a posting. Maybe every three feet just to be extra sure. In case you were wondering, the town did absolutely nothing. The bottom line was that you can't always protect people from *themselves.* Meaning, I assume, that stupid teens will do stupid things, and occasionally a very bad result will occur.

. . .

The first week in May our town holds this big community event at Jasper Blevens Park in the center of town. There are all kinds of crafts, food vendors, bands, novelty rides and entertainment.

So Devon, Greg and I rode our bikes there together. In the deep recesses of my mind it seemed like this was an important step for me in moving on. I had been here before with my parents, but never with Craig. For some reason, he thought it was a waste of time.

The first thing we did was ride around the sidewalk that encircles the park. The far end of the park has some isolated nooks and crannies. A lot of druggies, homeless and other "street people" congregate there. As we rode along we noticed a well-known homeless guy named Rich there. He was in his forties and always carried a beat-up Bentley acoustic guitar and wore a large silver cross around his neck. His guitar had writing all over it; his friends had signed it. One of the signatures read, "ZZ Top," so I guess some of them had gotten a bit creative.

As we rode by he called out, "Hi guys, enjoy the fair. God bless you."

I had always thought of homeless people as either a rough element or a pitiful mass of losers. This guy seemed, well, *interesting.* I stopped and called the other guys back.

"You're Rich, right?"

"I am. And who would you be?"

"Larry Pickard. And this is Devon and Greg."

"Oh," he said, looking at me more intently. He fingered the silver cross around his neck. "You're the one that got out alive."

I looked down. "Yeah, that's me."

"Let me ask you something. Have you ever wondered why the pond decided to take your friend that day?"

He made it sound like the pond had decision-making ability, and we were so bad that one of us had to die. It pissed me off a little. "It's Scobee's Pond. All kinds of weird shit has happened there. He got caught in an eddy."

"That's correct. But do you know *why* all kinds of weird things happen *there*?"

"No, not really."

"Well, I'm gonna tell you why."

I figured I was about to hear something far-out or ridiculous, but I wanted to hear it anyway. Greg and Devon had come closer.

Rich spoke in a very low, intense voice. "There are some things in nature that are *unnatural*. There's a stand of pine trees up in Maine. They *move* a little when no one's around. They have shown the ability to *communicate* to certain people. They have a *consciousness*. And most important, they can *sense* if people are going to harm them."

"What are you talking about?" I asked

"Did you and your unfortunate friend *disrespect* that pond?"

I knew that respect was a big issue with street people. "Disrespect it? We went there almost every day and just threw a few rocks in and left."

"Maybe a body of water like this one could take offense to that." He peered intently at me. "Anything else?"

I remembered all the times Craig and I had shot frogs there with our BB guns, and all the times we *yelled* at the pond that it was no good and we weren't afraid of it. "Maybe some other stuff."

"I see. Did you *kill* any of the pond?"

" How do you kill a *pond?* "

"Its plants. Its animals. Did any of them come to harm because of you and your friend?"

I could feel Rich, Devon and Greg staring at me as I looked down. "A few times."

"Maybe in this pond's *consciousness* you and your friend were *tormenting* it all those days you threw rocks at it and whatever else you may have done. Maybe that day was its first chance to get back at you."

"By *killing* Craig?"

Rich shook his head. "I'm not judging, Larry." Sounds of the festival drifted across Blevins Park. "I'll tell you something else, boys. There may be a lot more to that pond than the human mind can comprehend."

A repressed guilt over Craig's death had been revived, and I found it hard to speak.

Greg spoke up. "Whattaya mean?"

"You know how every now and then the water disappears and then comes back?"

We nodded.

"And that rowboat that was found with a book and someone's glasses in it?"

"Yeah," I answered, finally able to speak.

"Well, I got a theory that there is *another* part of the pond that we just don't know about."

"Where?" asked Devon.

Rich grabbed his silver cross. "Somewhere. Only God knows. That water *goes* somewhere. And I bet that other place is where that rowboat came from. Who knows what happened to the poor soul who was *in* it when *that* happened."

"You mean the pond *goes* to another body of water?" asked Greg. "Why would it *leave,* and then come back?"

"I'm tellin' you boys, this pond is *alive.* I would never go anywhere near it." He raised his silver cross and kissed it gently. "Like I told you, some things in nature are *un*natural." He looked all around, as though checking to see if anyone was watching or listening. "I gotta go meet some friends behind the fence down there. You boys take care, now. I would stay away from that pond."

He left, and we all sat on our bikes without saying a word.

. . .

None of us were in a festival mood after that, so we just rode home. The next day after church we met behind

Devon's house. There was a clearing near some pine trees where we talked or read comic books. Greg and Devon had apparently been talking after the fair and had some new ideas they wanted to "try out" on me.

"We should find out if anyone records when the water leaves and comes back," Devon began.

"Why?" I asked.

"So we can check it against when the rowboat was there. Maybe it really did come from somewhere else."

"That's not gonna solve anything," I said. "Besides, the sheriff already looked into it."

"Yeah, he looked around *here,* and Lake Palmer, but what if it was from somewhere even *farther* away?"

"And we should go and talk to Seb Scobee," added Greg. "See if he knows anything about the pond he's not telling."

"I don't want to talk to *him.* Besides, if he's got some secret he's not gonna tell *us.*"

"It's worth a try," said Devon.

"One more thing," added Greg. "We got to find out if anyone turned up someplace they didn't belong."

"What?"

"You know. Like those people they find wandering around in a daze and don't even know their names."

"What happens to them?" I asked

"I think they place them in some group home."

"Craig was fourteen last year, like me. Would he end up in an orphanage or something?"

"Maybe."

"Devon! Boys! Come here, please."

Devon's mother was calling us from their back porch. We ran over. She had a grim look on her face.

"Boys, the water's gone from Scobee's Pond. Someone called it in to the police. Mildred Calkins called. She said they're getting up a search party. I thought you might—"

"See you later, Mom," Devon called, as we all ran in the direction of Scobee's Pond, a half mile away.

When we got there it looked like a major recovery operation was forming. Police, fire, and ambulance, of course. And it looked like every winch-equipped truck in northern Virginia was there. How did they all get here so fast on such short notice on a *Sunday?* (I found out later that the sheriff had a contingency plan in place from last year.)

I had seen an empty Scobee's Pond a dozen times before, but always with Craig. It seemed spookier this time, for some reason. Maybe it was all that stuff Rich the homeless guy had said. Were all these men about to "disrespect" the pond by going down there now?

Fire and Rescue and volunteers were making their way down. I got a lot of sympathetic looks from people who knew who I was. I don't think anyone, ever, had set foot in the deepest part of the pond.

There's no sense in being dramatic. They didn't find Craig or any trace of him. There was no "passageway" or anything where the water could have gone. It felt like the final door in this mystery had been closed.

On the far side of the pond stood Seb Scobee, watching the proceedings with a somewhat impatient expression. I had walked around to that side during the search. I was no longer afraid of approaching him and asking if there was any secret knowledge he had. So that's what I did.

He gave me a scowl, which I assume he thought would make me go away. It was just the two of us. I was the only kid given free access during the search. When I didn't leave, Seb exhaled and came over to me. He spoke before I could even say anything.

"This is *bad water,* Larry, and that ain't no secret to anybody around here."

"When you say 'bad'—"

"*Evil.* When my great-grandfather bought this land back in 1890, he was told the same thing by the old-timer who sold it to *him.*"

I was about to ask him if there was secret information, but he started up again.

"My grandfather told me some stuff about this pond when I was a kid."

"What kind of stuff?"

"Oh, one day the pond is like this, and then it shrinks to about half the size. That was before it started disappearing. There were times you could walk across the pond, then all of a sudden it's fifty feet deep or more. This place is not of this world."

"Did you ever think of filling it in?"

"My father tried. *Once.* I was here watchin.' I was maybe twenty-one or so."

"What happened?"

"The machines they brought in, early 1940's, they couldn't get near the place. It's like they refused. *Machines.* They wouldn't budge once they got within twenty feet. One guy goes down by the water just lookin' around, and he slips and falls in. It took three guys to pull him out of two feet of water. It's like this God damn place was just itchin' to kill somebody that day."

He paused. "Ain't maybe ten people who know what I just told you. About four years later this guy is just back from the war and takes his girl up here. He was gonna propose to her that night."

"He came up here *at night?*"

"He just survived World War II, so I guess he was feelin' pretty confident. He wanted a little privacy, if you get my drift."

"I guess."

"So he pops the question, she says yes, and the guy's so excited he runs into the water, showin' off for her."

"And?"

"And he drowns. In *four feet of water,* he *drowns.* "

"He couldn't swim to shore?"

"He *knew how* to swim, but he was *unable* to. He's flailin' around, the girl's standin' on the shore screamin,' and he's tellin' her to stay the hell away or she'll die, too. He wasn't twenty feet from shore."

"What happened to the girl?"

"She left here long ago. And Cal Messner died last year, so forget about talkin' to *him,* too."

I remembered Cal Messner, used to see him around town. "Wasn't he the guy with half an arm?"

"Yeah, the guy that tried to catch The Long Lizard that time. And look what happened."

"The Long Lizard was around all those years ago?"

"Sonny boy, The Long Lizard was *always* around."

I stared at the ground. Part of me was feeling grateful that I was still alive.

Seb put his hand on my shoulder. "Lookit, Larry. I'm sorry about your friend. But we all kind of *know* what this is. If you want a long, happy life, just leave this place be and stay the hell away from it."

He turned and walked back toward his farm.

. . .

Seb Scobee walking away from me that Sunday in May of 1981 should have been the end of the story. But it was just a *hiatus.* A very *long* hiatus.

Devon, Greg, and I continued to be friends throughout high school. My *obsession* with Scobee's Pond gradually faded, although my curiosity about it never did. (Seb was right about almost no one knowing about the things he told me that morning.) But life goes on. We had girlfriends, good times, not-so-good times, and all that.

Senior year rolled around, and the class of 1984 made plans for their future.

Devon had wealthy, influential relatives up in Rhode Island, and they helped him get into Roger Williams College, studying criminology. He wanted to be an FBI agent. Sometimes I toyed with the idea of getting him to come back with an investigative team and finding out what happened that August day in 1980. But, there was no actual crime, so I guessed that wasn't going to happen.

Greg's parents were moving to the Brewster, New York area for his father's job, and he enrolled at a small university in Danbury, Connecticut to study history.

Me, I had no idea what I wanted to do, other than solve the disappearance of Craig Vernay. My grades were good enough to get into the University of Maryland. I figured I would start out in Liberal Arts and see where the wind blew me. It blew me into the waiting arms of Doris Falcone, a coed studying geology. We sort of found each other halfway through freshman year, and stayed together the rest of our time at Maryland.

Like me, she was an out-of-state student, but while I was only one state away, in Virginia, and the northernmost tip at that, she was from Carthage, Missouri. During summer, she went back to Missouri, and I came home to Virginia. We called and wrote at least three times a week.

It was the summer between junior and senior year that Seb Scobee passed away. One of his organs failed and he died within a week. His two sons, Seth and Steven, took over the farm.

The pond was the same as ever. The water disappeared two or three times a year and some animal from the outskirts of Hell lived there. No one went anywhere near it. Craig and my encounter that day in August of 1980 may well have saved someone's life. What happened that day was a story every kid in town heard early in life and often.

So, senior year again. Doris was after me to go into her father's business. He sold all types of medical equipment, from raised toilet seats to wheelchairs. Oh, almost forgot. We were engaged so it was not at all presumptuous of her. The more I thought about it the more it seemed like a good move. I would have to leave my home and move to Missouri, but it was a down payment on the American dream: a wife who loved me, a good job, and a chance at all the happiness a guy could want. We'd have a nice house, and according to all the studies, one-point-eight children. I told Mr. Falcone ("We're like family, son. Call me Art!") I would accept his offer come graduation, and Doris and I set a date for our wedding, in the autumn of 1988.

I mention this in retrospect. When I first got to college I was lonely and homesick. I noticed that many students had a particular *thing* that sort of defined them, set them *apart* from everyone else. My story of the incident at Scobee's Pond on August 23rd, 1980 became the thing that set *me* apart. I admit that no more than half the students I told that story to believed it. So, to half the kids I knew I was the guy with the incredible experience of the paranormal. To the other half, I was the pathetic sap who needed to make up a ridiculous story to get attention. Luckily, Doris was in the first group.

. . .

Believe it or not, things worked out exactly as Doris and I had envisioned. Except for the children. We had two-point-zero children. Doris's dad Art used me as his "advance man," visiting pharmacies and medical supply outlets with pamphlets and info on all the latest (and most expensive) medical equipment. Hell, I didn't even mind coming home from a long road trip and proudly announcing to Doris, Joseph, and Karla that I had sold seven dozen toilet seats that week.

"Hooray for Daddy!" they would all shout.

My little piece of paradise lasted fourteen years like this. I had a list of clients I paid visits to when I wasn't trying to get new customers. It was like a far-ranging, well-paying paper route. Back at company headquarters I had an office for planning and organizing, a file drawer, and a new 2002 computer that I was convinced hated me. And on my desk, next to a picture of the wife and kids, was a framed five-by-seven photo of Craig and me in our Little League uniforms from back in 1976. Craig Vernay was a dim, but cherished memory in a busy life. Sometimes what happened that August day seemed so vague that I wasn't sure it had actually happened.

. . .

Ganelli's Medical Supply Outlet was my favorite stop. It was in Hermann, almost an eighty-mile drive, but was always worth my while. The owner's son Gabe was in charge of purchases, and he was very generous with his father's money. The best part of my bi-weekly visits were his anecdotes. He always had some hysterical story that involved someone using some piece of equipment in a way it was never intended. These stories were usually gross and involved messy bodily functions, but I thought they were entertaining. I must admit I stole a few of them when trying to entertain possible new clients. Thanks, Gabe.

It was the middle of June that year, and I was showing Gabe a new souped-up enema device (please don't hate me because I have a glamorous job). Gabe gets this exasperated look on his face and says, "We better make sure we don't sell one of these to my cousin Ethan. He'd end up sucking out what's left of his brains."

That was moderately funny, and I asked, "Why, what's with your cousin Ethan?"

"Well, everybody knows Ethan. He's pushing forty now, but back when he was in school he was the biggest *reader* ever. Claimed he read two books a day. I don't doubt it for a second."

"Go on."

"There's this river about a mile out of town. Nice place, even though the water level in our part of the river rises and falls a couple of times a year for no reason."

Deep in my mind a warning light was going on and off.

"So Ethan's out in the middle of the river in his father's rowboat, as usual. *Reading,* of course. He *claimed* that some *force* sucked the boat under the water, with *him in it.*"

The warning light in my mind now had a buzzer with it. A loud one.

"He somehow got away from the suction, and he surfaces holding one of the oars. He holds onto it and kicks like hell and gets to shore. He looks back, he says, and the boat is *gone.*"

"Gone, huh?" I managed to say. The warning light and buzzer had been joined by a siren.

"Yeah. So he goes home, soaking wet, without his glasses, still *holding* the oar, and tries telling the story to my uncle Tony. Obviously, the asshole fell out of the boat and it drifted away."

"So your cousin lost the boat, and his glasses, and the *book*, I assume."

"Yeah, *and* the other oar."

Yes, and the other oar. On an imaginary piece of paper I had checked off all the boxes.   "So did they ever find the boat?" *Please say no.*

"Shit, no. Looked five miles down river. *Somebody* hauled it in. You know how people are."

I gathered myself. "When did this happen?"

"Oh, Christ, way back. Nineteen seventy-eight, seventy-nine. Ethan was probably sixteen. I was like seven then." Gabe shook his head and put an index finger in the air, the universal signal that the best was yet to come.

"I tell ya, I don't see the big deal in fallin' out of a boat, but Ethan was like … *shattered* after that. Quit school, wouldn't talk much, wouldn't *touch* a book." He shook his head in confusion and regret. "That is actually pretty bizarre *and* sad when you think about it."

"Is he still around?" I asked hopefully, trying to make it sound unimportant.

"Yeah, he works at a Mizco about a mile from here. I'll warn you, though, if you make *any* small talk with him, he'll start tellin' you the story."

That was *exactly* what I was counting on. "Thanks for the heads-up, Gabe. See you in a couple weeks."

. . .

Of course, I hauled ass over to that Mizco service station and convenience store.

I and everyone back home remembered the rowboat on Scobee's Pond. We remembered the reading glasses found in the boat, we remembered the missing oar, and we remembered the short story book by J. D. Salinger.

Ethan Ganelli was behind the counter when I walked in. He was very average-looking. He nodded at me, and since I just stood there, politely asked what he could do for me.

"You can listen to a little story from when I was a kid without interrupting." I started right in before he could even respond. I told him about Scobee's Pond, The Long Lizard, a quick summary of the other bizarre shit and moved swiftly into a trimmed-down version of what happened to my friend Craig and me on August 23rd, 1980, when we were fourteen.

While I spoke, I could see him practically tap-dancing back there, waiting to jump in with *his* story of what happened to him on the Danby River in 1979. He began to tell it, and then *I* jumped in and said, "In 1979, we found a rowboat out in the middle of the pond with an oar missing. Inside the boat was a pair of reading glasses and a sopping-wet copy of *Nine Stories* by J. D. Salinger."

He was speechless, and stepped back until he landed on his stool. "The water level on that section of the river rose and fell a couple times a year. Still does. Now I know why."

I confessed that his cousin Gabe had told me the rowboat story not half an hour earlier.

"Doesn't make any difference," he said, sounding vindicated. "*Nobody* knew what book I had with me. I never mentioned it. They were all busy thinking I had fallen out of the boat and somebody downstream stole it. To them, I was just an inept bookworm. And they all thought I went nuts after that." He swallowed and struggled to speak. "But I knew what happened, even if no one believed it. And it was so terrifying I just surrendered." He was choking on his own words at this point. "If there are forces in this world that can do things like that to a harmless nobody like me, I'd just as soon not even—" He sat back on his stool and buried his face.

'There, there, Ethan. It'll be all right.' No, I didn't say anything lame like that. I gave him a couple minutes to compose himself. We talked a bit more, comparing Scobee's Pond with that section of the Danby River.

"Virginia, huh? That pond is in Virginia?"

"Yes. It's got to be about a thousand miles from here." (I looked it up later. It's about 807 miles as the crow flies.)

"And the water just *goes away* a couple times a year, then *comes back* a day or two later?"

"That's right."

"They never found your friend, huh?"

"No," I whispered.

"Well, I almost ended up in Virginia, from what you're telling me. Maybe your friend ended up *here.*"

He said it almost as a punch line, or as a goof, not really realizing the possibility. I had not considered *that*— until now.

"Are you computer savvy?" he asked.

"Not really. But I have one in my office back in Carthage."

"Most people still think I'm a nut case who went crazy because I fell out of a boat, almost drowned, then made up a weird story about it, but I kind of kept up on technology from a distance."

"So what are you getting at, Ethan?"

"Why don't you do a search? You know. Put in something like 'missing persons in Missouri,' and the year it happened."

"What will that do?" I asked hopefully.

"It'll give you names and possibly photos of people that turned up here that year. He was what, fourteen? They would probably assume he was from around here. Maybe he had no memory. He would have been taken somewhere by child advocates, the state, something like that." He paused and lowered his voice. "*If* he *survived* what almost happened to me."

I was quite impressed by Ethan Ganelli, who was locally thought of as the village idiot, or worse. "You know, you don't sound like the helpless nut case that was described to me. No offense."

He was able to laugh and shrugged, opening a bag of chips. "No one really bothered with me after that. They just thought I was some pathetic, useless head case. The boss here gave me this job out of pity. I never picked up another book after that day. And I did not get past the eleventh grade." He tapped his temple. "But I was a smart kid, maybe *too* smart. I did not lose any of my *intellect.*"

"What *did* you lose, Ethan?"

He smiled sadly. "Everything else."

I could never let that meeting be my only encounter with Ethan Ganelli. Every two weeks, after visiting Ganelli's Medical Supply Outlet, I drop by the Mizco station and spend a few minutes chatting with him. He is a remarkable human being, to those who take the time to find out. Which is basically no one except me.

. . .

The internet back in 2002 was nowhere near as thorough as it is now. I was unable to get any solid information on people who turned up in Missouri out of nowhere. And I did not have time to ask around. Those toilet seats weren't going to sell themselves.

I continued to search now and then. It ended up being a sad, frustrating exercise I did every August 23rd. Nine more years passed.

In 2011, on August 23rd, of course, I happened on a site called *Missing in Missouri: Do You Know Me?* It had an expanded photo gallery of people that had not been identified. Most of them had been found dead. Only seven matched up with Craig for age, gender, and approximate time period. So I called up those photos on the computer that I was convinced hated me.

And there he was. It was Craig Vernay, all right. He had been found wandering along Route 73, about three miles from the Danby River. The date: August 25th, 1980, two days after the incident on Scobee's Pond in West Burlington, Virginia.

Details were scarce. A concerned motorist pulled over and tried to talk to him. Craig could barely speak and didn't seem to know anything about anything. Eventually social agencies stepped in and he was placed in a youth shelter, then with foster parents. He was now forty-five like me, unmarried, and a custodian at an elementary school in Monroe, just fifty miles from my happy home. His name was now Edward Green.

. . .

The school would not allow me to see Craig, even after I told them of his Missouri history (which they already knew) and his point of origin. I wasn't sure they even believed me, what with all the nut cases using schools to showcase their insanity. This was done through an outside intercom. They wouldn't even let me in the building. Fortunately, they said they would convey to him my wish to meet.

After a short wait they informed me he would come out during his lunch break (in an hour) and that we could meet *openly* in the parking lot in front of the school, in full view of the office staff.

So that is what happened on September 8th, 2011, two weeks after finding him on the *Missing in Missouri* site. He came out and walked over to me at the edge of the visitor's parking lot.

"Hello," I said quietly, holding back thirty-one years of emotional anguish.

I figured it would be best to address him by the name he had gone through most of his life with. "Mr. Green, I'm Larry Pickard, from Carthage."

"Nice to meet you," he said politely.

"Did the school tell you why I came?"

"No, they didn't. They just said a man was here to see me."

"Mr. Green, I have been looking for you since 1980, when you disappeared from West Burlington, Virginia." I purposely didn't give him any of the bizarre details. At any rate, when I said '1980' his face turned a bit pale. That was the year he had to start life over. I think he already sensed that I was someone from his unknown past.

He started to speak, but caught himself and stood silent, waiting for me to continue.

"Does the name Craig Vernay mean anything to you?"

"No, it doesn't." He *tried* to make eye contact with me, but couldn't.

"How about Scobee's Pond?"

"I don't believe so, uh, Larry." He did better this time, but I had mentioned a body of water. He knew, of course, that he had come from water.

I took out the picture of us together in our Little League uniforms and handed it to him. "This is us in 1976." He tensed up and tried a polite smile.

"Well, the kid on the left looks like you, and the kid on the right *does* look like me a *little*." He inhaled deeply, as if for resolve. "Who is it?"

Right then I knew there *was* no Craig Vernay in the world. This was Edward Green, middle-aged school custodian from Monroe, Missouri. "It's my best friend, Craig Vernay."

"That's nice. That you have a picture of your best friend."

There was only one thing left to ask. "You believe me, don't you? I got no reason to make this up."

He thought a moment, and looked at the pavement. "I, uh, can't *afford* to believe you. Do you understand?"

I did, actually.

"I've spent my whole life that I can *remember* right here. I can't start over. *This* is good for me, as good as it's gonna get. I just *can't* believe you. I am *not able* to believe you." He handed the picture back. "You keep this. I gotta get back inside. Sorry."

"Thanks anyway for your time. Good luck to you, Mr. Green," I said softly.

He started inside, but paused. "Uh, Larry, I'm just the custodian here. Nobody calls me '*Mr.* Green.' I'm *Eddie*".

. . .

On September 27, 2012, the water left Scobee's Pond and did not return. The Long Lizard was never seen again. In October of 2017, after several failed attempts, the area where the pond had been was filled in.

"WAITING FOR RALPHIE"
Aug. – Oct. 2017

We're learning about *irony* now in my College English III course. So here's an *example* of irony for you. The best parenting advice I've ever gotten was from someone *else's* parent.

. . .

Kids were laughing when I got called down to the office on the first day of school.   Unless being overly sarcastic with a droll sense of humor had suddenly become against school policy, I knew I hadn't done anything wrong.

"Martin," began the principal, Mr. Foss, as I took a seat opposite him, "we have a new third grade student here, and I would like you to take the initiative of his becoming acclimated here."

This was a common practice, assigning a kid a year or two older, and who lived in the same neighborhood, to kind of be a "buddy" to the new kid.

"Why me, Mr. Foss? I don't really—"

"Martin, I know that you are not the most outgoing student here. We feel that this experience and responsibility will be of benefit to you as well as the new student."

Normally, I'm pretty good at debate, but I just sat there. No sarcasm or droll humor came to mind.

. . .

I was instructed to go to Mrs. Heffernan's room. As I opened the door she was standing right there, doing her first math lesson of the new school year.

"Martin Williamson!" she exclaimed. "How nice to see you again. You must be a fifth grader by now."

"That's right, Mrs. Heffernan." We had gotten along fine that year. She lived down the street and had a big red Irish setter we all loved, usually stopping to play with him on the walk home.

Mrs. Heffernan motioned to a boy in the third row. "Ralph, would you come here please?" The boy swung out of his seat and walked briskly to where we stood. He was about average size for a third grader with brown hair that sort of *wrapped around* his head.

"Ralph, this is Martin. He'll be helping you and showing you around the school until you get used to everything."

"Hello, there," Ralph said, all prim and proper like.

"Hey."

Mrs. Heffernan handed me a paper with a list of places to take Ralph, explain a few school procedures, and answer any of his questions. So I showed him the cafeteria, the gym, and the library. Excuse me, the *resource room.* I explained all the things I was supposed to. He listened dutifully and nodded.

"Okay, Ralph, that's about it. Any questions?"

"Can I walk home with you, Martin?"

"Uh, I don't know if—"

"Will you wait for me after school, Martin? Mrs. Heffernan wants to give me some extra worksheets. You can wait outside her door."

I can? Gee, thanks, Ralph! I exhaled, hoping he would get the hint that I had better things to do than walk home with a *third grader.* "All right, Ralph. Just this once."

"Awesome!" he said. He ran down the hall, (which I had just told him was against school rules) turned and yelled, (also against school rules) "Call me Ralphie, Martin."

. . .

I could hear Mrs. Heffernan explaining the worksheets she was giving Ralph. It all sounded pretty straightforward. But no, Ralph kept asking her a million questions. 'Do I put my name on the left or right? Should I put the date? Do these count as homework or tests?'

By the time we got outside, the school was deserted. To top it off, Mrs. Heffernan's husband had Big Red inside when we passed by. Ralph was giving me chapter and verse on everything that had happened that day, including Ken Hildoski picking his nose during social studies.

"He wiped all of them under his desk," he added.

"Well, Ralph, that's how we do things here in Michigan."

"I'm from Ohio."

"Just goes to show you, Ralph, everybody's from somewhere."

"Call me Ralphie."

"What's your last name, Ralphie?"

"Farber."

"Wonderful."

"I can name all the Providences in Canada."

"They're *Provinces*, Ralphie, old boy, and no, you cannot."

"Alberta, British Columbia, Manitoba, New Brunswick, Newfoundland, Nova Scotia, Nunavut, Prince Edward Island, Quebec, Saskatchewan, Yukon Territory, and of course, Ontario."

I was somewhat surprised. "Very impressive, Ralphie, but to tell you the truth, I'm not a big fan of Canada. All they got up there are hockey players and hookers."

"My mother's from Canada."

Uh, oh. Think fast, Martin. "So, uh, what hockey team did *she* play for?"

"None. But she figure skated. And acted in school plays. Then she was a secretary. Then she met my father. He wasn't my father *then.* But then they got married after a long courtship and moved to Ohio."

"That's just fascinating, Ralphie. You'll have to tell me more some time, but that's enough for now. Really."

"I live at 257 Green Hill Road."

Great. Just two streets away.

"My mother said she would wait for me on our front porch."

"The nerve."

We ascended Green Hill Road, not really much of a hill, and at the last house on the left a woman was sitting on her open front porch. Mrs. Ralphie, no doubt. She smiled and waved, and good old Ralphie double-timed it to her, giving her a big hug. I gave a simple my-job-here-is-done wave and continued walking when Ralphie's mother called out, "Young man, could you come here, please?"

Terrific. She was probably gonna ask me a million questions like Ralphie did with Mrs. Heffernan. She stood and smiled as I approached, one arm still around Ralphie. She had black slacks with a yellow top, and looked to be older than most mothers of third graders. She had short dark hair and a beautiful smile. Wow. Didn't expect that.

"Hello, young man. I'm Carol May Farber, Ralphie's mother."

"Martin Williamson."

She extended her free hand and I shook it. She still wore that big, happy smile. It actually cheered me up just to look at her. I don't know.

"Martin, the school called and said you would be looking after my Ralphie until he knows his way around. So, thank you for all you did for him today."

Her smile was even *prettier* now. "Oh, you're welcome, Mrs. Farber. I was glad to do it." I *wasn't* at the time, but it seemed okay now.

"Do you live around here, Martin?"

"Over on Riano Avenue, two streets away."

"Hey!" Ralphie shouted, pulling away from his mom. "Maybe we can walk to school together. You'll be going right by here. Is that okay with you, Mom?"

"You should ask Martin, Ralphie, if he *wants* to walk to school with you."

I had begun thinking of alternate routes I could tell him I took. But there he was, looking up at me and asking, in his most polite voice, if I would walk to school with him. I made the mistake of looking at his mother. The smile had been replaced by a little tilt of the head and a hopeful look in her eyes.

I felt I could not disappoint *her*. What the hell was going on here?

"I'd be glad to, Mrs. Farber."

And that was how it all started.

. . .

Waiting for Ralphie became the most aggravating part of my life. The kid was what his mother called "a bit pokey" in the morning. I called it an annoying pain in my ass. His non-stop chatter and inane attempts at conversation were nothing; I always had droll or sarcastic come-backs that went over his head. But the waiting was a killer. I'm very driven, wound kind of tight, some might say. The only good thing was that while Ralphie was looking for his other shoe or his math book, his mother would talk to me, usually ask about my life.

I don't even like girls my *own* age that much, and here was this grown woman, over forty most likely, charming the hell out of me. I just didn't get it.

When Ralphie finally got his act together, Mrs. Farber would tilt her head and give us this cute little wave. I can't really describe it. It was just so *endearing.*

Ralphie was not so endearing. It seemed every day he would have a new topic to aggravate me. For several days it was his father Frederick, who was a sales representative for a company that sold heavy industrial equipment. He was on the road a lot and had originally been based in Toronto. That was where he met Ralphie's mother, who was a receptionist at a company on his client list. They hit it off, and finally married "after a long courtship" (Ralphie's words. Jesus, this kid.) and moved to the Akron, Ohio area when he was transferred. And now he was here in Minchner, Michigan.

This story was ten times longer than I just related. I had never looked so forward to getting to school, where I could jettison old Ralphie boy on the K-3 playground.

And suddenly at lunch I was catching it from my peers.

"Hey, Marty," said Ray Segarak, "I see you walking the new small fry to school this morning. You like hangin' with third graders all of a sudden?"

"I had to," I lied. "My parents made me," I further lied.

"Too bad, Marty. Not the best way to impress the girls."

"I'm tryin' to get out of it," I continued lying.

. . .

I knew there would come a time when Ralphie would not need me any more. But the good and bad of it was that the kid was so *clingy.* He was getting along just fine in his classroom. Sailing along, actually. I hate to admit it, but the kid was pretty sharp, and I don't mean being able to name all the "Providences" in Canada, where his lovely mother came from. He seemed like he was well above average in everything,

He knew a lot about the early days of our space program and could name the first man in space, (Yuri Gagarin) the first *American* in space, (Alan Shepard)the first American to orbit the earth, (John Glenn) and the first man to walk on the moon. (Neil Armstrong.)

Most of the time I would avoid talking on the walk to school or home. But that made things worse. A gap in conversation was usually followed by some school topic I wasn't up on at all. It made me wonder what the hell I had done for an entire year in third grade.

The good in all this was that Ralphie had attached himself to me, and I got to see his mother twice each school day. I know that sounds creepy, but it wasn't. She was just so *pleasant* and nice to me and asked about my school life, my likes and dislikes and all that, but not like a *parent* would. When *they* do that, they're looking for an opening where they can correct or criticize you. How do I know this? Guess.

There was a strict dividing line between walking Ralphie to and from school and the rest of my life. On weekends I didn't go anywhere near Green Hill. I did have a *few* friends that I hung out with, and we did the usual stuff: sports, games, exploring woods, and avoiding our parents and chores.

Okay, so Halloween is coming up and I know it would be social suicide to have *anything* to do with Ralphie that night. It was his main topic for at least three days before. I got chapter and verse on every costume he ever wore.

I went out with a couple of guys I always went trick-or-treating with, Pepe and Len. We went down Silano Drive, Rodgers Road, Moore Avenue, and back. I got them to cut down to Green Hill Road, and from there we worked our way to the top of the hill.

Guess where we ended the night. That's right. Two-fifty-seven Green Hill Road, the home of Frederick and Carol May Farber. And Ralphie. We had gone as The Three Musketeers, complete with billowy shirts and pants, big hats, masks, and plastic swords.

We knocked on the front door and Mrs. Farber answered. We went through the usual routine: 'Trick or Treat, blah, blah, blah.' Mrs. Farber was most gracious and complimentary, of course. We were about to leave when she said, "Martin, is that you?"

I took off my mask and she *giggled* like a schoolgirl. "I thought I recognized your voice, Martin. You couldn't fool me." I made an 'aw, shucks' gesture.

"Ralphie's not home yet. (Thank God) His father took him in the car. I can't imagine how much candy he's gotten. And how about you boys?"

"We did great. We had a lot of fun."

She gave me a sly smile. "And no waiting for Ralphie to throw you off schedule, right?"

Slightly embarrassing. "He's not so bad."

She patted me on the shoulder. "I've been working on him to be more organized."

No! screamed a voice deep within me. *Let him be disorganized. It gives us more time to talk.*

She told us to be careful on the way home, and we said goodbye and left. We hadn't gone five steps when it started.

"When did you get such nice manners, Marty?"

"Is that your *girlfriend* or something?"

"NO!"

"You know her, though, don't you?"

"Yeah, her son tags along with me going to school and going home."

"Oh, *that's* the third grader Ray Segarak said you hang out with."

"I do *not* hang out with him. He's a royal pain in the ass that I'm stuck with. My parents *make* me walk with him!" Good old parents. They *do* come in handy sometimes.

. . .

Fifth grade girls. They are so into themselves and doing exactly what the most popular girls do. After a while, I swear I can't tell one from the other. Mrs. Farber was different. Of course she was an adult, but she was little-girl sweet at times. I am happy to report that she was a failure at getting her "pokey" son to speed it up. Waiting for Ralphie continued to be the most frustrating and wonderful part of my day.

The school year rolled along, *slowly*. But as slowly as it seemed to be going, there we were at Thanksgiving. And there we were again, approaching the Christmas break. There was plenty of snow that year, and we were on our third snow day.

Pepe, Len, and I gathered at the top of Guerdat Hill for some white-knuckle sled rides. There were lots of other kids, even some girls. Somebody called out, "Let's try Green Hill."

"No way," I called out instinctively. "This is ten times better."

Within a minute, everyone was pulling their sleds down Calvin Street to Green Hill. I tromped along behind, grumbling. I had a feeling I was gonna get stuck with Ralphie Farber, and in front of kids my age!

When we got there, we found two younger kids sliding down Green Hill's gentle slope. In the distance a third sled contained one other boy with a woman pulling him up the hill. Our gang took one look at the slight incline and was disappointed.

"This is lame," one of the girls called out. "Let's go back to Guerdat Hill." They started tromping back down Calvin Street. I stood watching the kid being pulled up the hill.

"You coming, Marty?" asked Len.

I was stalling as the woman came closer with her sled passenger, now recognizable as Ralphie Farber. "Yeah, you guys go ahead. I'll catch up."

"Suit yourself."

It was obvious who was pulling Ralphie on his sled; the delightful Carol May Farber.   When Ralph recognized me, he shouted, jumped off his sled, and ran up to me. He almost ran right through me.

"Marty! Look, Mom, it's Marty! Marty, are you gonna slide down Green Hill?"

"I might give it one try."

"You should stay and slide with us!"

"We'll see."

Mrs. Farber had reached us. She had on a hooded jacket and a red hat. She gave me that unique smile.

"I didn't expect to find *you* out here sliding with the kids," I said, showing both surprise and admiration.

"I don't know if Ralphie told you, Martin, but I grew up in Ontario, Canada. I love being outside in the snow. It reminds me of my childhood."

"Did you live in Toronto?" I asked, naming the only place I knew in Ontario.

"No, a little town called Lindsey," she replied. "I did live in Toronto after graduation, though. That's where I met Ralphie's father."

I know. I heard the story a million times. "Oh, that's nice."

Even though Mrs. Farber was there, and acting like a kid with the snow, I really didn't want to hang around. The other kids were already at Guerdat Hill, and I told Len and Pepe I would be right there. But there was no quick escape. Ralphie kept coming up with different combinations of us to slide down the hill. One time I went down with Mrs. Farber holding onto me. That was pleasant, but Jesus! If any of the guys saw that, I would never hear the end of it.

Eventually I found an opportunity to excuse myself. Ralphie had lost a glove and both his boots were untied. I politely told Mrs. Farber I had better get back to my friends.

She was her usual gracious self. "Well, have fun Martin, and thank you for sledding with us. Ralphie, say goodbye to Martin." Ralphie was busy seeing how much snow he could stuff in his mouth.

When I got to Guerdat Hill, everyone was gone.

. . .

The last day of school before Christmas vacation is one of the best of the year. Fun activities, no work, goodies brought in from home, and MOVIES. They have to be more careful now about what movies they show, but you can't go wrong with *A Christmas Story.* They always had a backup movie just in case. I think it was one of the "Grinch" movies.

Me, I'm a *huge* fan of *A Christmas Story.* (You'll shoot your eye out!) There's always a channel that has it on a continuous twenty-four hour loop on Christmas Eve and Christmas Day. I practically have the whole thing memorized. I probably watch it at least three times every Christmas.

So I innocently picked up Ralphie that morning, and as I waited for him, as usual, I casually mentioned to Mrs. Farber what movie we were seeing. Suddenly I observed an angry look on her face for the very first time. She grabbed the nearest pen and memo pad and began writing—violently.

"Ralphie, come here!" she called.

He appeared from the hallway, a nervous look on his face. That made two of us.

"Ralphie, give this note to your teacher. You are *not* to watch the movie they are showing."

"What movie?" he asked, still nervous. Me too. What the hell was going on?

"That movie, *A Christmas Story.*" She turned to me. "Is there another movie that is being shown, Martin?"

"Yes, the Grinch—"

"Ralphie, you watch *that* movie."

I felt like Christmas itself was under attack, and by the *nicest* adult I knew. "Mrs. Farber," I managed to say, "what's wrong with *A Christmas Story?*"

"I'll tell you what's wrong with it, Martin Williamson."

(Using my last name was not a good sign.)

"It glorifies *guns*, for one thing, but even worse, it glorifies the obsession of a child. I don't want *my* son witnessing the obsessive, greedy behavior of another boy. I want Ralphie to be *centered* in life." Flustered, she stopped and then burst out, "And it glorifies *guns,* and *shooting,* and *bullying,* and *fighting.*"

Geez, I knew Canadians were inherently pacifists, but this was unbelievable. This was obviously a sore point with Mrs. Farber, so I just shrugged and said, "Okay." Besides, part of me didn't *want* to argue with her.

On the way to school I actually bothered to ask Ralphie why his mother was so against *A Christmas Story,* believing he might actually have some insight, some reason that she hadn't mentioned in her unexpected outburst.

"I don't know," he said, shrugging. "It's got guns and stuff in it."

Thanks for the great analysis, Ralphie boy. Then he went off on a long-winded talk about countries in South

America. Jesus, this kid. I liked him better when he was stuffing snow in his mouth.

I was not about to let this incident ruin the Christmas revelry at school. I dutifully stuffed *my* mouth full of brownies, cookies, and punch, and awaited the showing of my favorite seasonal movie, *A Christmas Story.* Good luck with the Grinch, Ralphie.

At last 9:45 rolled around, and the TVs were set to our closed-circuit feed of the movie. I was not going to let Mrs. Farber's comments ruin it for me.

But it did, at first. As I watched the opening minutes, all I could think about was a kid being *obsessed* and *greedy,* and *shooting,* and *bullying,* and *fighting.* But I quickly forgot all that as Schwartz "triple-dog-dared" Flick to stick his tongue on the flagpole. He got stuck, of course, and everybody left him there when the bell rang.

The teacher kept asking 'Where's Flick?' and everybody played dumb until a girl in the front row pointed toward the window, and everybody rushed over to see poor Flick stuck to the flagpole.

And that is when I got the most shocking surprise of my young life. The camera shot was showing amused kids looking out the window. And right up front was a little girl with short dark hair, big, expressive eyes, and a round, angelic face. *It was a nine-year-old version of Carol May Farber.*

The rational part of me said, *no way, not possible.* People's features change, it was thirty-four years ago, blah, blah, blah.

But my mind was blown. I knew there were more classroom scenes, so I watched intently. Several classmates of Ralphie Parker (played by the talented Peter Billingsly) were handing in their Christmas themes. And the dark-haired, big-eyed girl was one of them. I was even *more* convinced that it was Mrs. Farber. I found where she sat and *tracked* her. She was one row to Ralphie's right. I watched only her for the rest of that scene. (Wait a minute! She named her *son* Ralphie?)

A few scenes later the kids in the class were bringing presents up to the teacher. And there she was again, giving her teacher that unique smile I saw at least twice every school day. *It had to be her.*

I knew there was one more classroom scene (I told you I had this memorized) where the kids were called up to get back their themes. And nine-year-old Carol May Farber (I was 95% sure that it was her) went up to get her theme. As she left she gave the teacher a cute, casual wave. Just like Mrs. Farber gave Ralphie and me every morning! There couldn't be two people in the *world* that did that!

For the last half hour of the movie, I don't think I was really *watching* it any more. My mind was blown, like I said.

The movie ended with Ralphie Parker sleeping contentedly with his Red Ryder BB gun. There were still forty minutes of school left, and everybody was bouncing off the walls in anticipation.

Me, I was trying to figure out why Mrs. Farber did not want her son to *see* a movie she was *in.* A famous movie, no less. All that stuff she said about it, did she really *mean* it, or was it just an excuse to keep Ralphie from seeing her? Or was it an "adult" thing a fifth-grader like me wouldn't understand?

We walked home as usual, him blabbering a mile a minute about something or other and me ignoring him. When we got to his house, his mother was out on the porch. "Have a wonderful Christmas, Martin," she called out.

"You, too, Mrs. Farber." I said.

When I got home I did an internet search, and sure enough, even though Ralphie Parker's house and the downtown scenes were shot in Cleveland, the school scenes were shot in *Ontario;* the playground scenes in St.

Catherine's, and the *classroom* scenes in *Lindsey*, where Mrs. Farber grew up. *It was her, all right.*

. . .

One of the kids that had been in the movie as an extra had a long memoir on the internet. I read how they picked kids based on their pictures, (a sure thing for the sweet-looking Carol May) sent contracts to the parents, and paid each kid *one dollar*. Truckloads of 1940's style clothes and vehicles were brought in. They even had a stylist to give the kids 1940-ish haircuts.

Even though I had tuned Ralphie out on the walk home, I did remember that his dad was taking him to Detroit all week during the Christmas break. I never would have said anything to Mrs. Farber if Ralphie had been around, but *now* he *wouldn't* be around.

I had a full week to talk to my favorite non-parental adult, who happened to be *in* my favorite Christmas movie. The day after Christmas found me knocking on the door of 257 Green Hill Road. Only this time there would be no waiting for Ralphie. It never occurred to me that this might not be a topic Mrs. Farber would want to discuss, or that she would even want it known that she had been in the movie. I, too, was a greedy and obsessed young boy. Point made, Mrs. Farber.

She was surprised to see me and told me Ralphie was in Detroit with his father. How adorable. She thought I was there to see her son.

"I didn't come here for Ralphie. I came here to ask you something, Mrs. Farber."

"Really, Martin? Come in and sit down. How was your Christmas?"

"It was great."

"What can I help you with, dear?"

Besides being obsessed and greedy, I had no skills of tact and diplomacy. I was as blunt a ten-year-old as there could be. I sat at the table, smiled admiringly at her, and asked, "What was it like to be an extra in *A Christmas Story?*" Had she really thought I wouldn't recognize her?

She winced, surprised, and dropped into the nearest chair. She was searching for a reply. "You must be mistaken, Martin."

"I'm not, Mrs. Farber. I looked up all the places they filmed. You went to the Central Senior Public School in Lindsey, didn't you?"

"Yes, Martin, I did." She nodded resignedly. "And I *am* in the movie." She got very quiet, and her color seemed to fade. She looked sad suddenly, and bit her lower lip.

"What's wrong, Mrs. Farber? You seem upset. You said you didn't like the movie and Ralphie shouldn't watch it. I don't get it. I mean, I was *proud* that you were in it. That you could *do* something like that. You didn't seem—"

"Martin," she interrupted, "you have no idea how that movie affected my childhood." Her eyes were all red now, and she sniffled.

My God, what had I done?

"Will you swear you won't tell Ralphie?"

"I swear." I shot my right hand in the air for emphasis.

"We actually had a lot of fun filming, and being fussed over by adults. But as the days went by all I wanted was to be in the movies. And I had a lot of time to think about it, because they shot some scenes, then had to wait two months for there to be enough snow on the ground. They ended up using foam."

"What's wrong with wanting to be in the movies?" I replied, trying to be supportive.

"Well, Martin, as you can see, I am *not in* the movies."

"Oh, yeah."

"Here were these three boys, and *they* were in the movies."

She was referring to Peter Billingsly, Scott Schwartz, and R. D. Robb, as Ralphie, Flick, and Schwartz.

"I wanted that so badly," she continued. "And my parents and relatives and friends thought I could be in the movies, maybe even be a child star." She paused. "There were *expectations* of me, Martin. Do you understand what *expectations* are?"

Her voice had gone way up, and was trembling. I wasn't positive I understood what she was talking about, but I nodded anyway.

"There were only five scenes I was in, (I already knew that) so I figured I had to *do* something so that I could be in movies after this."

"What did you do, Mrs. Farber?"

"I was desperate. I wrote a note to Peter Billingsly and asked him if he could help get me in the movies."

"Why didn't you just ask Bob Clark, the director?" (showing off that I knew who he was)

"I was *nine* years old, Martin! To me Ralphie *was* the movie and my big chance."

"What did he say?"

"He wasn't *there*. They were redoing some of the audio. He was in the studio in Toronto. (*Didn't* know that.) So I gave the note to R. D. Robb and asked him if he would give it to *Ralphie*. I actually called him *Ralphie*. R. D. was going back to his trailer and he said 'sure' and put the note in his pocket."

"What happened?" I asked, kind of excited.

"*Nothing* happened, Martin. Every day I was waiting for Ralphie and I never even *saw* him again. Who knows if he even *got* that note? Those boys weren't responsible for getting me auditions or parts in movies."

"Yeah, right."

"Yes, and I just kept waiting for Ralphie to wave some magic wand and hand me what I wanted most of all in life."

There was silence in the Farber kitchen.

"What did you do after that, Mrs. Farber?" I practically whispered.

"I joined drama club and was in every play I could. People knew I had been in a movie and there came the expectations again. Parents, teachers, kids, everybody." She paused a moment, and raised her eyebrows. "And I was pretty good, Martin, but there I was acting in school plays, and there was Peter Billingsly making another movie." (I knew that, too.)

"Did you ever get any interviews, or auditions, or whatever you call them?"

"Martin, let's just say that those things never actually worked out for me."

"I'm very sorry, Mrs. Farber."

You know how on a dark day sometimes the sun comes out from behind a cloud and shines so bright that you completely forget how dreary it had been? That's what happened. Mrs. Farber sat quietly, but I could feel the mood changing. The sadness left her face, her color came back, and she smiled slightly. All of a sudden her smile grew, and she lit up the room the way only she could. The same smile that the people in charge of casting extras in *A Christmas Story* had probably seen.

"It's all right, Martin. (thank you, God!) After high school I became a secretary and moved to Toronto. I had a job with an industrial company and I met Frederick Farber. We got married after a long courtship, (where had I heard *that* before?) and after years of trying, I had my son Ralphie." She put a hand on my shoulder. "I just want you to know, Martin, that I am *very* happy in my adult life. I have a wonderful husband, an adorable son (debatable) and I love every day." She put her hands on my cheeks. Heavenly!

"My life is great now, Martin, because I am no longer 'waiting for Ralphie.'"

I *had* to ask. "But why did you name your *son* Ralphie? Wouldn't that just—"

"Martin, it reminds me to move forward in life."

"No more 'waiting for Ralphie'?"

She gave me the cutest wink. "No, Martin, 'waiting for Ralphie' is *your* problem."

She had me there. "Mrs. Farber, what was your last name, when you were in the movie?" I have *no* idea why I asked that.

"Tillotson. I was Carol May Tillotson."

What a great name, don't you think?

"And Martin, please don't say a word about our little talk."

"I won't. I promise."

"It did me good to tell someone." She exhaled deeply and put a hand on her chest as if relieved. "Eventually I will get around to telling Ralphie and my husband." (Jesus! *He* doesn't know *either?)*

I got up, and Carol May Tillotson, child actress, tussled my hair. I had no idea that what she was about to say would end up being so definitive in the years to come.

"Martin, don't go through life 'waiting for Ralphie' like I did. It never works, and it's not worth it."

. . .

I had planned to bug her that whole week, asking a million questions (sound like anyone?) about being in a movie that has become a classic Yuletide comedy. But I realized that she didn't need to go through that again, especially after she bared her deepest frustration to me, a fifth-grader. There was enough info on the internet to satisfy my curiosity. And she *had* sworn me to secrecy. I could never betray her trust.

But I never, *ever* forgot her last words to me that December 26th, 2017. It was the best damn advice I ever got.

So here we are, six years later. I'm a junior now, and Ralphie is a freshman. We don't walk to school anymore (thank God). He's *still* a pain in the ass, but on a much smaller scale. We're casual friends, I guess.

Last December, he stopped me in the hall and said, "Hey Marty, my mother was an extra in *A Christmas Story!* Honest, I'm not kidding."

Tell me something I *don't* know, Ralphie boy.

I only see Mrs. Farber once in a while, but we always give each other a heartfelt greeting. Good advice is priceless, you know. I also know that no matter what happens in my life, I will definitely *not* be 'waiting for Ralphie.'

"BACKFOLD"
Aug, - Oct. 2017

Ted Fowler sat in his recliner, checking the baseball scores, when his ten-year-old son Steven bounded into the room, dropped heavily to the floor, and opened his independent reading book.

Ted often wondered how his son could enter a room and be oblivious to everything around him.

And Steven Fowler *was* oblivious to everything else as he opened the novel *The Glimmer,* by Robert S. Banks, to two separate places, about forty pages apart. To Ted's amusement and curiosity, Steven now folded the intervening pages *backward,* inserting them into the spine of the best-selling Baroque period novel as he began to read the later pages.

Ted knew he could not watch this silently. He was very curious, and loved the way Steven explained things.

"Steven, what are you doing?"

Steven's head snapped up and located his father. "Reading, Dad. This is a great book."

"No, Steven. I mean, why are you reading the book with the pages like that?"

Steven held the book up. "You mean the backfold?" He pointed at it for emphasis.

"Yes, the-- what?"

Steven stood and held the book towards his father. "It's called a backfold, Dad. Mrs. Risley uses it to help us."

"Help you what? Ruin the book's binding?"

"No, it's to help us remember what we *already* read," he said, pointing at the earlier pages, "and to get us to extrapolate on what lies ahead," he added, touching the later pages.

"Oh," said Ted. He thought a moment. "You know the word 'extrapolate.'"?

"Sure, Dad, don't you?"

Ted Fowler looked at the unique page arrangement. "Of course."

. . .

Ted had no doubt that whatever method Mrs. Risley was using would be beneficial to his son. He was as resourceful a ten-year-old as there could be.

But the concept of the "backfold" intrigued him. Even the word itself conjured up images of dashing from the present to the future. But to Ted the present was working, paying the bills, keeping his wife Allison happy, and providing for his son Steven and his fourteen-year-old daughter Amy.

The future was watching his children grow up, graduate, go on to college, (how would they afford *that?)* then get married and move away. His eventual retirement, some thirty years down the road would ease the stress. He could watch a *lot* more sports on TV. But what else? Would his life eventually be empty? How much time in close proximity could he and Allison endure without getting on each other's nerves?

This made him think about his past, growing up in the east end on Cimarron Hill, two-and-a-half miles away. It was a solid middle class neighborhood with a dozen or more friends he had grown up with.

They had done everything together: camping, exploring the many woods near his house, football, baseball, basketball, playing cards and other games, or just hanging out and entertaining each other with all sorts of ridiculous exploits.

If he could do a real-life "backfold," it wouldn't go from the present to the *future,* it would go from the present to the *past.* His *own* past, the one lived on Cimarron Hill. He had often pushed it out of his mind. It was gone for good, the people in it were scattered all over, and he had *responsibilities* now. What good would daydreaming about incidents and people from years ago do him?

Still.

. . .

Last Christmas his daughter Amy had given him a journal. It was titled "Great Ideas," with a five-by-seven dark blue cover, and lined pages. She was always after him to "write down his thoughts," something he considered unmanly.

"Amy," he said to her a few days later, "do you really think I have any thoughts that should be on the pages of this beautiful book?"

"You hate it!" she blurted out. "Mom said you would." Her face reddened and she stomped upstairs and slammed her bedroom door.

"Ah, fourteen, what a wonderful age," Ted said to no one.

After dinner he paid her a visit in her room and apologized. "Amy, it's a wonderful gift. I just don't know what kind of "thoughts" should go in there. I would *hate* to use it for the wrong purpose and ruin it."

Amy got that faraway look he had often seen. "Dad, don't you *think* about things, *wish* for things, make *plans*?"

He didn't, actually. His thoughts involved worrying about nasty bosses, his wife's moods, and the demands of his children. "Yes, Amy. Of course I do."

"Then those are the things you should put in there."

Ted put the journal on top of his desk. Amy, oddly, did not mention it again. She had won a victory of sorts over her father and gotten an apology from him. For some teenage girls, that was the equivalent of a Super Bowl trophy.

Ted now unstacked the pile of work materials and other clutter that had been heaped on "Great Ideas" in the nine months since.

He still wasn't sure what he was going to write in the journal, if anything. But he knew that if he *did*, he was going to use a "backfold." Thank you, Mrs. Risley.

. . .

He thought it best to observe Steven for a few days. Most of the schoolwork he saw him doing on the living room floor was math and science. He did spy him twice with the novel, one time using the "backfold" method, and the other time reading it conventionally.

Just to make conversation he asked Steven how the book was going.

"It's going great, Dad. There's this big conspiracy to overthrow the king, but the three main conspirators are all working *against* each other."

"Really. Working against each other, huh? I noticed you used the word 'conspirators.'"

"Dad, I'm in *fifth* grade."

When Ted finally did start writing in the journal, he simply made an entry about all the kids he grew up with, and all the things they did together. A pleasant, general passage. He did not name any of his companions from that time period or recount anything in particular, but it was pleasant just the same.

Amy noticed him writing. As she left the room she said cheerily, "I told you writing would be good for you, Dad. Isn't it *therapeutic?*"

"I'm hoping it will be just that."

. . .

There was one major problem. Nothing in Ted's *present* was anecdotal. If there had been a *blueprint* of a white, male American middle class person's journey from childhood to age thirty-six, Ted was *it*.

Birth, early childhood, adolescence, teen, young adult, etc. had all been *standard issue* for him. The only exception was what Ted called "The Golden Years." From about age nine until twenty-one, the kids on Cimarron Hill and nearby streets lived a carefree, idyllic existence in a world of sports, games, activities, explorations, and evolving. Even conflict, but always resolution. Always good.

. . .

Ted cheated, sort of. He started a quarter of the way through the journal and wrote a flat, uninspiring entry of what had transpired that day. The highlight was the copy machine going berserk, spitting out finished copies and blank pages every two seconds. A co-worker had finally unplugged it.

Then, with relish, Ted turned to the two-page entry he had made at the beginning of the journal, an "Introduction to Childhood on Cimarron Hill." He decided to start with his earliest recollections, when it was just the Temmons brothers, himself, and his brother Dennis. When he had finished, he smiled in remembrance. He felt *warm* inside. Any had been right. Writing *was* therapeutic.

And to Ted, this *did* qualify as a backfold. His past and his present were represented, as opposed to his present and his future. You couldn't put yourself in your own future with any certainty, anyway. Yet, he could exist in his childhood and flip to what his future would *actually* be. It was confusing if you verbalized it, but in his perception, it was clear.

Ted did not want his family to know how *invested* he was in his childhood memories. After all, everyone had a childhood, and no one he knew seemed to be living in it as he was now. He knew Amy would respect his privacy. But Allison was getting tougher to gauge. With her it was unpredictable and inconsistent moods.

Many was the time he thought he had screwed up, only to have her laugh and wave it away as nothing. Other times he came home happy and innocent, only to have her tear into him with a vengeance.

No, his journal, half mundane day-by-day accounts, and half cherished memories from "The Golden Years," would be a secret.

. . .

The present-day journal entries continued to be a bland recounting of his daily life, which he had come to find unfulfilling. His wife and kids went about their daily routines as though he was not even there. The kids asked Allison for things they needed; money, transportation, permission, etc. He was just the guy that footed the bill. Ted did his best to keep his resentment in check. Many working men had the same situation.

The other half of the journal, the front half, began to take shape. He added characters as they joined the neighborhood and recounted incidents and games of baseball, football, and basketball in the streets all over the neighborhood and at Redmont Field, a huge, pasture-like area they often used. The stories were rich in detail and featured some of the funniest spectacles he had ever seen. Obviously he could not recall entire games, but to his astonishment, could still remember specific plays embedded in his memory.

Ted found he had to vary it. After all, how could he go on and on about sports games? There was the Temmons brothers' swimming pool and their patio with the picnic table and all the get-togethers there; playing cards, monopoly, and just acting as idiotic as possible.

A strange transformation began to take shape. The more *immersed* he became in his past, the more *tolerant* he became of his present. The journal entries from the past were a pleasant escape that gave him a better perspective on his family. When things got tedious or unpleasant, he could *escape* to his past. It *was* therapeutic.

. . .

Amy Fowler had stayed after school for Drama Club tryouts, and through some miscommunication found herself without a ride home. Ted answered the phone when she called and told her he would be there in ten minutes.

"So, did you get a part?" asked Ted, when Amy got in the car.

"I don't know yet. They're gonna post call-backs tomorrow."

"I'm sure you will. You were in, what, three plays in middle school?"

"*Six*. Hey dad, why are you going home this way?" Amy said, as their car seemed determined, with Ted's assistance, to head due east.

"Oh, I thought I'd give you a tour of the old neighborhood."

Amy had gotten *several* "tours of the old neighborhood," complete with the accompanying narration: where everyone had lived, where *this* happened, where *that* happened, and where the *other thing* had happened. She had homework and lines to memorize, but she interpreted this as her sometimes-distant dad to try to make an effort. And he *had* been writing like crazy in the journal, and seemed to be happier since. She decided to be a good sport. He was already reciting "The Cimarron Chronicles," as she and Steven called it.

". . . and right here is where—"

"That kid tied his brother to the telephone pole on Easter Sunday."

"You *remember* that one!" Ted shouted. He seemed genuinely pleased, as though a reluctant student had finally learned a valuable lesson.

Ted continued his guided tour of Cimarron Hill. It was a pleasant experience to share. But as he drove, he noticed that there was not a single person visible on the street of his most cherished memories. It was as though Cimarron Hill had been preserved as a drive-through museum.

. . .

It was a pleasant dinner that evening. Steven was always bubbly and brimming with stories and information from school, and Amy seemed happy, even though she felt under the gun timewise. Ted noticed that Allison was in a much better frame of mind lately. It seemed to coincide with his acceptance of his present life and his journal trips back to "The Golden Years."   If only he had found this new peace of mind earlier, he chided himself. At any rate, life was good on Wilson Avenue, and in his mind, back on Cimarron Hill.

For some reason, Ted couldn't let it be. He was compelled to "tinker." It started with him going out of his way on the drive home once or twice a week to drive up Cimarron Hill, or drive down Pratt Hill, which ran parallel and passed all the backyards of Cimarron Hill. He did this driving twenty miles an hour with his window down. It wasn't enough to *see* the old stomping grounds, he wanted to *hear* it, too. There was never anything to hear, though, and not much to see, either. The only person left from

"The Golden Years" was the Temmons' brothers mother, Lucinda, now past seventy, but with a sharp mind and the nurturing nature she had used on her boys, Tommy, Lonnie, and Roy. He entertained the thought of dropping in on her sometime.

The detours to Cimarron Hill became more frequent. Ted sometimes felt like someone cheating on their diet or sneaking a cigarette. But why *should* there be any guilt? He had put in the years there, he was *entitled* to drive by and just look at it, wasn't he? It's not like he was traipsing through people's yards or knocking on doors. Heck, he had even forgotten who lived in his old house now. Surely *that* was a sign he had moved on.

. . .

"Who is it?"

"It's Ted Fowler, Mrs. Temmons."

Lucinda Temmons smiled a motherly smile. "Teddy, how wonderful to see you. What brings you back to the old neighborhood?"

"I was just driving by and thought I'd say hello."

"That's so nice. Do you or your brother ever see Lonnie or Roy around?"

"Not usually. And we haven't seen Tommy for years."

"He's still teaching at Hofstra. His son is almost eight, now."

"Wow. Time flies. It sure is quiet up here, now."

"Yes, I miss all the noise you boys made. You had so much fun growing up here. You know, Teddy, I don't think there's a single kid on this street. It's almost *too* quiet, sometimes."

"A museum of our past," Ted said, proudly.

They made small talk for about ten minutes, then Ted realized it was time to go. He didn't want Allison or

Amy suspecting that he had been "carousing" here. He gave Mrs. Temmons one of those 'thanks for everything' hugs adults sometimes gave the elderly, and left. He walked out to the Temmons' driveway on Cimarron Hill, and as he was about to start his car his eyes fell on the blue cover of "Great Ideas." He had taken to bringing it to work and writing his present-day entries during his lunch hour.

He had never written a "backfold" entry anywhere but his study or the bathroom, but he felt so content in the Temmons' driveway at the top of his old street. He began to write about a typical football game on Cimarron Hill. He had just written John Martin's oft-repeated threat to his brother Frank after yet another dropped pass. From his open car window he *heard* the words he had just *written: "Frank, you idiot, I'm gonna kick your useless ass!"*

Ted's head snapped up and looked in his rear-view mirror, where he could see the lower part of Cimarron Hill, where the game would have taken place. There was a flash and a blur of blue and white. His eyes now focused on a quiet, deserted Cimarron Hill. But he had just *heard* John Martin! And the white tee shirts and jeans they always wore. (*a blur of blue and white.)*

A bead of nervous perspiration appeared on his forehead. I am *recreating* the *past,* for some reason, *by writing about it,* he told himself.

There was a tapping on his passenger window. Lucinda Temmons stood there, concern on her face. "Teddy, is everything okay? You've been sitting here for ten minutes."

"Uh, yeah, Mrs. Temmons. Just looking over some work stuff." He had to ask. "Mrs. Temmons, you didn't hear any kids yelling just now, did you?"

Her brow wrinkled in confusion. "No, Teddy, not a word, like always. Are you sure everything is okay,Teddy? You look kind of –"

"Everything's great, Mrs. Temmons. I better get going. Nice to have seen you again."

She waved as he backed his car onto Cimarron Hill, and he saw her walking back inside as he slowly drove down to where the football game would have been. And then he slowed down to ten miles per hour, past the Easton's former house across from him, and the Daignault brothers' house, Len and Charlie, the next house down from his.

He nearly drove past before he realized what he was seeing. He stopped and looked at the lawn of the former Easton residence. Two feet from Cimarron Hill lay a football.

. . .

Ted was both elated and confused. Allison and the kids didn't know what to make of it. The happy, semi-stunned Ted was new, and not at all unpleasant. He retreated to his study and categorized his backfold entries, including today's, which had just played a game of keep-away with reality. There were twenty-one of them, ten of which described baseball or football games. The others were get-togethers where something memorable or ridiculously zany happened.

He would do a backfold entry about one of *these* and see what happened. He had to keep reminding himself what had happened that afternoon: He *wrote* about an incident from the past and *recreated it.* There had to have been some *force,* some *energy* in play. He was a believer in the paranormal, and had read many accounts of it in non-fiction magazines.

A stand of pine trees in upper Maine *moved* and *communicated telepathically.* At a pond in Virginia the entire body of water *moved somewhere* and *came back,* and had been known to *harm* people it perceived as its enemies. Why couldn't *this* be real?

His backfold entries, if written in the area of where they originally happened, brought back some tangible proof of their long ago existence. That football on Easton's former lawn was his proof.

The next day he parked on Pratt Hill, which ran parallel to Cimarron. He parked facing uphill, adjacent to his former backyard, and in "backfold style" wrote about the famous Easter Sunday when Len Daignault tricked his younger brother Charlie into standing by a telephone pole one house down from the Temmons, then ran around him with a length of clothesline until poor, unsuspecting Charlie was unable to move. Charlie spent five minutes trying to escape, and the next half hour yelling, then pleading for Len to untie him. It wasn't something you saw every day in 1968; a kid tied to a telephone pole.

Ted looked up every few seconds to gaze at the pole, some thirty yards away. No shouts, no laughing, no flash and blur of blue and white. In frustration, he punched the gas and screeched to a stop next to the famous pole. In further dismay, he got out, slammed the door and strode over to the pole where the late Len Daignault had tied his brother, the late Charlie Daignault.

"Who was I kidding?" Ted muttered. His eye was caught by what looked to be a four-inch white worm. Ted bent down to it and laughed a satisfied I-knew-I was-right laugh. The white worm was a piece of clothesline.

. . .

"Two for two," Ted repeated aloud on his drive home. He had done two backfold entries in the old neighborhood, and believed some paranormal force had *recreated* those events in the exact spot where they originally occurred. Ted did not touch the piece of clothesline, and assumed that it, like the football, was gone now. His theory was that it took most of whatever force was in play just to get them to present-day existence. They were not souvenirs for the taking.

His question now was, could he keep recreating wonderful moments from "The Golden Years?" A second question: was he *imagining* it all, wanting it to be true so badly that he was seeing and hearing things that weren't there? That *did* happen to people that weren't grounded in their real life. Was he one of *those?*

It was time to make a total assessment. It was 1985, he was thirty-six with a wife and two well-adjusted children. His marriage was solid, his career going well. He *was* overly nostalgic about his childhood, but no big deal. Until recently. The "Backfold" concept had put him on a track *parallel* with reality. He was actively seeking out things that many psychologists would say was counter-productive.

The next big decision would be whether or not to continue. What if he stopped and could not start it up again? He didn't know if there were *rules* to this.

One other nagging problem: was there anyone he could *confide* in? Allison? She was a wonderful, loving wife and great mother, but would she be receptive to *this?* He pictured her either chalking it up to coincidence or assuming he was playing some elaborate practical joke. *Or* possibly thinking there was something wrong with a grown man claiming he had recreated moments from his childhood.

There were his children. Steven was simply too young. Amy would be excited and eager to believe him, but could you trust a fourteen-year-old girl with something this strange? What if she confided in a guidance counselor, and they thought that her father was *disturbed* or *unstable?* Or worse, they might think that of *her*.

A professional therapist would try to be objective and helpful. But didn't these people thrive on getting people to deal with *reality*, rather than feed what most people would consider a fantasy gone awry?

And who was left? The people who had lived the original experience with him. When you subtracted the few who were deceased, and those who had moved away, there were only a handful still *available*. And of those, maybe only a couple who would take him seriously.

There was his brother Denny. They were five-and-a-half years apart, which gave them little in common growing up. But that didn't apply any more. Denny was a grown man with a wife and stepson, and had always looked up to him. Maybe it was time for the Fowler brothers to team up for something truly—*amazing*.

Ted and Denny sometimes went months without talking to each other. One of them would call the other and they would catch up, of sorts. A few words about work, yard improvements, their deceased parents, and the occasional 'whatever happened to so-and-so.'

Ted used the phone in his study. He was not sure how he would explain what had happened—twice. He would just do it off the cuff. How could you script something like *this?*

The phone rang once. "Hello," Denny answered.

"Denny, it's Ted."

"Hey, Ted, how's it going, big brother?"

"Denny, there's some weird stuff happening in the old neighborhood."

"Weird, what do you mean?"

"I've been writing stories about things that happened back there when we were kids."

"You have?"

"I'm *in* the old neighborhood when I write the story."

"I don't get this, Ted. What do you mean, 'a story.'?"

"One of our funny adventures, or one of our football or baseball games."

"You *write* about that stuff?"

Ted wasn't happy about the 'why would you bother doing *that*' tone he detected. "Yes, Denny, it's very *therapeutic.*"

"Well, what's wrong, Ted, that you have to write our experiences down to *feel* better?"

Again, with the condescending tone. "Denny, how I feel is not the point. After I wrote the story, something *from* the story was there."

"Where?"

"Where the thing *happened.*"

"In the old neighborhood?"

"Yes. I wrote about one of our football games on Cimarron and I saw a football on Easton's lawn. And up by the telephone pole I found a piece of clothesline where Len tied Charlie that Easter."

Denny laughed involuntarily. "God, that was funny."

"Yeah, it was. But don't you think it's . . . *eerie* that when I wrote about something, a little piece of the story *appeared* there?"

"Ted, I don't know what to think about all this. Are you all right, going back up on Cimarron and writing stories about us and then finding stuff there? I mean, those things had to have been there *already.*"

"They *weren't,* Denny. There's no *kids* in that neighborhood. Where the hell did a *football* come from?"

"I have no—"

"Listen, Denny. There's some kind of . . . *energy* or *force* or *vestige* of us *still there.*"

"Ted, are you sure you're okay?"

This was a lost cause. "I'm fine, Denny. Let's forget this whole conversation, okay? Take care." He slowly hung up the phone.

. . .

An 8X10 enlargement of an old photograph hung on the wall of Ted's study. Ted and nine of his Cimarron Hill cohorts sat on the roof and hood of an old delivery van. The driver, Greg Duquette, had his head and arm sticking out the open window. The photo, taken by young Roy Temmons, was dated July 24th, 1969. Later that day, the first men to walk on the moon would return to Earth.

To Ted, this photo epitomized the joyous feeling of camaraderie growing up with his friends on Cimarron Hill. The old blue and white Chevy delivery van, rusting badly, its paint chipping off with the slightest touch, was used by Greg Duquette for his part-time job. He often *drove* to the baseball and football games on Cimarron Hill or Redmont Field.

Ted had selected the photo to be the topic for his third on-site backfold entry. He would write a brief bio on all ten boys in the picture, plus the photographer, Roy Temmons, "nominated" to take the shot since he was the youngest one there that morning.

As for the disastrous phone call to his brother the previous day, Ted had put it behind him. Yes, he knew how this sounded when he tried to explain it. And it *was* becoming the focal point of his life, but what the hell. He was *living* something out of *The Twilight Zone*. It was . . . *exhilarating*.

Before he could undertake this adventure into the past, the present beckoned. Allison gave him a shopping list, and Steven and Amy announced they were coming along to get some better snacks than what their mother had in the house.

A few minutes into the grocery foray, Ted heard his name called from the other end of the dairy case. He turned to see Lonnie Temmons walking toward him, a small basket in his hands. Lonnie Temmons was a somewhat minor player in the Cimarron Hill saga, but a player nonetheless. Ted handed Amy the list.

"Here, be a grownup. But a responsible one."

"Yes!" Steven yelled, taking off with the cart, as his sister double-timed it to keep pace.

As Lonnie came up to him, Ted shook hands and clapped him on the back. "Lonnie, long time no see. How's everything?"

A rueful smile from Lonnie. "Not so great these days, Ted."

"What's going on?"

"Jackie and I separated a few weeks back. She took the kids to Maryland. They're staying with her parents."

"Oh, Lonnie. I'm so sorry to hear that. I popped in on your mother a week or so ago. She didn't mention it."

"Yeah. She doesn't know yet. And here I am shopping for one. So anyway, Ted, how's things with you?"

For the next ten minutes, an overwhelmed and confused Lonnie Temmons was told the entire backfold drama, including Ted's latest plan to recreate the famous delivery van photo chapter.

Lonnie seemed fascinated by the theory that Ted was capturing residual energy from long-ago events. Ted remembered that Lonnie was always eager to get his approval. Maybe *now* that could come in handy.

"So, Lonnie, what do you think of my crazy *adventures* back in the old neighborhood?"

"Sounds like part of us never left. I'm in if you need any help."

Perfect, Ted thought. Lonnie could at least be a *witness. If* it happened again.

"I was gonna go up there later today."

"Give me a call when you're leaving. I'll meet you in our driveway. Where do we have to go?"

"Right in front of my house, remember?"

"What are you gonna do, exactly?"

"Just write about that day, how psyched we all were about the moon landing, how we all jumped on Greg's van and had Roy take a picture of us."

"Yeah, those were the best times. I was on the roof."

"Yes, you were. Then we all played football on Cimarron Hill. That day is so . . . *vivid* in my mind. I can still *feel* that day, Lonnie."

"It was the *perfect* day, Ted.*"

. . .

As Ted drove up Cimarron Hill an hour later, he could see Lonnie's car parked in the driveway, where he had written the first backfold entry. He hoped Lonnie was merely paying mom a visit, and not telling her what they were up to. He parked behind him and waited. After fifteen minutes, Lonnie walked down to Ted's car.

"You didn't tell your mother what we're doing here, did you?"

"No. She's upstairs cleaning. She can't even see the driveway from there. I just told her I stopped by to see how she's doing."

"Did you tell her about your wife taking off?"

"God, no. She would never have let me leave."

"Good thinking."

"So what do we do now, Ted?"

"Just follow me down to the front of my house and park behind me."

A minute later Ted sat with his journal open to the blank page where he hoped to recreate his most memorable day. Lonnie had joined him in the front seat. He looked excited.

"How does this work, Ted?"

"I sit here and write about that day, the van, all of us climbing up on it, and having Roy take the picture."

"Then what?"

"We go over and see what was left behind from that moment."

"What do you think it'll be?"

"I don't know."

"Somebody's shoe? A lock of somebody's hair?"

Lonnie was having fun with this. Ted could tell he was going for something clever and funny.

"I know. My *glasses!*"

"The ones you broke like once a month?"

They both laughed at the recollection of Lonnie Temmons' glasses, which seemingly contained more tape than plastic.

"Actually, Lonnie, glasses is pretty good, but I just thought of something else."

"What?"

"That delivery van Greg used was kind of the centerpiece that day. The quarter panels were rusted to hell and the blue paint was chipping off like crazy."

"That's right," Lonnie said, snapping his fingers. "Wherever he parked it left behind paint chips if somebody even *touched* it."

"And we were climbing *all over it* to get on the roof and hood!"

Without another word, Ted began. A pedestrian storyteller at best, he wrote with description and feeling as though channeling Kurt Vonnegut, John Steinbeck, and Raymond Carver.

It was the story of growing up in Ohio, U. S. A. They were happy, and free, and proud that a fellow Buckeye had been the first to set foot on the moon.

Somehow they all sensed that *this was the most definitive moment of their youth.*

Ted was no longer a thirty-six-year-old man with a wife, two children, and a job. In his mind, he was twenty again, and *felt* it, too. It was the greatest feeling in the world. It had all reached a climax on July 24th, 1969. He would live it to the fullest. He would sit down *where the van had been* and finish the backfold on the beloved spot.

Lonnie Temmons was aware of a change in Ted, who had the look of someone on a mission, or at the end of a long journey. When Ted flung open the door, he called out, "Ted, is it done yet?"

Lonnie focused on Ted, striding purposefully in front of the car. Suddenly, Ted seemed to lose the three-dimensional quality that entities possess. It was as though a two-dimensional black and white filter had been superimposed. *Bright light, a huge blur of blue and white, voices, laughter, and then dead silence.*

Lonnie saw nothing up ahead of him. What had happened? What was all that light and color and voices? Where the hell had *Ted* gone? He got out of the car and walked cautiously to the spot where a blue and white delivery van had parked sixteen years earlier.

A blue journal and disposable pen lay on the ground.

"Ted?" he called. Ted must have taken cover when all that light and color struck. What *was* it? He called Ted's name a few more times, then walked across the street to the edge of the water company's wooded lot and called some more.

"Ted, where the hell *are* you?" He paused and walked around both cars. "Not funny, Ted." He walked back toward where the van had been that morning. This was ridiculous, no unbelievable. No, it was *unexplainable.*

Lonnie looked down at the road where Greg Duquette had parked. Scattered along the edge of

Cimarron Hill, where the van's back quarter panel would have been, were chips of light blue paint. Lonnie picked up several of them, squeezed them as if the fate of the world depended on it. When he opened his hand, it was empty.

Lonnie Temmons, age thirty, suddenly turned into the shy, scared, fourteen-year-old he had once been. He ran towards his childhood home at the top of Cimarron Hill.

"THE HUNTER"
Aug, - Oct. 2017

It was nearly ten-thirty when an exhausted Keisha Weaver managed to drag herself off the bus and begin the longest fifty yards of the day: the walk to her old Toyota.

She knew she shouldn't complain. Many black single mothers did not have jobs, and here she was with *two:* helping at an off-the-books day care center mornings, and working the three-to-ten shift at a variety store. She took the bus to save the ten mile round trip in her car, which was on borrowed time.

She stepped off the curb to cross to the lot when she *sensed* a sudden whoosh of air behind her, then was bent backwards as one arm draped across her throat, the other grabbing her left arm.

"Don't scream, bitch, or you die right here!" a low, raspy voice ordered.

Keisha attempted to scream, but the arm across her throat tightened. The hand attached to that arm held a large kitchen knife.

"What I just tell you, bitch?"

She managed to nod her head in compliance.

"Tell me why I don't slit your throat right now."

As the arm across her throat loosened, Keisha managed to utter, "Please, mister, I got two kids home. They ain't got no father."

"They ain't gonna have no *mother*, either, you don't do what I says."

"I got money in my purse. Just don't kill me."

"I can take your money *and* kill you if I wants!"

"Yes, sir."

"Okay, now. I walkin' you across to that parkin' lot. Puttin' you in my trunk. You got *that?* "

"Uh huh." Out of the corner of her eye Keisha could see her own car. She refocused as her assailant walked/dragged her to a greenish car one row down from hers. It was then she saw another man, clad in jeans, a black jacket, and wearing a ninja-type ski mask. *Oh, God, she thought. There's two of them.*

Her assailant saw the masked man and stopped dead, pointing the knife in his direction. "What *you* lookin at? Get your ass movin!'"

The masked man raised his right arm. A nearby streetlight reflected off a large semi-auto pistol, pointed at the attacker. "Let her go right now," said a muffled voice.

Keisha felt the arm around her loosen but stood there, shaken and confused.

"Take off, lady," the masked man ordered.

Keisha ran for her car, fumbling with her keys and finally getting in. The masked man remained where he had been, still pointing the gun at Rod Crosby, who dropped his knife and raised his hands.

"Who *are* you?" asked Crosby.

The masked man took a step forward. "I am The Hunter." He lowered the gun, and as Rod Crosby started to relax fired three shots, hitting Crosby in each knee and one foot. He turned and ran.

Inside her car, Keisha Weaver dialed 9-1-1, and with Rod Crosby's screams in the background, began a rambling, confused narrative to the emergency operator.

. . .

When police had finally sorted out all the details, it was apparent that Crosby, a habitual and violent criminal, had been thwarted in his attempted abduction and disabled by three shots from a forty caliber semi-auto wielded by a stranger in black clothes and a ninja-type ski mask.

When the story hit news outlets the next morning, there were varied reactions. Keisha Weaver naturally viewed "The Hunter" as an avenging angel who had saved her from certain rape or worse.

The police, while relieved that Mrs. Weaver had come to no harm, were apprehensive about the possibility of a masked vigilante shooting people, even if they were criminals.

Women's Rights activists took an unveiled satisfaction that a scumbag who preyed on women got what he deserved. They went so far as to insinuate that despite the low voice of The Hunter, this could be the action of a former rape victim.

The majority of the city population fell somewhere between wanting to give The Hunter (with Crosby's and Weaver's testimony the nickname was arrived at in no time) a commendation and throwing him in jail.

Rodney Crosby and the criminal element of the city were infuriated. It was the duty of the *police* to enforce laws, and catch lawbreakers (meaning themselves) in the act. That was how the game was played.

It was odd how things unfolded the next week. People likely to be on the prowl at night found bars to hang out in, TV shows to watch, or gatherings with friends. Simultaneously, police patrols in unsavory neighborhoods had increased, as much to find The Hunter as to be a deterrent. The result was a very quiet week in the city of Ballin, Indiana.

. . .

Like every other Saturday morning since her family had moved to Ballin, nine-year-old Mary Lou Elkins rode her bike from her trailer park home to Faraday Park.

Mary Lou was unaware of the event that occurred eight days before. Her life had not been easy. A deadbeat dad and a drunken uncle were not even her biggest concerns. She had done without nice things all her life.

Her bike, many of her toys, and most of her clothes were from charity. Her mother and older brother struggled to earn enough to pay the rent and buy groceries. Mary Lou was likeable enough, but she had always been the new kid. By age nine kids could take one look at you and decide that they were not going to be your friend.

She was rough around the edges, but had always tried to befriend the girls whom she perceived as friendliest or most popular. That seldom worked when you were new and dressed in castoff clothing.

Faraday Park was a place she could just ride her bike, a quarter mile from the trailer park, and be alone on the swings with her thoughts. She had been in Ballin six weeks now, and already knew that the kids who would show here within an hour were all pre-schoolers, many of them also from the trailer park. Their moms were polite but distant, talking to each other, but not her.

The man who approached from Oscar Avenue waved to her. As he neared she could see a friendly smile on his face. Maybe *he* would talk to her. He looked all around as he neared. He was maybe the same age as her no-good uncle Freddy, had a curly black beard and hair, and wore black-rimmed glasses. He waved again, and this time she waved back.

"Excuse me," he said, "I'm looking for my daughter. She said she was taking a walk down here. You didn't happen to see her, did you?"

"There hasn't been anybody else here. Just me."

"Really?" The man wore a puzzled look. "I wonder if she took a walk into these woods."

"I don't know. I didn't see her." Mary Lou was confused and curious. She had never seen another girl here alone. She overrode the distant warning voice in her mind. "How old is she?"

"Your age, but with long dark hair."

That seemed even odder. She would have attempted to befriend a girl her own age. "What's her name?"

"Linda." The man seemed to think a moment. "Maybe you and I could look for her. I don't know these woods."

"I don't either. I've only been here—"

"Will you *please* help me look for her?"

Mary Lou jumped off the swing and walked briskly towards her bike. Maybe this is what her mother had cautioned her about. She could hear the scrunch of gravel behind her and felt a hand over her mouth and nose. An arm around her waist lifted her off the ground.

"Okay, blondie, now we do things the hard way," came a soft, threatening voice. He carried her towards the wooded area at the edge of the playground, leading to a trail that came out behind a senior citizen housing complex fifty yards farther in.

Mary Lou squirmed, swatted, and kicked at her abductor, but he had an arm and leg pinned against his body, his hand firmly over her mouth and nose. The difficultly she had breathing took most of the fight out of her.

At the entrance to the trail, bushes moved, and a man stepped into the path. The morning sun glinted off a silver revolver in his right hand, pointed at the kidnapper's head. He wore jeans, a navy hooded sweatshirt and a black ski mask. His eyes were hidden by reflective aviator-style sunglasses.

Norman Felandos could see *himself* in the sunglasses. He saw his mouth wide open.

"Put her down," came a gruff command.

Felandos dropped the girl like a sack of potatoes. She lay there, gasping for breath.

"Run home, little girl," said the masked man.

Mary Lou tried to scramble to her feet, but her limbs were not co-operating. She stumbled and landed in a sitting position. From there she got her first good look at the man who had saved her. She was not sure what was happening, except that she was going to be safe if she ran. She got as far as the last tree before the playground when her curiosity kicked in and she hid behind it and watched. The man who had grabbed her had his arms raised over his head.

"It's not what you think, man," Norman Felandos said, his voice wavering. "I know that girl. She's—"

"Shut your face. You're a predator. Unfortunately for you, *I am The Hunter*." The .357 revolver roared twice, one bullet hitting Felandos' right knee, the other entering the top of his left foot. Felandos shrieked in pain, fell onto his side, both hands on his shattered knee. His foot seemed to demand equal time, and his left hand grabbed for it. The man in the mask and sunglasses stood astride him, the gun pressed to his temple.

"Please don't kill me," whined Felandos, "I didn't mean any—"

A third bullet entered the back of his shoulder, and Felandos screamed again.

Behind the tree that marked the beginning of the woods, Mary Lou Elkins was trying to get her legs to run to her nearby bike. She finally made it, and pedaled as fast as she could, never looking back. The street-tough part of her was glad that this bad man had been shot, the little girl part of her had wet her pants.

. . .

Residents of the senior housing complex called police to report gunshots. Responding officers found Norman Felandos with three gunshot wounds, growing faint from loss of blood. The police canvassed the houses and trailer park in the surrounding neighborhood and eventually questioned a scared, reluctant Mary Lou Elkins. Her statement seemed to indicate that The Hunter had struck again, only with a silver revolver instead of the .40 caliber semi-auto.

Police were astounded. There had been two vicious attacks in the last eight days, and both had been foiled by a vigilante wearing a mask and calling himself "The Hunter." Even though two different caliber guns were used, it was determined that the shooter was indeed The Hunter, and not a copycat.

Police Chief Lewis Kersey immediately formed a task force of beat cops and his most experienced detectives. It was headed up by Chief of Detectives Wade Burrows, who convened a meeting of all seven members as soon as they had been freed of their other responsibilities.

"Okay, people," began Burrows. "I think the best way to begin is to start throwing your theories and suspicions around freely. I don't think we're gonna catch this guy in the act. We're gonna have to outthink him."

"We can't do *that* yet, Wade," said Detective Stan Simons.

"Why not?"

"His two attacks have nothing in common. Different weapon, different caliber, different time of day, different type of location, different *everything*."

"So you think we should wait until he hits again, Stan?"

"I'm not saying *that,* but our assumptions are limited right now."

"I think The Hunter *lives* in Ballin, and he or a loved one was the victim of an assault," said Leo Gendere, a patrolman. "Why else take such a risk?"

"Makes sense," said Burrows.

"He used two different types of handguns," said Detective Miles Fainer. "There's a chance he's a gun enthusiast."

"Okay, Miles," said Burrows. "But how the hell does this guy show up at the only two attacks in the city in the last eight days?"

"He's *Batman!*" shouted patrolman Dennis Redmond.

A hearty laugh was shared around the conference room table, quickly followed by silence.

"Look, people," Burrows said quietly, "regardless of who this guy has targeted, he's a menace. It's only a matter of time before he shoots an innocent person, accidental or otherwise. Or one of his shots is off and he kills somebody." Burrows inhaled deeply. "Let's start by checking out the gun club, and going into places where these potential perpetrators hang out; bars, clubs, tattoo parlors. Maybe the people The Hunter targets will have some ideas."

. . .

At the Ballin Gun Club members and their guests had to sign in with the date, time, and caliber handgun they were using. The few .40 caliber and .357 shooters were checked out by Detective Vance Murray and Stan Simons. Nothing matched. The canvassing of local bars, taverns, dives, and the like produced little co-operation and *no* theories.

It *was* insinuated that friends of Rodney Crosby, The Hunter's first victim, were going to do a little hunting of their own. Murray and Simons spelled out exactly what would happen to them if they did.

Detective Isabel Watkins, the only woman on the task force, checked women's rights groups and lesbian hangouts on the chance that The Hunter was an instrument of a feminist vendetta. That also failed to produce any leads.

. . .

The initial investigations of the task force took nearly two weeks, and in that time period there was no violent crime of any type in Ballin. Police chiefs in the two nearest cities, Stroli and Courston, reported that predatory-type crimes and felonious activities after dark had dropped to almost zero, with the exception of a few drunken, impulsive acts.

There was an almost imperceptible waiting game going on.

Patrol Officer Dennis Redmond, who had delivered the only levity at the initial task force meeting, was still thinking about The Hunter being a Batman-type figure. There had to have been something *extra* in The Hunter's modus operandi. It was humanly impossible for a person to *know* that two particular incidents were *about to happen*, eight days apart, at two different times of day in two different settings. What would give a person the information to *already be* at such locations? He *hadn't* shown up by chance or accident. He was *in the vicinity, waiting*.

To Redmond, there were three possibilities: The Hunter had been tipped off by someone with knowledge of *both* Rod Crosby *and* Norman Felandos, two men who had no friends or localities in common, or The Hunter himself knew both men and knew *what* they were about to do and *where*.

But the chance of either of these being true was as close to zero as it could be.

No, Dennis Redmond, a savvy street cop, had landed on a third possibility. It was this possibility that Redmond felt The Hunter Task Force should be made aware of. It was a gamble. If his theory was rejected or deemed ridiculous by his peers, it could damage his reputation and standing in the department, and ruin his chances of ever making detective. It *could* get him replaced on the task force.

. . .

The Hunter Task Force convened once again in the Ballin Police Department's conference room. Wade Burrows had asked Chief Kersey to sit in.

When everyone was seated, Burrows spoke. "Officer Redmond asked for this meeting. He says he has a theory we have not yet explored." He motioned to Redmond. "The floor is yours, Officer."

"Thanks, Detective," Redmond began. "We have all agreed that there is no conceivable way for The Hunter to know the precise time and place of the two crimes he interceded in. And yet he was *there*, waiting to do just that."

There were nods of assent around the table.

"Gentlemen, and lady, I believe The Hunter is some type of computer expert, or data analyst, and has access to, or has *created*, a database on violent crime in Balllin. I think his information is so sophisticated that it correctly predicted or analyzed *tendencies* and *probabilities* to the extent that he was able to show up at the correct time and place."

There was quiet in the room. Redmond tried to get a read on the reaction to his theory. He could see several people considering it as an interesting approach, but Vance Murray and Stan Simons looked as though they had never heard anything so idiotic.

"I don't know, Officer," said Simons, "where would anyone get enough detailed information? I think the application here is so improbable as to make it unworthy of our consideration."

"Stan," said Chief Kersey, "there *are* crime statistics that are compiled and occasionally released in the media. Could The Hunter have come across something like this?"

"Even so," said Murray, "why would anyone *bother* with that?"

Redmond was crushed. He thought his theory was a strong one, and yet two members of the task force had taken a shit on it.

"We can't focus on The Hunter's *motive* as a reason for discounting Officer Redmond's conjecture," Detective Watkins injected. "This guy has a thought process that is unknown to us. We *should* consider how The Hunter gets his intel."

Thank you, Isabel, thought Redmond.

"Maybe we *should* start looking at the type of person who would be capable of using crime statistics as a predictor," said Detective Fainer. "I doubt the low-life element we've been interviewing are capable of anything like *this*."

"You know," began Officer Gendere, "we normally have no contact with this type of person. Where would we begin to look?"

"Any advanced computer class in a high school could produce people like that," noted Miles Fainer.

"An office supply outlet would have people with advanced computer skills," added Isabel Watkins.

"Stores that *sell* computers," said Wade Burrows.

The brainstorming session added a few more examples of venues that could produce a computer expert.

"Wait a minute," shouted Officer Gendere. "We keep talking about a *computer* person. A computer is just a *tool.*"

"So are *you,* Leo," someone said kiddingly.

"Computer people are interested in *computers,* and what they can *do*," continued Gendere. "This is a *math* person."

The 'computer person' versus 'math person' debate went on for ten minutes. Finally, Chief Kersey asked for their attention.

"Listen, time is of the essence. This Hunter person needs to be caught ASAP. And as far as computer person or math person, you better start working *both* angles."

. . .

As it turned out, The Hunter gave the task force a sample size twice what they now had. Five days after the meeting, The Hunter struck again. A week later, he made his fourth incursion into the land of the vigilante. Both attacks were made by assailants who had targeted women at night.

The first was an eighteen-year-old high school girl who had a part time job at a pharmacy, the second was a forty-three-year-old school aide who worked at a grocery store two nights a week.

In both cases the women were accosted and in the process of being robbed when out of nowhere the man in the ninja mask appeared. The high school girl, Jen Mendelsson, said *her* attacker had a gun and was shot in the side without warning. The masked man pocketed the thug's gun and proceeded to shoot him in both ankles. "I am The Hunter," he announced, then ran across back yards to the next street. A survey of nearby homeowners revealed that people *heard* the shots, but didn't *see* anything. The perpetrator, Mike Negruzzi, refused to co-operate.

The other attack occurred in a shopping center, the grocery store being the only establishment that was open. Heather Olivier, a school aide, was held at knifepoint when

The Hunter made his appearance. The assailant, Willie Torrez, dropped his knife and turned to run, but was shot at five times. Four bullets hit him in the leg and hip. The shooter identified himself to Olivier as "The Hunter," told her she "should be more careful at night," and ran toward the entrance of the plaza.

Both Negruzzi and Torrez would recover, but their wounds were serious and possibly crippling.

. . .

"He's getting bolder, people," began Wade Burrows at the next meeting. "He's moving closer to actually killing someone."

"Well," said Vance Murray, "that Negruzzi was holding a gun on that girl."

"Are you *justifying* him shooting that guy?" snapped Isabel Watkins. "A bullet in the side more often than not hits something vital. And that girl is lucky she wasn't shot by either one of those two!"

"All right, everybody, listen up," interceded Burrows. "We've compiled a list of computer and math possibilities. Let's start dividing them up. It's a long, long list."

. . .

One problem with the long, long list was that it included establishments and institutions outside Ballin.

In the past, police had gotten tips from concerned citizens, but with The Hunter, tips were nearly non-existent.

A high school boy taking a make-up test in an empty classroom at Ballin High School said he saw a math teacher sneaking off behind the school and entering a wooded area by a parking lot. Police questioned the teacher, Mr. Seymour Franks, and had him lead them into the wooded area.

Franks acted as though he had been caught red-handed, and led police to a box he had hidden under some brush. Police were hoping that the box contained one or both of the handguns used in The Hunter attacks. Instead, the box held a stash of Cuban cigars, which Franks smoked during lunch and his free period. Police left in frustration after giving Franks a warning about illegal cigars, which they did not bother to confiscate.

There was a lull of three weeks in which The Hunter did not strike. Simple enough, there was *nothing* for him to strike *at*. Predatory crimes simply ceased to occur in Ballin. There seemed to be a ripple effect in Stroli and Courston.

To some members of the task force, what occurred next came as a surprise, but to others it was just a matter of time.

Two unemployed men in their twenties, Jacob Neils and Broderick Lewis, had broken into an abandoned commercial building in the early morning hours to steal copper tubing, which was a valuable commodity in the construction business. There were contractors who would pay good money for it, no questions asked. In the middle of their thievery The Hunter appeared, announced himself to Neils and Lewis, and shot each of them twice, once in each leg. He escaped without anyone else giving witness.

At the Allan B. Landon School for Boys, the only private school in Ballin, a routine investigation turned into something not-so-routine. A math professor, Dr. Leonard Dente, aroused suspicion by comments he made showing favor toward vigilantes in general and The Hunter in particular. He was brought in for questioning, during which he backtracked and tried to soften his stance. A judge sympathetic to the police signed a warrant for Dente's home and school computer.

The school computer was clean, but Dente's home PC had dozens of files on crime probability statistics, crime surveys, charts, and graphs, some pertaining only to Ballin.

When informed of what had been uncovered, Dente confessed, of sorts. He and two other math teachers had made a bet as to when and where The Hunter would strike next. Further investigation put all three men in locations other than where The Hunter had struck. Thorough checks verified that none of the three owned any firearms, and had no experience with them. The investigation ended before anything of substance got to the press. The task force had wisely not released any "person of interest" type statements.

Dr. Dente, Michael Searles, and Dr. Joaquim Messler were given reprimands by the Allan B. Landon School for Boys. Two other department members, Robert Knowles and Dr. Kurt Westerhoff, were found to have no involvement.

. . .

The Hunter was inactive for the next two months, but then, so were the people he targeted. The task force had done a thorough investigation of anyone suspicious, but most clues pointed to someone extremely intelligent and analytical, not a run of the mill criminal.

The only positive was that there was little in the way of a public outcry over the failure to apprehend The Hunter. In the conservative state of Indiana, apparently, violent criminals shot in the commission of their crimes went down easy with most of the public.

. . .

It started as a routine welfare check. A teacher had not shown up for school and did not answer his cell or home phone. A nearby patrol car took the call and went to his residence. As his car was in the driveway, the officers made a forcible entry, and realized by their lightheadedness that there was a carbon monoxide leak. The officers got out, assuming that no one could have survived several hours in these conditions.

Fire Department crewmen turned off the furnace, and took steps to dissipate the gas. A man was found dead in his bed on the second floor.

A team of detectives was called in to verify that there was no foul play.

Both the house and furnace on 76 Eldrick Drive were old, and a heating and ventilation expert at the scene found cracks in the heat exchanger and flue pipes. The air filter was filthy, and the house contained no CO_2 detectors. In short, everything that *could* contribute to a fatal incident was in play.

The investigating detectives were Stan Simons and Miles Fainer. Although on The Hunter Task Force, all its members were assigned to pick up the slack due to inactivity on the case.

The victim was identified as Dr. Kurt Westerhoff, age 45, a mathematics professor at The Alan B. Landon School for Boys. The name immediately rang a bell with both detectives.

"That school where the math teachers had that bet when The Hunter would strike next," said Simons.

"Yeah, he was one of the two that had nothing to do with it."

"Wow, we just investigated this guy and here we are identifying his body," added Fainer.

They moved to the basement to finish the investigation. The H and V crew was just leaving.

"I don't think you'll find anything down here other than a killer furnace," one said.

"I don't either, but we have to check the entire place," said Fainer.

The detectives did a cursory search. Miles Fainer noticed a door that led to what was commonly known as a "mud room" in houses built in the early 20th century.

"Let's take a quick peek in here," he said.

Fainer had to use some force on the ill-fitting door. The room was dark but there was a light switch nearby. He flipped it, and almost forgot to breathe.

"Holy *shit,* Stan. Come look at this!"

What the two detectives were looking at was The Hunter's workshop.

The room had been refurbished with tables, a chair, a file cabinet, and a couple of throw rugs. There were charts, graphs, algorithms, and other mathematical probability tools from wall to wall. A computer sat on one table.

Simons and Fainer donned gloves and quickly opened the file cabinet drawers. In one drawer was a silver Taurus .357 revolver and a Sig-Sauer .40 caliber pistol, with ammunition for both. The bottom drawer held a beat up S & W .38 revolver, once belonging to Mike Negruzzi.

"My God, Miles, it's *him*! We found—"

"Shhh," hissed Fainer, his index finger on his lips.

"What? We solved the case. We solved the freakin' *case!"* Simon exclaimed, sounding like a ten-year-old whose team had just won the championship.

Fainer seemed to ignore Simons, and scanned the room quickly. He wore a grim expression before speaking in a hushed tone. "Listen up, Simons. Here's what we do. We go upstairs and get rid of everybody. Then we come back here and clean out this room. Charts, graphs, guns, computer, *everything."*

"What?"

"Let's say we go back to Burrows with what we just found. He'll have a big press conference announcing that The Hunter has been found dead."

"Miles, we solved the case. We solved it because we were *thorough*. We did our job. So what if we caught him by accident? Yes, the guy was some incredible math genius, but he didn't have the common sense to keep his house safe."

Fainer put a hand on Simon's shoulder. "Stan, we've known each other a long time. We both know what's important, and it's not Wade Burrows patting himself on the back."

"Miles, it's on record that we were the ones investigating here today. Our names will be—"

"Damn it, Stan. You're not getting it! The minute the public knows that The Hunter is dead, all the violent crimes he *prevented* will *start up again!* The scumbags who have been too afraid to do *anything* will be back. And they'll be worse than ever, because they're *frustrated.* They've been held in check by this guy for months. How many innocent people, mostly women and children, will pay the price for us reporting what we just found?"

Stan Simons seemed to be replaying what was just told him by a man he respected. He decided that Fainer was legally wrong, but morally right. And *factually* right, too. Violent offenders were not known for moderation. They wouldn't go back to crime a little at a time. It would be people acting out knowing that no man in a black ninja hood was going to interrupt their crime and shoot them.

Simons looked at Fainer as though he was a teen needing guidance. "So what do we do, Miles?"

"Like I said before, we clear the scene, and we sneak all this stuff out. I'm sure there are trash bags around someplace. We destroy all his charts and other data. We take this computer, smash it into a million pieces, and then *burn* it." Fainer was checking off boxes in his mind. "We take these three guns home and they never see the light of day again. We can destroy them later. I doubt if they can even be traced. I'm sure Westerhoff didn't get them legally."

Simons examined all three weapons. "Serial numbers are filed off."

Fainer shook his head in amazement. "This guy had to have been a god damn genius."

He and Simons looked again at the data in front of them. In addition to being advanced mathematical notation, it was in a code of Westerhoff's own creation. Some symbols did not even *exist* in any alphabet or numeric system. They had been *created* by Westerhoff. It would take a codebreaker *and* mathematician working together months or *years* to crack.

In Fainer's mind, there was one more box to check off. "Then," he added, "we search this house top to bottom for any copies or backups. We got a lot of work here, Stan. Let's get started."

. . .

With the exception of a memorial service at the Alan B. Landon School for Boys, the September 29th death of Dr. Kurt Westerhoff went largely unnoticed. He was a transplant from Kansas, unmarried, with no known family. He had no criminal record, nor had he been a victim of any crime. His motive died with him.

Simons and Fainer often speculated to each other in private what it might have been. They came to the conclusion that the late Dr. Westerhoff was a mentally-disturbed, anti-social loner with repressed violent tendencies, and *not* a champion of the victimized. They theorized that he carried out the shootings just to see if his data was correct, *and* to see if he could actually get away with it, which he *had*.

By January, months of inactivity by The Hunter was just too tempting for Miles Coogan, a nineteen-year-old mechanic. Like other criminals in the area, he surmised that The Hunter was laying low.

His target that evening was 65 -year- old Emma Daigle, who had just left an all-night pharmacy, where she had been waited on by Jen Mendelsson, saved by The Hunter the previous year.

Coogan dashed out from between parked cars, pushed Mrs. Daigle down, and grabbed her pocketbook. He turned to run, but his path was blocked by a man in dark attire and a ninja-type ski mask.

"No!" said Coogan in disbelief.

"Yes," said the masked man, and shot Coogan in his left knee and right arm. He walked over to where he lay and slammed him in the head with the black .45 Colt he held. He brought the pocketbook to Mrs. Daigle, helped her up, and nodded politely.

He paused to stand over Miles Coogan, groaning with pain, looking down at him.

"I am The Hunter," he stated, and fled from the parking lot towards the unlit section of the street.

"SIMPLE GIFTS"
2017-2018

My name is Faith Lauffenburg. I was born on May 15th, 1992. When I was nearly two-and-a-half years old, my sister Joy was born on November 1st, 1994. The twins, Hope and Patience, were born a year-and-a-half later, on May 24th, 1996. I had just turned four. A year and nine months after that my youngest sister, Serenity, came into the world on March 4th, 1998. We were born in Lennoxville, Kentucky.

We received our gifts shortly after turning fifteen. There was no defining moment in receiving these gifts. There was merely an *awareness* of something different in us.

I was given the gift of reading. Not the written word. People. No matter what is on your face or in your voice, I can read your heart.

My gift is the reason Mother no longer speaks to my aunt Johanna. Her words and demeanor were pleasant, but in her heart she harbored a bitter hatred towards my mother. When I informed Mother, she had no recourse but to believe me.

Joy's gift is the power of persuasion. She is indefatigable in her ability to turn a person's desires and opinions to align with her own.

Hope and Patience are "The Doers." No matter what needs to be accomplished, Hope knows *what* to do, and Patience knows *how to do it.* It is strange at times to have these young ones giving instruction to their parents and older sisters.

Serenity has extraordinary sensory abilities in both sight and hearing. This may seem of secondary importance, but it has helped us to thrive on an almost daily basis. Serenity can see the smallest geographical detail on a distant hillside, and can hear deer running or a bear thrashing through the woods hundreds of yards away. We are never without fresh game during the hunting season, and a lost four-year-old who wandered away from his family's farm was found safe under a pile of brush that searchers had passed by. Serenity saw and heard him from an overlook nearly two-hundred yards away.

At first glance one might think that we Lauffenburg sisters are like the Amish or the Amana, with our old-fashioned first names and being home-schooled, but we went to public school through third grade before Mother undertook to educate us, using state guidelines. We attend school plays and sporting events, and therefore have a small circle of friends and acquaintances. We have a phone, a television, and indoor plumbing. My father owns a pickup, which he uses to get work as a handyman. He makes an adequate living. Mother runs her own business from our home, sewing hand-made items she sells locally, although by word of mouth she occasionally gets orders from out of town, and even back East. A lady in Connecticut orders a pair of hand-sewn slippers every year.

• • •

It was a joyous occasion in late March of 2013 when Serenity proudly announced she had received her special gift. She took us outside and told us a truck was heading up Duxbury Road, where we live, about a mile-and-a-half from the town proper.

We stood by the road, shivering in the early spring chilliness.

"Don't hear a thing, daughter," Father said.

It was thirty seconds before the rest of us heard the sound of the truck's engine.

"Yep, you was right, girl," stated Father, and went back inside. The rest of us remained, in a mood of celebration and waved enthusiastically to the driver. He looked surprised to see a congregation of females cheering him on.

That night, after supper, Mother put a record on the phonograph and made us listen to an old Shaker hymn, "Simple Gifts." She told us it was in appreciation that we all now had our special gifts, and signaled the end of another day in our household, like the playing of "Taps" on a military base. The lyrics of the hymn are steeped in humility and religion, but we are nothing like the Shakers, who practice a very fundamental manner of worship.

We don't know why we were bestowed with a special "talent." Mother would not say much about it. And yet she knew that we would receive these talents at age fifteen. Father said even less about them and seemed to almost disapprove.

We girls knew that Mother was the driving force behind the gifts. Even when Joy and I were the only ones with them we discussed it among ourselves. We would try to bring it up at "school" when we all sat around the kitchen table, but our mother would make us get back to our lessons. She was a very competent teacher, and I once asked her if she had ever considered teaching as a profession. She seemed almost repulsed.

"Teach *other* people's children, Faith? I could not even *consider* such an idea."

. . .

We often wondered why we attended public school through third grade. We had several theories. One was that it is difficult to teach very young children, and Mother wanted trained professionals to "break us in." Another was that she wanted us to see both the good and bad in people. Serenity, jokester that she could often be, said that by fourth grade we would be of some actual use around the house. Joy's particular theory was that nothing *really* horrible could happen through third grade. After that, she maintained, the odds were ever-increasing of coming in contact with someone who might be a bad influence.

One day when we were feeling bold we listed our theories on a sheet of paper and asked Mother point blank why we attended public school as far as grade three only.

She looked at our list and seemed to be deep in thought while we five looked expectantly at her and each other.

"I am proud of you girls to have cared enough to ask such a question." She paused, probably for dramatic effect. "All four of your 'theories,' as you call them, are correct. I am giving you the rest of the day off from your studies as a reward."

The twins and Serenity squealed with happiness and burst from the table, but Joy and I noticed a peculiar half-smile on Mother's face following her praise and our "reward."

If you are thinking that I could easily read our mother's true thoughts in the matter, you are wrong. My parents and sisters were a blank slate to me. (We were equally immune to Joy's powers of persuasion.) I think it was a Divine reckoning that I could not know what was in my mother's heart. We were often told by our parents that God has a plan, and it is seldom obvious to us mortals.

This had already been demonstrated by what happened to Peter Blankenship, a boy Joy and I had known from school. He was the most brilliant student anyone had ever known. At age fourteen he was hiking in the hills the day after a big rainstorm. The erosion on the hillside loosened a large boulder, which careened down an embankment and hit him while he was walking up one of the trails, killing him instantly. The three younger ones were upset, but Joy and I were devastated. All the great things Peter was destined to accomplish were wiped out in an instant.

We were given the "all part of God's plan" talk by Mother while we mourned him. Eventually our mourning abated but not the sense of loss. I still wonder why God deprived us of the greatness that Peter certainly would have brought to this world.

. . .

Our father, Herman Lauffenburg, was a stoic man of few words. He smiled when the occasion called for it, but I do not ever remember hearing him laugh. He did not say much to us other than asking how we were doing with our studies, especially when we were in public school. Once under Mother's care, I guess he assumed he need no longer inquire.

He was an extremely skilled carpenter, and by necessity had taught himself plumbing and electrical abilities by observing others he worked with on various jobs.

His work is seasonal and therefore he is quite busy in spring and summer, less so in autumn, and without much work in the winter, except for repairs. But the winter slack is taken up by our mother, who sells more in December than any other time, it being the Christmas season. Father is free to hunt more at that time, providing her with more deerskin and such.

There are men who come to our house on occasion. We assumed it was to engage Father's services in building or repairing something. But we no longer think that. When these men come Father goes out back with them, up a hillside on our property and talks to them there, about twenty yards away. Joy and I once gave Serenity a chocolate bar if she would circle around in the woods above them and listen in. (She was eight years old then, and none of us had our gifts.)

At about the time when we figured Serenity was closing in, we observed Father snap his head around and look in her direction. He had *sensed* movement (*not* a gift, just ability honed by years of hunting) and seen a flash of white in the distance (her stockings) and called to "anyone out yonder" to make themselves known. Serenity got up and walked toward Father and the other man, looking as guilty as any child who has been caught red-handed.

"What would you have been doing out there in the woods, girl?" he demanded

"Nothing, Father. I was just taking a walk."

Even Joy and I were not convinced by her words and body language.

"That is not where you would go to walk, young miss," he said sternly.

Now we could hear him plainly, which meant that his previous conversations on the hillside were in hushed tones.

"Were you trying to listen in on my conversation with this man who is my *guest?"*

"Yes, Father."

"And *why,* child?"

"I don't know, Father."

We could tell that our eight-year-old sister was about to cry, and surmised that the next words out of her mouth would be our names.

"I was bored, Father, that is all."

"You are bored, you say? Well, there's a remedy for that. Go in the house and for the rest of the day you are to help your mother with any tasks that need to be done."

"Yes, Father. I am truly sorry."

"Just go now."

Later that day we got her aside and gave her more candy for not informing on us and asked what she managed to overhear.

"Not a word."

We had a sisters' gathering the next day. At that time we decided we would no longer engage in any spying on our parents, whom we loved dearly. We were just curious about adult relationships, even more so, of course, when we were purposely left uninformed. And Mother had not, at this point, had "the talk" with us, in which we were informed that something "special" would be occurring after our fifteenth birthday.

Ironically, in seven years, Serenity would have had no trouble hearing Father and his visitor. And she would not have had to risk detection. She could have squatted down on our back porch and easily heard every word that was said. In further irony, she would most likely have been caught doing *this* by our *mother,* whom I sometimes believed had her *own* gift of seeming to know when any of us were up to no good.

Had Serenity been successful that day, it would have answered a lot of questions we all had much earlier than when we actually got those answers.

An aside on the gifts Joy and I possessed with regard to our families. I repeat: they simply did not work on them. Mother called it the "Divine Safeguard." As far as Serenity's super-sensitive hearing, she had to concentrate on an area in order to hear anything. Otherwise, I suppose she would go mad with the multitude of sounds coming at her. Father's secret conversations with men on the hillside ceased once he knew of Serenity's gift.

. . .

On May 15th, 2013, my twenty-first birthday, our family had a small observance in my honor. Mother had baked her special cobbler that she makes on all of our birthdays. We do not receive presents, just the well wishes of our parents and sisters.

"You don't get rewarded just for having lived another year," Father once said.

Then Mother went to our phone and made a call. We girls rarely used the phone. Not in public school any more, we had little use for it. Father used the phone for his work, and Mother did as well for her sewing business.

We were all still at the table, finishing the last of the delicious birthday cobbler.

"Deandra, this is Ellen." Mother began.

We all stopped chewing to listen in as unobtrusively as possible. We had never heard of anyone named Deandra.

"Deandra, Faith has turned twenty-one today."

A pause while Mother listened to Deandra's reply.

"Very good. Tomorrow at noon, then."

Mother hung up the phone and looked at the five of us, peering inquisitively at her. She gave us a sly smile and winked, something we had never seen her do.

"Girls, we are going to have a little adventure tomorrow."

While Hope, Patience, and Serenity were peppering Mother with questions, Joy and I looked over at Father, who exhaled loudly and shook his head slightly.

• • •

Father used the truck the next day to get to a job about three miles up the road. So at 11:30 that morning the six of us trooped down Duxbury Road for the mile-and-a-half walk to town.

It was obvious we were going to see this Deandra Mother had spoken to on the phone, but why? Mother had made it clear she would not be answering any questions ahead of time, so we made small talk with each other. Mostly we teased Joy about the boy who had flirted with her at the high school baseball game the week before.

"Maybe we'll see your new boyfriend, Joy," teased Serenity.

"You shush now, Serenity," Joy retorted.

"I bet you can convince him he's in love with you," she continued.

"That will be enough of *that,*" snapped Mother. "The gifts you girls have been given are not for frivolous endeavors." She stopped and glared at all of us. "This is a serious new phase of your lives. Do you understand?"

We all nodded and said 'yes, Mother' in a subdued tone.

"Nice going, Serenity," whispered Hope.

We got to town and walked toward the Center Shops, a part of town we had hardly ever been in. Mother stopped at a small shop with a sign that read *Dee's Curios and Specialties.* It was a toss-up whether you would call it "rustic" or "ramshackle."

. . .

Mother entered first, the door hitting a small bell above it, like in the old TV movies. A woman approached her, hugged her ardently, and began to look at the five of us.

She introduced herself as Deandra Hardy, and spent a few moments looking each of us over, showing both excitement and anticipation.

We were doing the same thing, of course. She was perhaps between forty and forty-five, dressed in an outlandish print full length dress. She wore a tan bandanna, hiding most of her short light brown hair.

She went to Joy first. "Joy, right?"

"Yes, ma'am."

"Call me Dee."

"Yes, Dee."

She held up a section of Joy's shoulder length hair. "My, my, almost blonde, aren't you?"

"Yes, ma'am, I mean Dee."

She did the same to each of us, commenting on Serenity's dark brown hair and darker complexion, and noting that even though Hope had dark, short hair and Patience had light brown hair worn longer like Joy and I, they were remarkably alike in features. I don't know what she was expecting, Hope and Patience being twins.

She concluded her "inspection" by complimenting us on our beauty and stature, something we had never heard from *anyone,* including the boy who was sweet on Joy, and our own parents.

She then led us all to the back of the shop, which included such treasures as old lamps, backscratchers with plastic hands, ancient musical instruments, and piles of magazines and books. There were three chairs and two stools, and she asked us to sit. Serenity and Hope got stuck with the stools, which looked decidedly uncomfortable.

She stood in front of us, Mother at her side. "Girls, your mother and I have known each other our entire lives. We were close friends as children, and have become even closer as adults, despite living entirely different lives. There is nothing we would not do for each other."

We were curious, but slightly uncomfortable. There was something serious coming, we were sure of it. And I *could not* "read" this woman, which was the most discomforting aspect of all.

"Girls, you have been bestowed with certain abilities that defy convention."

Mother leaned over to her and whispered something.

"*Gifts,* girls. You have been given special *gifts.* Your mother has made great sacrifices on my behalf, and I have sought to repay her."

The pause Deandra Hardy gave made me think she had acted on stage.

"Faith, Joy, Hope, Patience, and Serenity, I am responsible for your gifts. *I* have given you your special abilities."

"You did *what?*" Serenity blurted. "How? Why?" continued our olive-skinned little sister.

We expected Mother to scold Serenity for her impolite outburst, but she looked at Deandra, obviously deferring to her dear friend.

Deandra closed her eyes, and spoke in a loud whisper. "The 'why' will be made known to you in due time. As for the 'how', I can only tell you that not everything in this world is *of* this world."

She seemed deep in thought, then managed a smile. "It was very gratifying to finally meet you." She came over and gave each of us a big hug, then hugged Mother again. "I will see you all again soon. Have a wonderful day."

Mother pointed us towards the door, and gave a nod that meant we should say a pleasant good-by to Deandra Hardy, which we did.

As we were leaving, I happened to notice a tapestry on a wall near the front window. It was titled, "Simple Gifts," and below it were the eight lines to the old Shaker song, the song we had heard each night for nearly two months.

The song spoke of humility and piety, and being accepting of the Lord and our fellow man. I did *not* see a kinship between those humble words and our special gifts, given to us from a strange woman I could not read.

We started to head towards Duxbury Road, but Mother called to us, and had us walk in the opposite direction. "One more little surprise, girls."

(My God, what next?)

We walked around the corner, and Mother led us into a quaint little drugstore, announcing that we were going to be treated to ice cream and sodas, something we had not had in months. At the counter were a dozen stools. Hope cringed. Mother laughed and said, "Let's sit in a booth, shall we?"

After giving our orders to the waitress, whom I recognized from Lennoxville Elementary School, Mother said, "Girls, let's enjoy our treat. We can discuss today's events when we get home, and not *until* then." She looked directly at Serenity. Like I said, I believe Mother had her own gift.

. . .

As it turned out, Mother had mislead us. We thought there would be an intense round of questions and answers. But she insisted we wait for Father, who was leaving his job early for the sole purpose of explaining this strange situation.

Father arrived home at just past three, having forfeited at least two hours wages. That, and the fact that he simply did not have "talks" with us verified that this was indeed, a serious matter.

He had his usual glass of homemade cider, and nodded to Mother, who ushered us into our seats at the kitchen table. Father stood at his place and seemed to be thinking.

"Daughters, today you met Deandra Hardy. She is an extraordinary woman who has endured much sorrow and injustice in her life. She and your mother share a bond of friendship and sacrifice the likes of which I have seldom witnessed."

He paused. It was obvious he was leading up to something. It was also obvious how difficult this was for a man who rarely spoke except to answer a question or correct one of his children.

"This family owes its very *existence* to her." There were wide eyes and open mouths all around the table. Mother nodded. "A good Christian repays his debts, does he not?" We all nodded and said 'yes.'

"From this moment on, you are at the service of Miss Hardy. What*ever* she asks of you, you will obey without question and without hesitation. Is that clear to everyone?"

"Yes, Father," we answered.

. . .

There was a sisters' meeting the next day. Mother knew what we were up to, but acted as though she didn't. One thing did not make sense. Miss Hardy had said that over the years Mother had made great sacrifices for her, and yet Father was telling us our family would not exist as such if it wasn't for Deandra Hardy.

"So, who owes who?" I asked the others.

"We owe *her,"* replied Patience.

"She seems nice," said Hope. "We *should* help her. She is Mother's very dear friend."

"Then how come we never *heard* of her until the day before yesterday?" asked Serenity.

Joy said, "All those men that came to see Father, all those secret conversations on the hillside. I wonder if there was any connection."

We were still so confused we could not decide on a course of action other than to obey Father. We also had little or no information, and that was driving Hope and Patience crazy. What we *did* know was that we would be making a return trip to *Dee's Curios and Specialties.*

We walked to church together that Sunday, as we always did. Father maintained it was good exercise, and good for one's soul, but the main reason was that he did not want us riding in the back of his pickup in our Sunday clothes with all his tools and such.

At the conclusion of the service, Father told Mother he would see us at home, then waggled a finger at us, saying, "Remember what I told you girls Thursday."

Father walked off in the direction of Duxbury Road, while Mother took us along side streets until we were in front of *Dee's Curios and Specialties.*

Deandra Hardy met us at the door, and ushered us into a back room, where she had set a table and served us girls tea and donuts, while she and Mother drank coffee. She hugged us all lovingly and complimented us profusely.

"It's time to tell you girls a long, sad story. Before I start, is there anything any of you would like to ask me?"

Of course there was! We had a *thousand* questions!

"Dee, do you have gifts, also?" Joy asked.

"I do not, my dear girl. I am solely a giver. And now I ask that you would use *your* gifts to help me."

"Help you what, Dee?" asked the precocious Serenity.

Deandra's visage turned stern, nearly angry.

"Nice going, Serenity," whispered Hope.

"It's all right child," she said, smiling at Serenity, whose eyes were wide as saucers. "You have been taught to be good people, have you not?"

"Yes, Dee," we answered.

"Well, what else could you be with my dearest friend as your mother."

Mother nodded humbly.

"A good person does not turn a blind eye to injustice, for if they do they are helping to perpetuate it."

We nodded silently.

"Girls, we are going to right a grievous wrong that was committed many years ago. The wrong was inflicted on my older brother Theodore."

Completely out of character, my three youngest sisters started asking a myriad of questions out of turn.

"Who did it, Dee?"

"What did they do to your brother?"

"How are you able to give gifts, Dee?"

The poor woman. I will relate the story she told when she was finally allowed to speak.

. . .

Deandra Hardy was from Lennoxville originally. She and Mother became close friends in their schoolgirl days. Dee's older brother Theodore had political aspirations. The family moved to Lexington, where there seemed to be more opportunities for him.

Theodore was a Democrat, (Kentucky is by and large a conservative Republican state) and after several years of successful law practice and community service, ran for mayor of Lexington, our largest city. He won a close, bitterly-contested election over the incumbent mayor, Roland Peterson. Peterson was anything but a gracious loser, and used every political connection he had to make Theodore Hardy's time in office difficult.

Peterson had planned to use his mayor's office as a springboard for a run for Governor of Kentucky. But first he needed to discredit Theodore Hardy and to get re-elected mayor.

Theodore was only thirty, a newcomer to politics, and not one who practiced back room dealings that many politicians did. He was naïve, and did not realize the lengths that men like Peterson would go to ruin him.

Unfortunately, he *also* had his sights on Frankfort and the Governor's mansion. He honestly felt that he could be a great leader of our state. In a leap of faith, he did not seek re-election for mayor so he could devote all his efforts to running for Governor.

Peterson jumped at the chance to get his power base back, and won the next mayoral election in Lexington. From there, he and his henchmen planned the political downfall of their most hated enemy.

Deandra did not go into specific details, but over the next few months, her brother's quest for the Governor's seat against incumbent Republican Samuel G. Dillane was plagued by constant innuendo of wrongdoing as mayor of Lexington. Included were allegations of misappropriated funds from the Highway Department, political favors to persons of dubious character, and supposed trysts with women involved in drugs and prostitution. Nothing was ever proven, but the constant drone of these allegations had a very negative effect. He went from frontrunner for the nomination to being censured by his own party, and dropped out of the campaign in disgrace.

His return to private law practice in Lexington was a disaster. People in Lexington would have nothing to do with him. Even local Democrats considered him toxic. His law practice dwindled to nothing. He became a man without friends, money, or standing.

It was during this time period, still a couple of years before my birth, that he began to drink heavily. Deandra, perhaps my age at the time, tried to help her older brother, trying to get him to attend AA meetings, reassuring him that she believed in him, and that he must stay strong and re-establish himself.

But nothing helped, and his downward spiral continued. On November 11th, 1990, he was killed in an auto accident when his car plummeted off a bridge. Upon investigation, it was determined that he had intentionally driven off the bridge.

Deandra was devastated, and knew that Roland Peterson was responsible. She could not stay in Lexington, and returned to her childhood home of Lennoxville, where she re-established her former close friendship with my mother. And in that homecoming, she somehow discovered the strange power within her: the power to empower *others.*

It is very important to note here that in this long, sordid story of backstabbing and betrayal, Deandra Hardy did not once mention the name of the man who was to blame. She merely referred to him as "that vile man." At the end of her long discourse, she revealed the name Roland Peterson to us. Our jaws dropped.

More than twenty years later, Roland Peterson was not some over-the-hill politician. He was the two-term current Governor of the state of Kentucky.

. . .

We have five months to accomplish our objective," Deandra stated, sounding like a general planning a military campaign.

Hope and Patience leaned forward in their chairs. This was their territory.

"What's our objective, Dee?" asked Joy, who seemed the most accepting of our mother's dear friend, and seemed to be Dee's favorite.

"The ruination of that vile man who sits in the Governor's chair, where my dear brother would have served with honor."

"So we are working to get Governor Peterson out of office in the coming election?" asked Hope.

"That's one way of putting it, child."

"He's way ahead of Artemis Folliger in the polls," said Joy, who had always been interested in politics. "It's sixty percent to forty, but maybe Folliger can close the gap."

"A twenty point lead spells a landslide victory for that vile man!" Deandra shouted. "This is not a show of hands on the school playground. This is over a million voters in one-hundred-twenty counties. Mr. Folliger has *no chance* of winning this election *if* events take their normal course."

It was obvious that Deandra Hardy was going to make sure that events did *not* take their normal course. And *we* were going to be instrumental in that.

. . .

It was nearly two hours after sitting down in Deandra Hardy's back room that we finally got home. A sister's meeting was planned, but we never got that far. We were again made to sit at the table. Mother also sat while Father stood and looked at us intently.

"Faith, tell us all what you have agreed to do for Miss Hardy."

I was calm for having been put on the spot. "My sisters and I, using our special gifts, are to help bring about the impeachment, resignation, or indictment of Governor Peterson before the election." I recited it word for word as Dee had said it.

"That is correct," Father replied. "And this plan has been in the works ever since he was elected Governor. There have been many benefits to this family due to your special gifts, thanks to Miss Hardy. We shall be her arm of retribution. That is, *you* shall."

Father paused, and actually smiled slightly. "I can tell you now that the men who came to see me all those times were sent by her. They were men she could trust and who knew about your gifts and her plan. She did not want to contact your mother directly, so she sent them to *me,* assuming you would think it had to do with my work. You were taken out of school to minimize your contact with any child or adult who might know something we didn't want you to know yet." He smiled again as he looked at Serenity. "My dear girl, it was for the best that you did not overhear my conversation that day years ago."

. . .

Things got hectic and complicated after that. Deandra and her cousin Edward showed up at our house the next day with a pile of statutes and documents for Hope and Patience to read and *learn.* Joy and I were being driven all over the state by Edward to various campaign headquarters. It was soon decided that we would hit the streets to talk to people *convincing* them to vote for Folliger. We were backed up by information gathered by Hope and Patience showing that many of Governor Peterson's actions favored an elite few.

Kentucky is a very diverse state. You had the upper crust of Lexington and "horse country," where most of Peterson's support lay. But there are many other groups: poor farmers, rich farmers, chemical workers, miners who risked their lives every day, hill people who didn't care who was Governor, and everyday merchants, police, teachers, and the like. Joy and I felt like we were doing a whistle stop campaign for the Presidency.

We did this for seven weeks non-stop, and the next poll proved that Joy's gift was a powerful one. Folliger had gained substantial ground on Governor Peterson, with an "undecided" element that had not existed before.

Deandra Hardy called us to her shop on another Sunday morning. "My cousin Edward was only a teenager when my brother Theodore took his life. He is more than just a chauffeur for Joy and Faith. He is going to do some looking into the past of that vile man."

"Where would he look, Dee?" asked Hope.

Dee scowled. We knew we were about to hear another scathing indictment of Governor Peterson. "This man did not become the evil scum he is during my brother's gubernatorial campaign. He was a devil from the outset. Of that, I am positive. Edward will act as a private investigator. I must keep my distance. That vile man and his associates know who I am from long ago."

"How will he do that?" asked Patience.

"Old girlfriends, high school and college peers, former associates." Deandra smiled a cunning smile. "If you shake enough trees in that vile man's past, some rotten fruit is bound to fall."

Serenity sighed loudly. She seemed to have been forgotten in all the planning and action. Dee noticed immediately.

"Don't worry, young one. You will have a very important role eventually."

Serenity smiled, and Dee went over and gave her a big hug. "At the end of this venture, we will need you to hear what needs to be heard."

"You can count on me, Dee."

"Good. The race is getting closer. This man cannot accept a fair, close campaign. Watch for him to speak and act like the vulgar, dishonest person that he is. And when he does, I believe things will get even tighter."

. . .

Although the race grew closer, there were setbacks. Hope and Patience had gone over Governor Peterson's record and could not find anything illegal. Dee's cousin Edward had found and interviewed as many people from Peterson's past as he could, and while it was obvious the man was a self-centered, power-hungry user of people, there was nothing that could be brought to light to cause him public humiliation, censure by the legislature, or indictment by the law.

"The cleanest dirty scumbag on the face of the earth," Dee remarked.

The twins, now seventeen, had closely examined everything Peterson had done or said he would do, and spent ten days writing a platform for Mr. Folliger, who had closed to within nine points in the polls. I was so proud of those two. Dee sent it to his campaign manager. Within a week we started to notice some of their ideas being put forth by Mr. Folliger, a capable speaker with a background in business, and a three term mayor of Lutz, a medium-sized city west of Frankfort.

One Sunday afternoon, Dee summoned Joy to her shop, while the rest of us remained home. I had long suspected Dee of having a special affinity for Joy, but I didn't think it very polite of her to make it so obvious. When Joy returned home, she was pale and had a headache that drove her to tears.

"Too much candy and ice cream," whispered Serenity.

We asked Joy about her day alone with Dee, but she was very vague. "We just talked about life, things in general. It was a very pleasant day."

"Then why were you so sick when you got home?" asked Hope.

"I guess it was just the excitement of the day."

. . .

Artemis Folliger continued to make slow, steady progress in the polls, but Dee said that wasn't good enough. "He's a Democrat, relatively unknown, and running against an incumbent whose main constituency is well-spoken and deep pocketed. But," she continued, "a man like this can be made to become his own worst enemy."

"How?" asked Joy.

"He must show his true colors in public, my dear Joy."

Meanwhile, Dee's intrepid cousin Edward had made a connection with Folliger's campaign manager, Teresa Turcotte, a city council member from Folliger's home town of Lutz. He had met with her twice and informed her that he had a "network of supporters" responsible for drafting the platform that had served Folliger so well. Turcotte was impressed, and after that Edward Hardy had her ear. We were assured by Dee that there was *no* mention of five sisters utilizing special gifts to get her colleague elected, and to make sure the incumbent Governor went down in disgrace.

Edward took us girls to a campaign stop in Tonnet Falls the next week to hear Governor Peterson speak. He had been advised that he should start playing to crowds other than his upper crust supporters. So here he was in coal country, Tonnet Falls, which had experienced a major mine disaster the previous year.

Edward left us in back of the crowd, but led our sister Joy up front, where Peterson was pressing the flesh of people we knew he had contempt for. Joy had been instructed to shake Peterson's hand and say 'pleased to meet you, sir.' She and Edward remained in front, the rest of us feeling left out.

Peterson went into a spiel about caring for all the people of our great state. Then someone from the front of the crowd yelled out, "Governor, what would you do to prevent the tragic circumstances that killed fifteen of our miners last year?"

We were sure the voice was that of Edward Hardy.

Peterson looked annoyed as he said brusquely, "There is nothing to *be* done. Our mines are as safe as we can make them. Mining is dangerous. There will always be risks and loss of life. We must make sure that that is an acceptable level of loss."

There was a gasp from the crowd and a smattering of boos. Peterson was aware he had made a huge gaffe in the presence of people who had lost fathers, sons, brothers, and husbands in the Tonnet Falls mine explosion. Like a seasoned politician, he backtracked on the heartless, cruel statement he had made, then moved on to the rest of his prepared remarks.

Newspapers throughout the state had a field day. Many ran front page pictures of the fifteen dead miners with the headline, *'An Acceptable Level of Loss?'* The poll that came out two days later showed Folliger within two points of Peterson, with a "three to four point margin of error."

"We are about to see the reaction of a desperate man," said Dee.

"How can you be so sure, Dee?" asked Serenity.

"I know how he thinks, my dear. He would never let on that he is worried. This vile man has gotten his way his entire life. I'm sure he feels he is *owed* the office."

"What do you think he'll do, Dee?" Joy asked.

"I'm not sure, but it will be something that would make one think that he has the election in hand."

. . .

Artemis Folliger was starting to believe he had an even chance to win the election, although he was still between one and three points behind, depending on which poll you read. With Peterson's horrible pronouncement at Tonnet Falls in mind, Folliger challenged Peterson to debate him.

Folliger showed gumption in issuing the challenge. He was close, but a poor performance at this late date would all but end his chances. He had to hope that

Peterson might slip up again, with only a week until election day.

Teresa Turcotte met with Peterson's campaign manager, a slick PR man named Will Kozmanski. They picked Blandenburg, a city about halfway between Frankfort and Folliger's home city of Lutz. Governor Peterson, with a lot at stake and a lot to lose, accepted the challenge with a wave of his hand and a confident smile on his face.

It was further agreed that both candidates would check in at *The Bluegrass Lodge* the day before and have a luncheon together, with campaign issues off limits. Peterson believed that this would show voters that he, too, could be a regular guy.

As soon as Dee learned of this, she sent Edward to Blandenburg that very day. He arrived at our house after eight that evening and handed an envelope to our mother. He talked to her in hushed tones, and Mother nodded. She removed a photograph from the envelope, but would not allow any of us to see it.

The next morning found Mother hard at work, making a dress that looked like something a maid or waitress would wear, in a size that would only fit Hope or Serenity. When Father came home, Mother took him aside and showed him the photo. Father went out to the garage where he had a work space, and returned to our living room an hour later, handing Mother a small object which she put in the envelope that contained the photo. Later that day Edward came to our house and gave Mother a large zippered satchel.

It was obvious by now that Dee's objective to get Governor Peterson impeached, indicted, or get him to resign was unattainable.

"Yes, I have failed in that," she admitted, "but the debate is coming, and I must prepare Joy and Serenity for their very crucial roles that day."

"What about the rest of us?" asked Hope.

"Your part in this is complete," Dee answered, "and it was done to perfection. We could not have gotten this far without you, my dears."

. . .

On the morning of the debate, Edward arrived at our house at eight-thirty. Father was building a fence on the outskirts of town and had already left. I went to use our bathroom and heard voices laughing inside.

"Who's in there?" I asked.

"We'll be out in a minute," answered Mother.

Five minutes later Mother emerged, followed by two people I initially did not recognize. After staring at them while they giggled uncontrollably, I realized it was Joy, wearing a dark brown wig and makeup, and Serenity, dressed as a maid from *The Bluegrass Lodge,* complete with an identification badge, (which Father had made) a *blonde* wig, and makeup. She looked years older than her actual age of fifteen-and-a-half. They both flashed cell phones in my face, which we were not allowed to have.

"What is going on?" I demanded.

"Can't talk right now, my dear," Serenity said, in a snobby woman's voice. "I must get to my job at *The Bluegrass Lodge.* Be a good girl now and look after the twins." She and Joy giggled as they bounced out the door to Edward's car.

By now Hope and Patience were watching, their mouths agape.

"Mother, what is happening?" I pleaded.

She sat the three of us down and explained. Edward was driving the girls to Blandenburg, where both candidates had spent the night. Serenity would go into *The Bluegrass Lodge,* slip into a bathroom, and change into the maid's uniform, which Mother, working from the photograph Edward had taken, had duplicated right down to the light green cuffs on the sleeves. Her ID badge was also authentic-looking, and read "Pamela." She would find Governor Peterson's room, easily identifiable by a Kentucky state trooper stationed at the door, and pretend to work, going up and down with unattended cleaning carts, brooms, and the like. She would listen to any conversation coming from inside the room, an easy task for her. If she heard anything important that Peterson was planning, she would call Joy on the cell phone and report it. Joy would then call Edward, who had convinced Teresa Turcotte to give him access to Mr. Folliger as he made last-minute preparations for the debate, which would be held at noon in the town square.

Patience remarked, "We could have helped with this, you know. Lately all Dee's attention has been on Serenity and Joy," she complained, sounding like a miffed ten-year-old.

Mother smiled, patted Patience's head, and told us that the gifts of Joy and Serenity would be needed that day, just as our gifts were needed previously.

. . .

It was nearly seven that evening when Edward dropped off Joy and Serenity. We had all watched the local news at five and knew that Artemis Folliger had thoroughly bested the Governor in the debate, making him look like a petulant, spoiled elitist.

Folliger came off as a concerned person who could raise the quality of life in Kentucky. I am sure he convinced a lot of people on his own merit, but he had the help of Joy, who "worked the crowd" during the debate, and of course Serenity, who had made small talk with state trooper Bartoszek while listening to Governor Peterson,

Will Kozmanski, and other aides come up with what they believed to be "traps" for the challenger.

As Serenity herself told it, (after Father insisted both she and Joy "remove those wigs and devil's war paint") she was in constant contact with Joy, who passed the information on to Edward. Folliger and his advisors had prepared rebuttals to all of Peterson's inaccurate accusations.

"And I used *both* my gifts from Dee," Joy said proudly.

"You don't have *two* gifts," I said.

"But I *do*. Dee gave me the second gift the day I spent with her. It was quite intense. That's why I was so ill when I came home. But it was worth it."

"And what gift *was* it?" I asked, a shade of jealousy in my voice.

"I can't tell you."

Anyone watching television footage of the debate could not help but notice that the fiery, bombastic Roland Peterson, his political career on the line, seemed listless and not fully engaged as he read his prepared remarks and leveled inaccurate charges at Artemis Folliger, who countered them with ease. We could not help but wonder if Joy's "second gift" had a part in any of this.

A week later, Folliger won the election 52.4 percent to 47.6 percent. Peterson grudgingly conceded, and scurried off to his Lexington area home, leaving the day-to-day chores to his Lieutenant Governor, Charles Crowder. Peterson made an appearance perhaps once a week, looking lost and disinterested.

. . .

The final chapter of this long saga came several days later.

Dee and Edward arrived at our house shortly after our evening meal. Both Mother and Father acted as though they were expecting them.

After hugs and handshakes among the four adults, we all sat at the kitchen table. It was Father who began. "Girls, your mother and I found out early in our marriage that her eggs were not going to allow us to start a family. But Deandra offered to give us the family we had prayed for."

Joy and I knew immediately what this meant. Hope and Patience were working through the details, while Serenity looked extremely puzzled. Mother leaned over and whispered in her ear. Her eyes widened and her jaw dropped.

"Are we all on the same page, now?" asked Dee, smiling. Everyone nodded. "Your mother would get the family she and your father deserved. And I would get the satisfaction of knowing that my fertility allowed me to be the biological mother of all of you. Since I was not married and had no prospects, this was my only path to motherhood."

It was starting to sink in. Although she did not raise us, and had only known us six months, Dee was our *real* mother.

"Why did we get the gifts, Dee?" asked Serenity.

It seemed an odd question, in light of what had just been revealed.

"It was all part of our agreement, a pact we made," she said, looking with admiration at Mother, who smiled in appreciation.

Hope and Patience were busy whispering to each other behind cupped hands. Hope stood up, a resolute look on her face. "Dee, we were all born after your brother's death. Did you give us the gifts so that you could get revenge on Governor Peterson?"

"Of course not, my dear," Dee answered, seeming unflustered by the tone of the question. "I was grateful to your mother for giving me the opportunity to be a mother, and I further agreed to stay out of your lives until the first born turned twenty-one. I gave you the gifts so that you all could be special, and prosper, and help others."

Yes, Dee, I was thinking. *We certainly were able to 'help others,' mainly you.* I happened to glance at my sister Joy. She rested her head in her hands and stared at Dee with pure adoration. Hope and Patience seemed to be taken aback by everything, and Serenity still looked lost and confused.

"Well," said Mother, "I am glad, Dee, that we finally got everything out in the open, and I can assure you that my girls were glad to have used their special gifts to help you."

"Our girls, Ellen," Dee corrected. *"Our* girls."

"Yes, of course, Dee. *Our* girls."

"Ellen?"

"Yes, Dee?"

"You realize there is one more matter that must be settled."

Mother looked confused at first, then Dee's meaning came to her. "Dee," she said, "you can't be serious. We were young then. We said a lot of things that didn't make sense."

"And we *agreed* on all those things, Ellen. Do we *continue* to keep to the agreement?"

Father stood, anger on his face, but Mother headed him off. "Let her speak, Herman. She is correct. We agreed to this. A good Christian keeps her word."

"She does, Ellen," said Deandra Hardy.

"Go ahead, Dee. Tell the girls the last thing we agreed to *twenty-three years ago."*

"Thank you, Ellen. My dear girls, your mother and I agreed that when all of you had your special gifts, and the oldest of you was twenty-one, we would tell you of your unique situation. And we agreed that *on* that day, which is today, you would be given the opportunity to decide whether you will stay with the parents who have raised you, or come to live with me, from whose egg you originated. If you choose to leave, your parents have agreed that they will not stand in your way."

Now, *all* of us had that same stunned, confused look that Serenity had.

Dee, followed by Edward, headed for the door. Reaching it, she turned to us in yet another dramatic gesture. "I will be back in three days, girls, for your decision."

That evening at bedtime, Mother played "Simple Gifts" *twice*.

. . .

There is no need to relate any scenes that took place over the next three days. Joy wanted to go, the twins and I wanted to stay, and Serenity did not know what to do.

Dee returned to our home three days later as promised. Edward was not with her. She had walked the mile-and-a-half from town.

She did not seem surprised to see Joy waiting in our kitchen, bags packed and ready to go.

"Leave those here for now, Joy. I will send Edward to pick everything up later." She turned to Mother. "Ellen, I would like to leave here with your blessing."

"Isn't a blessing *your* department, Dee?"

"Not any more. I seem to have used up what was left of my own gift in bestowing a second gift upon our daughter Joy. God's will, I presume. It was not of this world to begin with, as I often said. At any rate, I would hope we all can see each other often and remain friends."

"If it is God's plan, Dee, it will happen. That is all I can say for now."

We had all been standing in the kitchen witnessing this exchange. Serenity, who had experienced three days of worry and tears, came over to Dee and gave her a hug.

"Part of me wants to go with you, Dee, but part of me wants to stay here."

"I understand, child. It would be difficult for someone your age, but your sister is nineteen, and has chosen her path. A time will come when you will do the same."

None of us was sure what Dee meant by that.

There was a question I could not hold back. "Dee, why won't you or Joy tell us what her second gift was?"

Dee smiled slightly and put her arm around Joy, who had gone to her side. "No one must know except Joy and me. May God bless all of you." She and Joy headed out the front door to begin their walk to town.

We sat at the table in silence. Father, who had said his own goodbye to Joy that morning, arrived home and sat with us.

Finally Mother spoke. "I never thought she would do it, but we agreed. I let her bless you with the gifts. It seemed, after all, that they were simple gifts."